MW01114676

Silver Butterfly

Silver Butterfly

Janet Logan

Five Star • Waterville, Maine

This novel is a work of fiction. Names, characters, places and incidents are either the product of the author's imagination, or, if real, used fictitiously.

First Edition
First Printing: August 2006

Published in 2006 in conjunction with Tekno Books.

Set in 11 pt. Plantin.

Printed in the United States on permanent paper.

Library of Congress Cataloging-in-Publication Data

Logan, Janet.
Silver butterfly / Janet Logan.—1st ed.
p. cm.
ISBN 1-59414-491-5 (hc : alk. paper)
1. Widows—Fiction. 2. Restaurateurs—Fiction.
3. Restaurants—Employees—Fiction. I. Title.
PS3612.O395S56 2006
813′.6—dc22 2006007958

Dedicated to the memory of
Eugene J. Benge,
my father, my first writing teacher, and author
of seventeen business and self-help books . . .
with love and gratitude.

PROLOGUE

Brooklyn, New York

Serena D'Agostino and Steven Katz stood near the Red Ball moving van and watched a brawny black man wheel the maple bureau from Steve's room across the sidewalk and up the wooden ramp. It took its place near the furniture from Steve's parents' bedroom. Moments later, when the dining-room breakfront went by, its leaded glass doors taped shut, Serena began to cry.

"You promised me you wouldn't cry," said Steve. He jammed his hands in the pockets of his cut-off jeans, rocked back and forth on his sneakers and jingled the loose change.

"I know I did. I just can't help it!" she wailed. "I feel as if my heart is breaking into little pieces."

Steve pushed a hand through his dark curly hair. "We're only moving to New Jersey."

"*South* Jersey," Serena corrected him mournfully. "Right across from Philadelphia!"

It might as well be Moscow!

"I'll call you every Sunday," he promised, "and we'll talk like always."

"It won't *be* like always! You won't be here in July for my fourteenth birthday! And you won't be here with me to start Erasmus Hall in September. You'll be going to some high school in South Jersey!"

Steve put his arms around her and hugged her tight.

"I know. I know. I wish my dad's company didn't

transfer him to New Jersey, but he's gotta go where the money is. It's a big promotion for him; he's gonna open a new branch of Hudson Construction . . ."

"Oh, Steve, I'll write to you!" Her silver-gray eyes gazed up at him. "Will you write back?"

"Sure I will!" He yanked her long dark-brown braid as if trying to stop a train. "What didja think—I'm gonna forget you?"

"You better not—and I'll never forget you either!" She picked up the bottom of her tie-dyed T-shirt and wiped her eyes. "I'm not gonna say goodbye, Steve, because I know we'll be together again someday."

Together, they watched the moving van disappear around the corner onto Flatbush Avenue.

CHAPTER 1

New York City

"Do you have an appointment?" the receptionist asked.

Serena, standing tall before the desk, shook her head.

"I'm afraid I don't. One of my friends—Melanie Fox—recommended Mr. Franklin, and I was hoping he might be able to see me this afternoon. Perhaps I should have called first, but I was . . ."

Her voice began to slide downhill and she had a feeling that she was going to disgrace herself and cry, right here in the lawyer's office. She guessed the receptionist had seen a lot of clients cry in front of this desk. The young woman nudged a box of Kleenex toward her, but she ignored it.

The receptionist asked for her name.

"Serena Epstein."

"You're very, very lucky, Mrs. Epstein. We just had a cancellation five minutes ago. Please have a seat. Mr. Franklin is with a client now, but he'll be able to see you in a few minutes. May I get you a cup of coffee?"

"No, thank you."

Still battling the inclination to weep, she sat down on a graceful antique chair upholstered in crimson needlepoint which contrasted pleasingly against her navy-blue cashmere coat. When she removed her sunglasses, she glanced in the mirror across from her chair, and realized that anyone could see she'd been crying. A lot.

"You have beautiful hair, Mrs. Epstein. It looks like silver silk."

Serena looked at the brass nameplate on the receptionist's desk. It said *Penny Sawyer.*

"Thank you, Penny. You should've been a poet."

Penny giggled.

When Serena entered Mr. Franklin's office ten minutes later, a middle-aged man a little taller than herself came out from behind his desk to greet her. His salt-and-pepper hair was perfectly styled, and his charcoal-gray suit, white shirt, and red tie were immaculate.

There was a faint odor of cigarette smoke in the air, and she recognized the popular breath mint he'd used before her entrance.

"Penny tells me you're a friend of Melanie Fox," he said. He shook her hand, smiled reassuringly, and held a chair for her.

"Now, Mrs. Epstein, tell me why you're here, and I'll try to help."

His blue eyes, behind rimless glasses, were kind, but she found it hard to talk to a stranger about her problems.

"I've never filed for a divorce before so you'll have to forgive me if I'm a little reticent. You see, my husband is the one who wants the divorce. He told me to get myself a lawyer."

"I see. Why do you believe your husband wants a divorce?"

"Our son Mark . . ." She stopped speaking and closed her eyes for a few seconds; took a deep breath, and began again.

"Our son died in an automobile accident six months ago." The words came out in a short burst, like pellets from a BB gun. "Burt—that's my husband—gave him a sports car, a Corvette, for his twenty-first birthday."

Edward Franklin was making notes on a legal-sized yellow pad.

"Had your son been drinking?"

She nodded.

"They'd both been drinking—Mark and Judy. That was his girlfriend."

"Judy died also?"

She nodded again, and could not hold back the tears any longer.

"It was such a *waste*, such a terrible *waste!* Two young lives ended before they had really begun."

"How did it happen?"

"Mark ran a red light and crashed headlong into a big truck, an eighteen-wheeler." She was sobbing now. "Judy was killed instantly. Mark died the next day."

"How did this tragedy affect your marriage, Mrs. Epstein?"

Serena eyed the box of Kleenex on the lawyer's desk, and finally reached over to pluck one.

"My husband blames me for the accident," she said, mopping her eyes. "He won't sleep with me, he won't eat with me—he says he can't stand to look at me. He—he doesn't want to live with me anymore."

Mr. Franklin stopped writing and laid down his pen. He gazed across the desk at her face, which she realized was now contorted with anguish.

"Why does he hold you responsible for the tragedy?"

"He says I was always too permissive with Mark, did not discipline him enough. He thinks I made him into a mama's boy."

"Where was he, while all these alleged transgressions were occurring?"

"Burt is the CEO of a large corporation. He's always worked long hours—he travels a lot on business . . ."

"Are you telling me he had a less than satisfactory relationship with his son?"

"Not exactly. It was more like—they didn't have any relationship at all. They were like strangers."

"I see. Why do you think he gave Mark such an expensive car for his twenty-first birthday?"

"I guess he thought it might make up for—all those years of not being there."

She paused to pluck another tissue from the Kleenex box and dab at her eyes.

"Mark was a tall boy. He played basketball in high school, but his father never came to see him play. He promised to come to Mark's high-school graduation, but at the last minute there was an emergency, a strike at one of the company plants, and he had to fly to Houston . . ."

"Mrs. Epstein, I have no degree in psychology, but it seems to me that your husband felt enormous guilt about Mark's death and cannot bring himself to acknowledge it."

Serena's right hand twisted the diamond-and-emerald wedding band on her left ring finger as she listened to the attorney's words.

"Don't you think it's possible that your husband has transferred his guilt to you because he cannot accept it himself? If Mark's death becomes your fault, he does not have to deal with it."

"You're saying he's lying to himself?" she asked.

"I think it's very likely. He says he 'cannot look at you.' Don't you think he knows you did his job as well as your own while Mark was growing up? What he's really saying is that he cannot look you in the eye!"

Serena dropped both tissues into a wastebasket and nodded wearily.

"I suppose you're right. You probably *are* right, but it doesn't change anything, does it? Mark is still dead, and my husband still wants a divorce."

Ed Franklin picked up his pen again.

"I'd like very much to represent you in this matter, Mrs. Epstein."

Cherry Hill, New Jersey

It was just before noon, and Steven Kingsley was sitting in his walnut-paneled office, studying the check register in his computer. His balance didn't agree with the bank statement, and he'd just found the problem: a funds transfer had been entered twice in the register. When he heard a commotion in the lobby area of his restaurant, he lifted his head and listened for a moment. When the voices grew louder, he left his office and hurried toward the source of the altercation.

He saw his wife, Anne Marie, in her dark-gold velvet hostess gown, talking to a very angry woman wearing a full-length mink coat. A young teenaged girl, apparently her daughter, was crying.

"I'm Steven Kingsley. What seems to be the problem?"

"Are you the manager here?" demanded the irate woman.

"I'm the owner. Please tell me what's going on."

"My name is Ellen Stanford. I came here three weeks ago to arrange for a bridal shower for my older daughter. This woman . . ."—she paused to indicate the hostess—". . . accepted the reservation. She assured me that everything would be ready—the table would be set up, there would be an appropriate centerpiece, and I ordered a specific luncheon menu . . .”

She stopped speaking, shook her head, and took a deep breath. Her face was flushed with anger. Her voice had gone up an octave as she spoke, and her younger daughter was now sobbing.

“I *told* you we should have had it at the country club, Mom! Why wouldn’t you listen to me?”

Steven Kingsley, a handsome man with brush-cut gray hair, flung a worried glance at his wife.

“I haven’t heard yet what the problem is, Mrs. Stanford.”

“The problem is—the shower is set for one o’clock today. My younger daughter and I came a little early to decorate the private room we were promised.”

“And . . . ?” Steven prompted her.

“. . . and *nothing has been done!* This woman, the hostess, doesn’t seem to remember taking the reservation. In fact, she doesn’t seem to remember me at all. I simply cannot believe this is happening! I ordered a cake, chocolate with white frosting, to be inscribed ‘A Time for Love.’ ”

The younger daughter’s sobs were growing louder.

“Mr. Kingsley, twenty guests are supposed to arrive at twelve-thirty! My daughter and her fiancé will be here at one o’clock!

“I have a copy of the contract, as well as the receipt for the American Express card I used to pay for this shower! If everything is not provided—*just as I ordered it*—you are looking at one hell of an ugly lawsuit!”

Steven Kingsley smiled, but a muscle was twitching next to his left eye.

“Mrs. Stanford, if we fail to provide any part of the

promised services for your daughter's shower, there will be no charge for the event. Come with me now, and let me show you the private room where it will take place."

As he escorted the woman and her daughter through the restaurant, he called over his shoulder, "Anne Marie, I want you to go *immediately* to the kitchen and tell Anton to bake a chocolate cake, and to decorate it as Mrs. Stanford has just described."

"What did she say? About the cake, I mean?"

Steve smiled through gritted teeth.

"A chocolate cake, white icing, inscribed 'A Time for Love.' Got it?"

Anne Marie was close to tears.

"Yes, Steve."

For the next hour, as shower guests began to arrive, nearly every employee of the King's Feast worked feverishly to set up the room for twenty-three people with a white tablecloth and red napkins. Steve rush-ordered a centerpiece of red and white roses from a nearby florist which was picked up by his son Cliff, the assistant manager.

Anton, the dessert chef, had a dark chocolate cake in the oven. By the time the luncheon attendees were ready for dessert, it would be cooled and covered with white frosting; "A Time for Love," would be written in script with red gel.

Mrs. Stanford could not fault the speed and efficiency with which everything was accomplished. Steve Kingsley rewrote the luncheon menu, with her concurrence, making a few changes dictated by the food items available that day in the kitchen.

By one-ten, when the bride-to-be arrived with her future husband, everything was in readiness and Mrs. Stanford and her younger daughter were both beaming.

⋆ ⋆ ⋆ ⋆ ⋆

Steve retired to his office and collapsed on one of the visitor chairs. He would not berate Anne Marie, in front of their employees, but when they left the restaurant tonight he needed to have a serious talk with her. This was not the first time she had neglected to write down a reservation in the book, but it was certainly her most disastrous memory lapse to date. He wondered if the hostess job was too stressful for his sweet, gentle wife. He'd been thinking about hiring a second hostess to eliminate some of the pressure. Perhaps the time had come to take action.

He picked up a copy of today's *Camden County Courier-Post*, and glanced at the Situations Wanted. One ad attracted his interest. It read:

RESTAURANT HOSTESS: 10 years experience. Attractive, reliable.

Will consider 5-star establishment only. Salary negotiable.

There was a telephone number listed at the bottom of the ad. Steve Kingsley picked up his office phone and dialed.

CHAPTER 2

New York City: One Year Later

"How does your fiancé feel about your working for a divorce lawyer?" Serena asked. Her silver-gray eyes regarded the receptionist with warm curiosity.

Penny laughed.

"It doesn't seem to bother him," she said. "He knows I make a good salary, and that has a very soothing effect."

They both laughed.

Their conversation stopped abruptly when they heard voices raised in anger coming from Ed Franklin's office. The decibel level increased, and Serena recognized Ed's normally deep voice. It was an octave higher than usual. And loud.

The other voice belonged to a woman.

"Is that a client in there with Ed?" she asked at last.

"No, it's his ex-wife," Penny told her. "She's a real bitch."

Because Ed never talked about himself, Serena hadn't known he was divorced.

"How long have they been apart?" she asked.

"I never asked him. I've been with him for five years, so it's been at least that long."

They both winced when they heard Ed's ex-wife's coloratura screech: "Well, I hope you don't think you're coming to the reception!"

And Ed's baritone roar: "Since I'm paying for it, I'll goddam well come if I feel like it!"

Both women were startled when Ed's office door burst open, and a small skinny woman flounced into the reception area on high-heeled sling pumps. Her beige wool suit was perfectly tailored, but the color had been a poor choice. It did little to enhance her saffron complexion. Her cheeks were mottled with mauve spots, evidently flushed out by the argument. Her hair, dyed black, boasted a white streak down the middle. It looked like a skunk pelt resting on her head.

Without glancing at Penny or Serena, she opened the outer door and slammed it behind her so hard that the Kleenex box on Penny's desk jumped. Moments later, Ed appeared in his office doorway and smiled apologetically at them both.

"Sorry you had to hear that. Even when she was younger, Margaret was never a runner-up for Miss Congeniality."

He held the office door open. "Would you like to come in now, Serena?"

When she was seated in front of his desk, she asked anxiously, "Are you all right, Ed?"

"Yes, I really am. I—ah—would you mind terribly if I smoked a cigarette?"

"Go right ahead, if you think it will help. I know from experience how nerve-wracking an exchange like that can be."

"The good news is that I seldom see my ex-wife anymore." He withdrew a cigarette from a pack on his desk. "She's another man's problem now."

"Someone else married her?"

Embarrassed, she realized she had not edited the amazement out of her question.

Ed Franklin laughed.

"I know. It surprises me too. Every day I thank God for sending Stuart Rhodes to break up my happy home."

Again, Serena could not conceal her surprise.

"*She* asked for the divorce?"

He chuckled. "Yep. I was the cuckolded husband. She claimed I was never home, so she found a more constant companion on the golf course at our country club. I had the good sense to let her divorce me seven years ago."

She smiled shyly. "I'll bet she regrets it sometimes."

"The only thing she regrets is that I'm going to walk down the aisle with my daughter when she gets married next month. She wanted Stuart to do it, but Phyllis is Daddy's girl. She wants me. Margaret was hoping I'd say no, but of course I said I would. That's what the argument was about."

"I didn't know you had a daughter," said Serena.

"Yes, Margaret's a mother hen with one chick. Phyllis is—ah—petite, like her mother. She's thirty-one years old, a very nice girl but not a beauty, and I think Margaret was afraid she'd never find a husband."

"I hope she's found herself a good man."

"His name is Chester Abbott—he's a pharmacologist."

Serena nodded, and Ed cleared his throat and picked up her folder from his desk.

"Enough distractions for one morning! You asked to see me today, so you have the floor now."

"Yes." She looked down at her ringless left hand. "Ed, I'm at the end of my rope with this divorce. Why is it taking so long?"

"Your husband and his attorney are unwilling to give you any of the concessions we've asked for. As you know, you and Mr. Epstein acquired a lot of valuable items during your marriage—houses, cars, a boat, investments—and you are entitled to a share of all of that. I have been fighting for your right to receive them in the settlement."

Serena leaned forward in her chair.

"I know what you've been doing. I'm not faulting you, Ed! You're an excellent lawyer, but not one of those 'valuable items' you mentioned means anything to me since Mark died."

Ed got up from his desk and seated himself in the second visitor's chair next to hers.

"That sounds very brave, my dear, and I know you mean every word you're saying, but I'm concerned about your future. How do you expect to survive without any money?"

Serena lifted her chin.

"I may be fifty-three years old, but I'm not afraid of work. My parents, may they rest in peace, owned a restaurant in Brooklyn at one time. During my teenage years, I worked in that restaurant every weekend. I'm a good cook, I know how to order food and supplies. *I know the business.* I'd like to open my own little restaurant."

"You need money in order to open a restaurant, Serena," Ed advised her patiently. "Even a little one."

She smiled. A small, secret smile.

"My parents left me some money. Burt can't touch it. I can use that to buy a place and get it going."

"But you haven't been a teenager for—quite a while," Ed reminded her, frowning a bit. She hadn't mentioned the inheritance before today.

"You've been living as the wife of a corporate executive for—how many years?"

"Thirty years."

"Running a restaurant is hard work. Do you really feel able to take on so much responsibility?"

"Ed, *I'm looking forward to it!* My life has been a living hell for the past year and a half. Burt refuses to move out of our house, and he treats me like a piece of furniture. He sleeps in Mark's old room, and sometimes he brings women home and has sex with them there. He won't talk to me about anything, and if I try to say something to him he just says, 'Tell your lawyer to speak to my lawyer.' I just can't take it anymore!"

Her voice broke, and she started to cry.

"Let him have everything! I don't care! I just want it to be over with!"

Ed's face revealed the distress he felt, hearing about her wretched life.

"You realize, don't you, that Burt has been doing these things deliberately, trying to wear you down? Do you really want to let him win?"

Another small smile. A weary one this time.

"Ed, neither of us can 'win,' because we both lost our son. If it eases Burt's pain to keep all our possessions, let him have them."

"As your attorney, I must advise you against doing this, Serena! I'm deeply troubled about you."

"Don't be. I know what I'm doing."

Ed moved his chair so that he was almost facing her. His left knee was touching her right knee.

"I just want to make certain you understand that you could regret your decision in the years ahead. And it will then be difficult, if not impossible, to reverse it."

"This is what I want to do. I will not change my mind. And I promise you, I will not regret my decision."

Ed took both her cold hands into his warm ones, and looked into her huge silver-gray eyes.

"In all my thirty-five years of practicing divorce law, I

have never met a wife like you, Serena. If this is what you are determined to do, I will accede to your wishes."

Cherry Hill, New Jersey

"I want you to fire her, and I want you to fire her right now!" shouted Anne Marie. She stood in her husband's walnut-paneled office in a new hostess gown. This one was the color of ripe apricots.

Steven Kingsley knew enough to keep his voice quiet, low-pitched. Shouting back would only fuel the disagreement.

"I have no grounds to fire Juliette. She's performing all her duties quite well."

"Better than me?"

Her big brown eyes, filled with tears, were pleading now. He could feel a crushing ache in the vicinity of his heart as he prepared to answer her question with a lie.

"No, of course not! I only hired her to help you out, honey, because the job got to be too much for one person."

"I used to do it by myself."

"Our business has grown a lot in the last two years. Hey, that's why we had to move to a bigger place!"

"A bigger place . . . ?" Anne Marie echoed.

"Sure. Six months ago we moved *here,* honey. Don't you remember?"

A vacant stare from the big brown eyes told him she didn't remember. He tried to close the discussion.

"*So.* That's why we need Juliette. To help you out."

As soon as she heard the woman's name, it was as if he'd set off a fire alarm.

"She's not helping me out, she's trying to take my job! I

see how she looks at you! And you're sleeping with her, I know you are!"

His wife was screaming now, and Steve gritted his teeth. It took all his self-control to keep from raising his own voice, but he knew he had to remain calm if he was going to succeed in allaying her fears.

"Why would I sleep with her—or any other woman—when I already have the prettiest girl in town?" he asked. He walked around his desk and tried to put his arms around her. She pushed him away.

"You're lying! I want her out of here *today!*"

It was nearly three o'clock, but there were still a few customers in the restaurant lingering over a late lunch. His office was near the lobby, and he didn't know whether those customers could hear what his wife was saying, but he did know he had to think of some way to resolve this escalating problem.

Anne Marie had hated Juliette at first sight. Mostly, he realized, because Juliette was tall, with an abundance of curly red hair, and a shape that looked like a centerfold for *Playboy.* The hostess gowns she chose were designed to showcase her lush body.

Steve had never touched that lush body. He had never called her *honey* or *doll,* or in any other way indicated that he was interested in her sexually.

Juliette, on the other hand, found a dozen reasons every day to squeeze past him, touch his arm or his hand, and gaze at him through the thick lashes that fringed her green eyes. He had made a decision not to dignify the situation by speaking to her about it. *Stop touching me and giving me the eye!* How ridiculous would that sound, coming from the boss? He noticed that she played up to male customers who came in alone or with a group of men, and concluded that she was just a born flirt. It probably meant nothing.

"I have never been unfaithful to you, Anne Marie," he said softly. "You should know by now how much I love you!"

"If you love me so much, you'll fire Juliette," she insisted, but her lowered voice told him she had heard his declaration of love.

When she went to the ladies' room to repair her makeup, Steve called their family doctor. He described what had just transpired, along with other incidents over the past year.

"Why don't you bring her in to see me, Steve?" Dr. Wolf suggested.

"Can I bring her right now?"

"Yes, bring her this afternoon. I'll tell my receptionist to expect her."

When Anne Marie returned from the ladies' room, Steve was holding her coat.

"Where are we going?" she wanted to know.

"I'm taking you to see Dr. Wolf. I'm worried about you, honey. You're stressed and over-tired. I think you need a physical examination."

Her pretty face puckered in a frown.

"I'm not sick."

"You haven't had a physical in—what? Maybe five years?"

"I guess it has been that long, but I feel okay. Really I do!"

"As you get older, it's a good idea to let a doctor look you over at least once a year."

"I'm only fifty-three. That's not old."

"No, it's not," Steve agreed as they walked out to the parking lot. "This is just a precaution."

* * * * *

It was a sparkling cold winter day. Sunshine reflecting off the snow banks along the road made the sky seem bluer and their Cadillac whiter, as Steve drove them to the doctor's office on Main Street in Moorestown.

The receptionist invited Anne Marie to enter the inner sanctum as soon as they walked into the waiting room, a courtesy that did not go unnoticed by the fifteen or so other patients assembled there. After the door closed behind her, they continued to direct dirty looks at Steve. He ignored them, removed his coat, and picked up a copy of *People* magazine.

Half an hour later Dr. Wolf appeared in the doorway and beckoned to him. Steve tossed aside the magazine and hurried inside. He followed the physician into his office.

"Where's Anne Marie?" he asked.

"Still in the examining room. Getting dressed by now, I would imagine. I wanted to talk to you alone."

"Why?" Steve's heart began beating faster. *Brain tumor?* Would that explain her continuing erratic behavior, her pathological jealousy? Maybe even the memory lapses? Would she need surgery?

"What is it, doc? What's wrong with my wife?"

"Her vital signs are good, Steve. She needs to have some more tests. I want to rule out a couple of villains before I make a diagnosis."

"Do you think she has a brain tumor?"

"Probably not."

"So what kind of villains are we talking about?"

"I'll know more after I see the test results."

CHAPTER 3

Brooklyn, New York: Six Months Later

Serena's Kitchen

Serena stepped back on the sidewalk to admire the freshly painted sign on the front of her newly renovated restaurant. Above the sign was a blue-and-white banner proclaiming that tonight was the Grand Opening.

Blue-and-white-checked gingham café curtains hung in the windows. Inside, eight booths and eight tables stood on a brand-new floor tiled with white vinyl. The kitchen, visible from the dining area via a wide pass-through, was spotless and filled with stainless steel equipment for storing and cooking food.

She had hired two waitresses, Mimi and Angela—local women. She would do the cooking herself.

The little restaurant was in the same Flatbush neighborhood where Serena had been born and raised. The first customers, who arrived just after five o'clock, were elderly people who had been her parents' friends. She greeted each one with a hug.

By seven o'clock nearly every table was occupied. Serena was busy in the kitchen filling the orders as they came in when Angela appeared and announced, "There's some old guy out there who said to tell you hello."

"Probably another one of my parents' friends," Serena guessed. She was stirring a pot of spaghetti sauce and browning meatballs in an iron skillet. A huge pot of water was simmering just under a boil on a back burner, awaiting whatever variety of pasta she chose to drop into it.

Angela shook her head.

"I don't think so. This guy is wearing a business suit that prob'ly cost more than my house, know what I mean?"

Serena walked to the pass-through and peered into the dining area. "Point him out to me," she said. Angela pointed, and Serena squealed.

"Oh my God, it's Ed Franklin!"

She darted out of the kitchen, and Ed stood up when he saw her approaching.

"Looks like I'll have to take back all my caveats," he told her, smiling broadly. "This vegetable lasagna is the best I've ever tasted—and judging by the size of the crowd, I'm not the only one who feels that way!"

She blushed and said, "I'm glad you're enjoying your dinner. It was nice of you to come for my grand opening."

It occurred to her that driving through rush-hour traffic from Manhattan to Brooklyn had probably not been an enjoyable experience.

"I wouldn't have missed it." He pointed to the empty chair opposite his. "I don't suppose you could sneak out here and have dessert and coffee with me . . . ?"

She shook her head.

"Fraid not. I have to get back in the kitchen. But please come back anytime, Ed, you'll always be welcome."

Later, when he asked for the check, Angela told him "the boss" had said his dinner was on the house. He scowled, and left a fifty-dollar bill on the table. Angela marched into the kitchen, holding the bill between her thumb and forefinger as if expecting it to disintegrate at any moment, and asked Serena what she should do with it.

"Keep it. You deserve it," Serena told her.

"It's too much! Let's split it."

"If you don't want to keep it yourself, why don't you buy something for your kids?"

Cherry Hill, New Jersey

On the Monday following their office visit, Dr. Wolf called and asked Steve to come to his office alone. He thought he'd been prepared for anything: Parkinson's, cancer, coronary artery disease. Anything except the two words the doctor pronounced.

Early Alzheimer's.

When Dr. Wolf warned him her short-term memory problems and erratic behavior would get worse, Steve was forced to make an agonizing decision. It would not be possible for him to let her continue working at the restaurant.

If he told her to check the salad bar, she would come back to the office two minutes later and asked him what he had told her to do. Or worse, she would forget that he had told her to do anything, and he would be unaware that the salad bar was not properly stocked until customers began to complain that there was no more lettuce—or cucumbers—or cottage cheese.

The reservation book was another fiasco. She would take a dozen reservations on the phone and forget to write them into the book. Then, when the parties arrived and had to wait a half hour or more for a table, they complained—or opted to go elsewhere.

Telling his wife that she could not be the hostess anymore had been one of the hardest things he had ever done in his life. She had cried, promised to do better, begged for another chance—but he had remained firm. He knew she was no longer employable, even in her own husband's restaurant.

And just as she had feared, Juliette took over her job, and was performing efficiently.

After the first few days of enforced retirement, Anne Marie had started driving to the restaurant around lunchtime every day wearing one of her hostess gowns and trying to resume her former duties. That was when he had taken away her car keys. Then she began arriving by taxi every day, and he had to ask Cliff to drive her home. He knew it wasn't fair to Cliff to use him as a chauffeur, but he could not allow her to remain in the restaurant. She argued with Steve and fought with Juliette, creating embarrassing scenes in the office, the kitchen, and the dining room.

Beverly, one of his waitresses, suggested that Anne Marie might be lonely.

"You're in here every day by ten or eleven in the morning, and you hardly ever get home before midnight," she pointed out. "Cliff and Lisa both work, and your daughter-in-law, too. Why don't you hire a nurse, or a companion? Someone to look after her and keep her company?"

Steve thought it was an excellent idea. He called an agency that specialized in home care. The woman he spoke to suggested he come in and interview several applicants.

Late that morning, while Cliff was driving his mother back to Moorestown, Steve drove to the agency in Cherry Hill and interviewed three women—two LPNs and a nurse's aide. All three were in their early forties, a bit younger than Anne Marie. All three were personable, and had experience working with Alzheimer's patients. He chose a pleasant woman named Vivian. She was not pretty enough to make Anne Marie jealous, and she seemed capable and mature. He explained that it would be a "live-in" job, that she would have her own room and adjoining bath, and asked if she could start immediately.

The following morning, Friday, Vivian was there at nine o'clock with her luggage. Steve introduced her to Anne Marie and explained that this woman was here to keep her company. He did not mention that she was also a nurse.

Anne Marie glared at her.

"I don't need anyone to keep me company. What I need is my hostess job at the restaurant. Everything would be okay if you would simply fire the slut and give me back my job."

He gave Vivian a despairing look, and said to his wife, "Now, Anne Marie, we've talked about this before. That job got to be too much for you, remember?"

"No, I was fine." She turned to the nurse and said, "I used to be the hostess at his restaurant. I used to wear pretty dresses every day and greet all the customers. And then he hired some girl who looks like a *Playboy* Bunny to take over my job."

"Dammit, that's not the way it happened!" Steve exploded. He didn't want the nurse to think he was some kind of lecherous old goat.

"Why don't you go on to work, Mr. Kingsley," said Vivian soothingly. "Your wife and I need time to get acquainted. Please don't worry."

He kissed Anne Marie, and as he walked out the door he heard Vivian say, "Do you like to play cards?"

And Anne Marie answered, "No, I like to play hostess."

He'd warned Vivian that he rarely got home before midnight, and that he would appreciate her remaining awake until he got home even if Anne Marie was asleep.

When he unlocked the door that night at eleven forty-five, Anne Marie was sleeping soundly and the nurse was in the TV room watching Jay Leno.

"How'd everything go today?" he asked.

"Pretty well, I guess, for the first day. Your wife kept asking me to drive her down to your restaurant, but I told her I couldn't do that."

He nodded.

"So what did you do all day? Play cards?"

"No, we watched television. We took a little walk."

"Did you have any problems with her?" he asked anxiously. She didn't sound very enthusiastic, and he was afraid she might be ready to quit. After one day.

"No, sir. Don't worry. She just has to get used to me."

The next day, Saturday, was exceptionally busy. There were two bridal showers in the afternoon, a baby shower and a retirement dinner in the evening—besides their regular customers. Steve even thought about taking a taxi home from the restaurant himself, because he was so exhausted by the end of the evening.

His son Cliff, who had stayed to help him lock up the building, said, "Let me drive you home, Dad. You're dead on your feet."

"It's out of your way. You'd have to double back to Delran."

"Please, Dad. I really don't mind."

He finally consented, and fell asleep in the car on the way to Moorestown. When Cliff's car pulled into the driveway just before one o'clock, he said, "You better wake up, Dad. The front door of the house is standing wide open."

"*What?*" Steve was instantly awake, and both men raced into the house.

Vivian was sound asleep in the TV room. When they woke her up, she was embarrassed and defensive.

"I was awake. I must've just dozed off for a few minutes," she muttered, blinking as she stumbled to her feet.

All three of them hurried upstairs to make sure Anne Marie was asleep in her bed. She was not there, nor was she in any of the other bedrooms.

"Jesus Christ!" shouted Steve. "Where the hell could she have gone?"

They searched the entire house from top to bottom. Anne Marie was not there.

"Maybe she was kidnapped," said Cliff. "I think we should call the police."

Just then there was a knock on the front door, which was still standing open. They dashed into the front hall and found a stranger standing there with Anne Marie. She was barefoot, but wrapped in a blanket.

"My name is Horace Ewing," said the stranger. "I live on the next block. I was out walking my dog before bedtime, and I found this lady in front of my house without any clothes on. I went inside and got a blanket for her. I was pretty sure this was where she lives. You own that restaurant in Cherry Hill, right?"

"Yeah. Right." Steve was simultaneously relieved, appalled, and miserable.

He stared at his wife, who had dropped the blanket and was strolling into the living room, completely naked. Vivian hurried after her and tried to head her toward the stairs. Steve handed the blanket back to the good Samaritan.

"Uh—hey, thank you, Mr. Ewing. We were just about

ready to call the police." He lowered his voice. "She has Alzheimer's disease."

Horace Ewing seemed shocked.

"She looks too young for Alzheimer's!"

Steve nodded. "When the doctor told me, I said the same thing."

All three of them could hear Anne Marie arguing with Vivian when they reached the top of the stairs.

"Where is my hostess gown?" she shouted. "I have to get dressed for work."

After the door closed behind Horace Ewing, Steve turned to Cliff with tears in his eyes.

"Son, what am I going to do about your mom?"

CHAPTER 4

Lawrenceville, New Jersey

Steve watched his wife in the rearview mirror, sitting in the back seat of the white Cadillac between her son and daughter, as he pulled his car into the circular driveway of the group of buildings known as Tall Pines. Azaleas, impatiens, and pansies bloomed in the center of the circle. It was a nursing home cheerfully disguised as a resort hotel.

Anne Marie was crying like a little girl.

"I want to go home! I don't want to stay in this place! I won't come to the restaurant anymore, I promise! *Please, please, just let me go home!*"

Steve, behind the wheel, was sweating profusely although the weather was cool for early June. Now that they were actually here, he wasn't sure he could go through with his decision. He looked over his shoulder at Cliff and Lisa. They were both crying, too.

"Shit," he said under his breath. He was going to have to be the bad guy, the bastard who put his wife in a nursing home.

He and Anne Marie had been high-school sweethearts. There had been strenuous opposition from both families when they began to date. His family was Jewish and devoutly religious; hers was Italian and devoutly Catholic. Sort of a Tuscan rewrite of *Abie's Irish Rose.*

He'd never forget how proud he'd been the night he took her to the senior prom. She'd looked like a movie star in her pink chiffon dress, wearing his pink camellias on her wrist—and guarding their secret within her womb.

Later, when her family learned that Anne Marie was pregnant, they had insisted on the wedding which took place two weeks after graduation, at St. Andrew's church. Steve did not agree to convert to Catholicism; therefore, the couple knelt in front of the altar rail—not behind it—to repeat their marriage vows. No one on Steve's side of the family had attended the nuptials. Instead, on the day of the wedding his parents had begun sitting *shivah,* seven days of mourning for their son, who was now "dead" to them.

When Cliff was two years old, Steve and Anne Marie had taken the child one Sunday to visit his paternal grandparents. Cliff had been a handsome little boy, dark-haired and rosy-cheeked, and Anne Marie had dressed him in a sailor suit. Steve had hoped the sight of a beautiful little grandson would soften their hearts.

Steve's father opened the front door, and when he saw who was standing on the doorstep he said, "To the wrong house you come." He closed the door. And Steve never knew whether his mother found out they had been there. He had not tried again to reconcile with his family. Both his parents passed away a few years later, before Anne Marie gave birth to Lisa, their second child.

Without the Catholic Church's approval, Steve raised his son in the Jewish faith, but allowed him to accompany his mom occasionally when she went to church. Those occasions were usually special holidays, like Christmas or Easter. When Lisa was born, Anne Marie stated that she should be brought up in *her* faith, and Steve agreed. It seemed like a fair compromise.

Two years before Lisa was born, Cliff made his Bar

Mitzvah. When he was twenty-two, he had attended his little sister's First Holy Communion.

If there is a God, Steve mused, He must have a quirky sense of humor. His son Cliff had dated a bevy of beautiful Jewish girls while he was a student at Cornell University's School of Food Service Management. When he flunked out of college after one year, Steve had given him a job as his assistant at the King's Feast. Later, Cliff fell in love with Cheryl O'Keefe, a petite blonde from an Irish Catholic background who worked as a hairdresser at a little beauty shop in Delran. Like his parents, Cliff and Cheryl were married in St. Andrew's church. In front of the altar rail.

Steve and his wife had been through a lot together, and neither of them had ever regretted that they married each other. In fact, he'd always thought their marriage had been specially blessed—until that terrible day when she'd been diagnosed with Alzheimer's.

He didn't know how he was going to live without her. On the other hand, he didn't know how he could have continued to live *with* her. Alzheimer's disease had crept into Anne Marie's mind and stolen his wife. He would have paid any ransom to get her back, but in his heart he knew that the sweet, gentle girl he'd married was gone forever.

Two white-coated attendants emerged from the administration building to escort Anne Marie to her new living quarters. "Escort" was a euphemism. She continued to look over her shoulder, weeping and pleading, as she was led away. The administrator had advised him against prolonging the pain of separation by going with her to her room on the first day. When she disappeared inside the building, Steve put his head down on the steering wheel and cried along with his two children.

Brooklyn, New York

"He's here again," Angela told Serena breathlessly. "I swear he likes you."

Serena laughed, and gently turned over the last breaded veal cutlet in a pan of bubbling olive oil.

"He likes my cooking, that's all."

"Maybe he likes the cooking, yeah, but he likes the *cook,* too!"

Angela emphasized her last words with a particularly Italian gesture, made by putting her thumb and other four fingers together to form a point, and bobbing it up and down in front of Serena's face.

"Okay, I hear you! Take him his soup now, Angela, and stop trying to play cupid."

After the waitress hurried away with a bowl of escarole soup, Serena stepped over to the pass-through and peeked out at Ed Franklin, sitting in a booth by himself with his *Wall Street Journal.* If she bet a million dollars that he was her only customer who read the *Wall Street Journal* while he was eating his dinner, she knew she would win the bet.

He looked up and caught her watching him; he grinned and beckoned. After she removed the veal cutlets from the pan, she left them to drain and made her way to his booth—hoping she didn't reek of garlic and oregano.

"So how's the soup?"

"Delicious. Can you sit down for *one minute?* I have something to ask you."

She slipped into the booth, facing him, and said, "Okay, I'm sitting. You have forty-five seconds left."

"You've been feeding me several times a week since you opened the restaurant. The restaurant is closed on Mondays, am I right?"

"Yes, you're right. Was that the question you wanted to ask me?"

"Serena, I'd like to take you to dinner next Monday night."

She felt herself blushing with pleasure.

"I'd like that. Letting someone else do the cooking!"

"I don't know where you're living. Where shall I pick you up?"

"Right here. There's an apartment above the restaurant, and that's where I live." She laughed at his astonished expression. "Think of all the money I save on commuting to work!"

"May I pick you up around six? Is that too early?"

"No, six would be perfect. I'll see you then."

She slid out of the booth and hurried back to the kitchen, where Angela was waiting to pounce on her.

"He ast you out, right?"

"What are you now, a gossip columnist?" asked Serena.

"Don't gimme that. I bet he ast you out."

Serena's smile and telltale blush was her answer.

"See? What'd I tell you? I told you he likes you!"

Her first date in thirty years! What to wear? It was early June, the weather was pleasantly cool, and she had plenty of clothes to choose from, souvenirs of her former life with Burt Epstein. She was almost sure they'd be dining in Manhattan, so she selected a black linen suit, and black alligator pumps with a matching bag. To soften the monochrome look she wore a petal-pink silk blouse with a décolleté neckline, and pink opal earrings.

"You look lovely, Serena," Ed told her when she came down the steps from her second-floor apartment to meet him. He took her arm while they walked to the curb where his dark-blue Lexus was waiting. As he held the door for her, she wondered whether Angela was watching through binoculars from her two-family house across the street. The thought made her smile, and Ed—seeing it—smiled back.

As the Lexus moved slowly across the Williamsburg Bridge, Serena inclined her head to gaze at the island of Manhattan in twilight. She felt Ed watching her.

"Do you ever hear from your ex-husband?" he asked suddenly.

She turned back to face him, eyes twinkling.

"Funny you should ask. I heard from him today; he called to invite me to his wedding."

Ed almost drove off the bridge into the East River.

"His *what?* Did you say wedding?"

"Yes, I knew you'd be shocked . . . the ink is still damp on the divorce decree."

He glanced quickly at her hands, and saw only a ruby ring on her right hand.

"You once told me you were going to give him back your wedding band and engagement ring, and remember? I told you not to do it. I'll bet you did it anyway."

"Yes, I did. But don't worry. Burt is environmentally aware. *He's recycling them.* I think that was the real reason he called. He knew I would never come to the wedding."

"Are you sitting there telling me he is using *your* engagement ring and *your* wedding band for the second Mrs. Epstein?"

She nodded. "They're gorgeous rings. Why put them in a safety-deposit box?"

"Dammit, Serena, you should've kept them!"

"They meant something to me once, Ed. They don't anymore. I would never have worn them again."

Ed shook his head.

"You never fail to amaze me, my dear. So who gave you the ruby ring you're wearing tonight?"

"My parents. For high-school graduation. The ruby is my birthstone."

After a long moment of silence, Ed burst out, "Doesn't it make you just a little bit angry to think of another woman wearing the rings he bought for you?"

"Angry? No, I don't think so. How could I be angry at a woman I don't even know? And I'm sure Burt didn't tell her the truth about where the rings came from."

"Maybe you should tell her!" Ed was still outraged.

"But I won't."

"Perhaps you believe God will punish your husband?" Ed suggested, obviously trying to make sense out of beliefs and values that he did not share.

"I don't believe in God. I stopped believing the day my son died."

Beside her, Ed's profile was a grim silhouette in the deepening dusk. She raised her eyes and saw the first star in the evening sky above them.

"Let's talk about something else," he murmured, sounding angry. "I owe you an apology for bringing up an unpleasant subject."

"Good evening, Mr. Franklin! Your table is ready," the maitre d' exclaimed, bowing to Serena before leading them to an alcove where a table was set for two and a magnum of champagne rested in an ice bucket.

While she was married to Burton Epstein, Serena had dined in many of New York's finest restaurants, but tonight was her first visit to Lutece.

Their waiter was as obsequious as the maitre d'.

"May I suggest the seared lobster for you and your exquisite lady, sir?" he asked, bowing to Serena.

She stifled an overwhelming urge to laugh. If this waiter could have seen Ed's "exquisite lady" twenty-four hours ago, ladling mushroom sauce over fettuccine noodles and squirting whipped cream on saucers of strawberry Jello, she was sure the sight would have brought on cardiac arrest.

"I'll have the seared lobster, Heinz." Ed closed the menu. "Shall we make it two, my dear?"

"Certainly," she agreed. Then, unable to resist her devilish impulse, she widened her eyes and added, "I never knew Sears sold lobsters!"

Heinz directed a disdainful stare at an area just above her left shoulder, seized the menus, and stalked away to the kitchen. As soon as he was gone, Serena released a howl of laughter. Ed smiled, looking a little bewildered.

"Oh," she cried, wiping her eyes on the damask napkin, "if only I'd had a camera!"

Now understanding that she'd made some sort of joke, Ed joined in the laughter.

CHAPTER 5

Two hours later they were back in Ed's dark-blue Lexus, traveling east along Fiftieth Street. Ed put his hand over hers and squeezed it gently.

"Did you enjoy your dinner?"

"I loved every forkful of that lobster. And that baked Alaska we had for dessert . . . it just melted in my mouth!"

"A dessert made with ice cream is supposed to do that," Ed remarked solemnly.

"Ed! You made a joke! You're getting to be a regular Robin Williams!"

"Robin Williams has nothing to fear from me," he answered, but she could tell he was pleased with himself.

"My co-op is a few blocks from here. Would you like to go there for an after-dinner drink, or would you prefer 21?"

Serena had been to 21 many times with Burt.

"I'd like to see where you live," she answered at once. "What do they call it? A bachelor pad?"

He grinned.

"My place would more likely be called a Spartan pad," Ed confessed.

Another little joke! Serena was enchanted and clapped her hands. "I can hardly wait to see the Spartan pad! Does it have Greek columns?"

Ed frowned thoughtfully.

"Maybe a couple, downstairs in the lobby."

When they got on the elevator in his building and he

pressed the P button, she asked, "Does the 'P' stand for Pad?"

He chuckled. "Actually, it's for Penthouse."

It was a beautiful apartment on the twenty-first floor: living room, dining room, kitchen, three bedrooms, three and a half baths, and a wraparound balcony.

The apartment owed its Spartan appellation to the fact that there was almost no furniture. A king-sized bed in the master bedroom and a television set. His underwear, sweaters, and socks were stored on shelves in one of the closets. Another bedroom had become his library; it boasted a desk, chair, and computer—plus bookshelves holding more than a thousand books. In the living room were a leather recliner, a floor lamp—and another television set, the kind you might see in a sports bar. The kitchen was equipped with state-of-the-art appliances and a tiny table with two chairs.

"So. What do you think?" he wanted to know.

"The apartment is gorgeous. The view is magnificent!"

"How about the furniture?"

She giggled. "How long did you say you've lived here?"

"Seven years. Almost eight."

"When you got your divorce, didn't Margaret let you take anything except your law books?"

"Yes, she let me take that leather recliner, because she'd always hated it. But how would you characterize the whole place?"

She giggled again. "A work in progress."

He grinned. "I asked for that, didn't I?"

He poured a small snifter of apricot brandy for each of them. They walked out onto the balcony and stood looking at the diamond-studded view of Manhattan at night.

"How would you like to take on the job?" he asked, gesturing over his shoulder at the apartment behind them.

"What job?"

"Furnishing my apartment."

"You must be kidding! I'm not a decorator."

"I know that, but you're a woman with extraordinarily good taste. Look how you renovated that restaurant of yours!"

She really laughed then.

"Are you telling me you want blue-and-white gingham café curtains and a plastic booth in your dining room?"

"Of course not. But I doubt that's what you would choose."

She sobered a bit. "No. But you could hire an interior decorator to make all these decisions. You don't need me!"

"You're wrong about that, Serena. I do need you. I know I'm a pedantic sort of man, and perhaps that's why I enjoy your company so much. You're like no woman I've ever known before. You're kind, you're cheerful, and I wish I had your irrepressible sense of humor. When I'm with you, I feel optimistic about the rest of my life. That's why I'd like to share it with you."

Serena took a gulp of apricot brandy and stared at him. "Ed, are you asking me to . . ."

"Yes, my dear, I'm asking you to marry me. I think I fell in love with you that first day you came into my office. You looked so lovely, and so very sad. I remember thinking I'd like to teach you how to smile again, because when you do, your smile could light up this entire city."

He waved at the glittering panorama below his balcony.

When he put down his snifter on the wide cement railing, she saw that his hand was trembling. He took her drink out of her hand and placed it next to his.

He held out his arms. Still in a trance, she moved forward until they closed around her.

"Ed, we hardly know each other," she whispered.

"I know all I need to know about you, my dear. What do you want to know about me?"

"Well, for starters, how old are you?"

"I'm fifty-six . . . three years your senior."

"What kind of name is Franklin—English?"

"Yes, my father was of English extraction, my mother's family was Dutch."

"I guess that means you're Protestant, right?"

"Yes. I was raised as a Presbyterian, but I rarely attend church services. What about you?"

"I guess I'm what you'd call a half-breed. My father was Italian, Dominic D'Agostino, and my mother was Jewish. Her maiden name was Miriam Singer. I was born in Brooklyn—Flatbush—and that's where I grew up. That's why I opened my restaurant there."

"Your parents' marriage must have raised quite a few eyebrows, particularly since it took place more than half a century ago when mixed marriages were less commonplace than they are today."

She smiled. "Eyebrows may have been raised, but voices were raised higher than eyebrows. Mom told me there was a lot of yelling and foot-stomping, but eventually both families learned to get along okay. I had two sets of loving grandparents, growing up. That doesn't always happen, you know, in a mixed marriage."

"Were you brought up as a Catholic or a Jew?" he asked.

"In the Jewish religion, it is believed that the mother's religion should prevail, so my brother and I were raised in the Jewish faith."

She stopped and smiled, reminiscing.

"Some years, when Christmas and Hanukkah were celebrated at the same time, we had a Christmas tree in the corner of the living room and a Menorah on the windowsill."

"Does your brother still live in Brooklyn?"

A shadow passed over her face.

"Jerome was a few years older. He died in Vietnam when he was twenty-one. I was a teenager."

"I'm so sorry. Your parents . . . are they still living?"

She shook her head. "They were never the same after Jerry died. My mother was still alive when Mark was born, though. She was crazy about that child! Thank God she didn't live to see *him* die at twenty-one."

Ed pressed her closer. She lifted her face for his kiss. He pressed his lips to hers briefly, then laid his cheek against her hair.

"I haven't heard you say you'll marry me."

The top of her head felt like a launch pad for rockets. She remembered laughing at old black-and-white movies she'd seen in which the heroine listens to a marriage proposal and twitters, *Oh! This is so sudden!* She'd never laugh at such movies again, because that's exactly what she felt like saying at this moment.

Instead, she asked, "What about my little restaurant?"

"You could keep it and hire someone else to run it if that's what you want to do. Or you could sell it, and put the money in certificates of deposit."

"Let me think about all this, okay? This past year and a half has been traumatic for me, Ed: losing my son, getting a divorce, starting a new business. I need a little more time to decide what I want to do about my future."

"Take all the time you need, my dear. You're worth waiting for."

Cherry Hill, New Jersey: Six Months Later

Steve trudged into the restaurant at eleven-thirty on a Tuesday morning. Dark circles underscored his eyes.

"Hi, Dad," said Cliff, coming out of the office.

"How many times do I have to tell you the salad bar should be set up and ready to go by eleven-thirty? It hasn't been set up yet!"

Some greeting. "The salad bar is Juliette's job," Cliff muttered. He and his father, both with alpha personalities, quarreled sometimes about work-related issues. These unsettling incidents seemed to occur more frequently since his mother had gone to live at Tall Pines.

Steve went into the office and shut the door. Cliff found him there five minutes later, sitting at his desk and staring into space. He seemed unaware of Cliff's presence.

"Hey, Dad. Did you go see Mom yesterday?"

"Don't I always go see Mom on Monday?"

"Yeah. So how is she? Was she glad to see you?"

"Now there's a stupid question! Of course she was glad to see me!"

Steve slid open the middle drawer of his desk and slammed it shut. "Is Juliette setting up the salad bar?"

"I guess she is."

"Don't guess. Go check it out."

Cliff opened the office door and started to leave, then turned back to face his father.

"Dad, how was Mom yesterday, really? Tell me the truth this time."

Steve stared back at his son and shook his head.

"She didn't know who I was."

Several days later, Steve went into the kitchen when he

arrived and found the food preparation tables rearranged.

"What the hell is going on here?" he shouted.

All activity ceased and in the silence that followed, one of the chefs answered, "Talk to Cliff. It was his idea."

Steve found his son in the storage room, taking inventory of their paper goods and other non-perishable items. "Cliff? *My office!*"

"I'm almost finished here, Dad. I'll be there in about ten minutes."

"When I tell you I want to see you in my office, I don't mean ten minutes from now!" Steve barked. "I mean *this minute!*"

"Dad, I've tried to overlook your bad moods lately because I understand how upset you are about Mom, but . . ."

"Mom has nothing to do with this. This is business! What the fuck is going on in my kitchen?"

A crimson flush stained Cliff's face. "I rearranged the tables to make the preparation process more efficient."

"And where did you get that half-assed idea?"

Cliff tightened his grip on the clipboard and took a step toward his father. His voice was low-pitched, but his eyes were shooting sparks.

"I got that *half-assed idea* from one of the courses I took at Cornell!"

Steve took a step toward his son.

"Are we talking about the Food Management course you flunked out of after only one year? I guess I should be happy that you remember anything you learned that year, after all the money I spent on your tuition! I may not have gone to Cornell University, but I think I know a little more about managing a restaurant than you do, sonny boy!"

Cliff gave up on restraint and shouted, "I'm not your

sonny boy, Dad, I'm thirty-four years old, and I think I deserve a little respect!"

"Oh, you do, do you? Well, I've got news for you! If you want my respect, you'll have to earn it!"

"I've taken just about enough shit from you, Dad! It was *your* idea for me to work here as your assistant, but you treat the busboys better than you treat me!"

"When I asked you to work here, I thought I was going to teach you how to run a restaurant, but instead of that, you keep trying to teach *me* how to run a restaurant!"

"I'm not trying to teach you how to run this place, Dad! I was trying to help you run it *better!*"

Steve's face was almost purple with rage.

"*Oh?* Poor old Dad's way isn't good enough anymore? It was good enough to pay for your fun-filled year at college, though, wasn't it?"

Cliff hurled the clipboard against the wall. It fell, clattering, to the floor.

"You know what, Dad? You and your fucking restaurant can both go to hell! I *quit,* effective right now!"

"You'll never get another job that pays you what I'm paying you, you snot-nosed kid!"

"Well, I'd rather clean toilets than work for you one more day, you son of a bitch!"

Ten minutes later, Cliff's yellow Porsche burned rubber as it left the King's Feast parking lot.

And in the walnut-paneled office he'd shared with Cliff for the past fifteen years, Steve sat behind his desk with tears rolling down his cheeks.

When Anne Marie was the hostess, she'd always known how to referee their arguments before they got to the second round. Today they'd gotten to round ten—and he, Steve, had been the loser.

CHAPTER 6

Cherry Hill, New Jersey: One Week Later

"Hello, Cheryl? Is Cliff there?" Steve sounded like a pre-adolescent boy whose voice is changing.

"Oh hi, Dad." A long moment passed. "I won't lie to you. Cliff is here, but he doesn't want to speak to you."

"Okay. I just wanted to make sure you and Cliff will be coming to the house for Christmas Eve and Christmas Day, like always. Lisa is bringing a new boyfriend with her. He's a young lawyer from the office where she works, and when I spoke to her on the phone she told me she wants to introduce him to her family."

"What happened to the dentist she was seeing? I thought that was pretty serious."

"I thought so, too," said Steve. "I think this guy—his name is Gary—sort of swept her off her feet. She says he reminds her of me!"

Cheryl laughed. "Fathers and daughters! I must admit I'd like to meet him, but I don't think it's going to happen this year, Dad."

"Still mad at me, huh?"

"He's starting a new job, the first of the year," Cheryl told him.

Steve knew she must've heard his swift intake of breath.

"Doing what?"

"He'll be driving a bus for Reindeer Coach Lines."

"A bus driver?" Steve exploded. "I don't believe it!"

"But it's true. He told me he'd never come back to the King's Feast."

"Ah, Cheryl, I wish I could live that day over again and not say any of the things I said. I don't know what the hell got into me."

"You've been very upset about Mom, I know that much," Cheryl suggested.

"Yeah . . ."

Anne Marie had encouraged Cheryl to call them *Mom* and *Dad* when she married Cliff, because both her parents had died when she was a teenager.

". . . but I know that's no excuse for taking it out on Cliffie. I hope he knows I still love him."

"I think he knows. And I'm sure he still loves you, too, Dad. You know what they say about blood being thicker than water. It's going to take time, that's all. Maybe a long time."

Brooklyn, New York

"Have you made any plans for Christmas?" asked Ed.

Tonight they'd dined at 21. Their Monday-night dinners had become a weekly ritual.

They were sitting in the living room of Serena's tiny apartment. She'd managed to furnish it comfortably with the help of a few pieces of furniture from her former apartment in Manhattan, items that the second Mrs. Epstein hadn't wanted to keep. Serena was sitting at one end of the gray velour couch, and Ed was stretched out along the rest of it with his shoes off and his head in her lap. She was gently massaging his face and forehead.

"Eddie, I haven't had time to think about Christmas;

I've been so busy with the restaurant."

"I'll be glad when you sell that place," he murmured, adding hastily, "if you're still sure that's what you want to do."

"Oh, yes. I can't see myself married to you, living in Manhattan, and coming over the bridge to Brooklyn every day to run a restaurant."

"As long as you see yourself married to me and living in Manhattan," he said.

The massage stalled.

"Hey, don't stop! That felt good."

She got her hands moving again, letting her fingertips slide through his immaculately clean salt-and-pepper hair and knead his scalp.

"Maybe I should get a job as a masseuse."

He laughed. "Okay, as long as I'm your only client."

She glanced at her watch. It was nearly midnight and time to tell him her news about the restaurant.

"The realtor called today. Nick Marrone made an offer."

Massage forgotten, Ed sat up.

"No kidding! How much did he offer?"

"He met my asking price. I guess I should've asked for more."

"Oh, take it, dearest! Call the realtor tomorrow and tell him you'll take it!"

She smiled.

"No . . . what I'm planning to do is call him and tell him to notify the other three people who looked at the place that I have a firm offer at the asking price. Maybe I can get a little more if I do that. What do you think?"

"I think I'm going to marry a very savvy lady."

He swung his feet down to the carpet and added, "You didn't answer my question about Christmas."

"Oh. I don't have any plans, Ed. Do you have something special in mind?"

"Yes, my daughter Phyllis and her husband would like to meet you. They've invited us to come for Christmas dinner."

"I think you told me they live in Cold Spring Harbor, am I right?"

"Yes, they have quite a big house out there."

"They must be planning a big family," Serena guessed.

"I hope so," he said with a big grin. "I'd love to have a couple of grandkids."

"Christmas dinner out on Long Island sounds good to me," said Serena, pleased that she would be meeting Phyllis and her husband on Christmas. He hadn't mentioned her since the wedding in June, and after her one glimpse of his ex-wife, she wasn't sure whether his relationship with his daughter and new son-in-law was flourishing. She had refrained from asking him about it because she thought it might be a sensitive subject.

"Okay, I'll let them know we'll be there." He leaned over and gently kissed her lips before adding, "I guess I should warn you that Margaret and Stuart will be there too."

Teeth brushed, face washed, Serena lay in bed waiting for sleep to come. A succession of disturbing images came instead, shoving sleep aside.

It was natural that Ed's daughter would want her mother and stepfather to visit her on Christmas, she admitted. Having seen Margaret that one time in Ed's office, she had little desire to see her again. Yet, perhaps she was judging her unfairly. She herself would not want to be judged by her demeanor after an argument with her ex-husband.

Would his daughter welcome her, she wondered, or

would she see her as an interloper? It was possible she did not like Margaret's second husband, since she'd preferred to have her father escort her down the aisle at her wedding.

Serena was almost certain Ed was planning to give her an engagement ring for Christmas. He'd been dropping sledgehammer hints about it. He was a generous, good-natured, and kind person. She did love him. He'd become an important part of her life, and yet—something was missing. Ed was a good lawyer; he hadn't become a wealthy man by being mild-mannered and polite in courtrooms. It was only around her that he behaved that way, like a teen-aged boy with his first girlfriend. Was it because his wife had damaged his masculine self-esteem when she dumped him in order to marry someone else? It was hard for her to believe that, because he was a nice-looking man, intelligent and successful. A good catch!

He had told her he loved her on their first date, six months ago; and he had repeated it many times over since then. He had bought her a ruby and diamond watch for her birthday in July, and often brought her flowers. He praised her looks, her taste, her cooking, her business acumen . . .

Why had he never tried to have sex with her?

Was he just an old-fashioned guy who wanted to wait until they were married? Was he afraid he would be unable to perform? Or was it something else?

Burt had always been sexually aggressive, before and after their marriage, but of course they'd been much younger then. She didn't know how to handle this problem. She'd thought about trying to initiate sex with Ed, but she felt shy about doing that . . . and she had a feeling he might be embarrassed, or offended, if she took the initiative.

Would their marriage be a sort of brother-and-sister arrangement? After all, she was fifty-four years old now and

Ed was fifty-seven. Maybe people of this age aren't supposed to be interested in sex anymore. Was she depraved because she was having these thoughts?

Moorestown, New Jersey

"Happy Hanukkah and Merry Christmas," said Steve, walking through the great room with outstretched hands to greet his daughter and her new friend.

"Daddy, this is Gary Barnett. He's an attorney in the office where I work."

"Do you celebrate Christmas or Hanukkah, Gary?" asked Steve, shaking the young man's hand.

"Hanukkah, sir. I was born in Israel."

"I'm a Jew myself—as I guess Lisa must've told you—but my wife, Anne Marie, is Catholic so we've always celebrated both holidays. The kids didn't seem to mind!"

He laughed, and the young couple laughed with him.

"Where're Cliff and Cheryl, Daddy?"

Since Lisa no longer lived at home, Steve had put off telling her about his fight with Cliff, half-believing that his son would relent and show up tonight with his petite blond wife.

"They may not be coming this year, kitten."

"Not coming! Why not? Are they sick?"

"Not as far as I know," Steve replied, wishing now that he had mentioned his quarrel with Cliff before. Lisa had always adored Cliff, but because of the considerable age disparity between them, they moved in different circles and seldom called each other. He hadn't anticipated that Cliff and Cheryl's absence would be awkward to explain, after—no doubt—she had prepared Gary for their traditional family get-together.

"*So?* Why aren't they coming, then?" she demanded.

"Cliff and I had a little disagreement, that's all."

"What about?"

"I—ah—don't think we should spoil the evening by subjecting Gary to the details of a family squabble."

"Daddy, I know it must have been more than a squabble, if Cliff and Cheryl aren't here tonight!"

Steve sighed.

"Okay. Cliff quit his job at the restaurant because he thought I was picking on him."

"Were you?"

"Yep."

"*Why?*" Lisa was horrified.

"We're too much alike, I guess. He kept trying to initiate his management ideas, stuff that he learned when he went to Cornell—and I resented it. I saw it as a criticism of my own management ideas. I pulled rank on him once too often, and he walked out."

"Daddy, that's awful! What's he going to do now?"

"Cheryl told me he has a new job, starting January first, driving a bus for Reindeer."

"Driving a bus? What about the year he went to Cornell? Couldn't he get another restaurant management job?"

"When he left me, I think he was fed up with restaurant work. Try to look at it this way: he'll probably be the best-educated bus driver Reindeer ever had."

He turned to Gary. "This is not the way our traditional holiday evenings used to be, but my wife is now in a nursing home with early Alzheimer's . . . and my family seems to be falling apart. Anne Marie was a great little peace-maker."

"Please don't apologize, Mr. Kingsley. I have a family too, and I do understand."

"That's good," said Steve, trying not to look at Lisa's stricken face. "So come in and sit by the fire, both of you, and have some egg nog."

CHAPTER 7

Cold Spring Harbor, Long Island

"You weren't kidding when you said your daughter and son-in-law have a big house," Serena exclaimed as Ed's dark-blue Lexus moved up the driveway in front of a gray stone mansion boasting four marble columns. "I expect Rhett Butler and Scarlett O'Hara to step out on the veranda to greet us."

Ed chuckled. He was getting used to her sense of humor.

"If you're expecting Rhett and Scarlett, you may be in for a surprise," he said dryly.

A middle-aged man in a butler's uniform appeared in the driveway and came over to the car.

"Merry Christmas, Mr. Franklin. Let me take care of your car."

"Thank you—and a Merry Christmas to you too, Vernon."

Ed helped Serena out of the car and handed the keys to the servant.

"This is my fiancée, Ms. D'Agostino."

Serena shook his hand and said, "Merry Christmas, Vernon. What a pleasure it must be to work in such a beautiful house!"

He smiled and bobbed his head.

A slightly overweight woman in a maid's uniform opened the door for them.

She took their coats and said, "Please go right on in. They're in the library."

"Thank you, Darlene. Are Mr. and Mrs. Rhodes here yet?"

"Yes, Mr. Franklin. They arrived about an hour ago."

With her heart bumping against her ribs, Serena allowed Ed to escort her into the library where a huge Christmas tree dominated the room. It sheltered a pile of gifts, already opened.

"Serena, may I present my daughter Phyllis and her husband, Chester Abbott? And this is Phyllis's mother, Margaret, and her husband, Stuart Rhodes. Everybody—this is my fiancée, Serena D'Agostino."

After a moment of silence during which everyone inhaled or exhaled, or both, Stuart Rhodes said, "Why, you sly old dog, Ed! She's lovely!" He stepped forward and kissed her cheek. Judging by his breath, Serena suspected he had begun drinking before he got out of bed that morning.

Margaret, clad in a bright-green velvet pantsuit that made her look like an affluent leprechaun, appeared next to her husband and said, "*D'Agostino?* Isn't that a curious name?"

"It's not curious, it's Italian," Serena told her.

Ed stifled a grin.

Phyllis Abbott was wearing a black satin evening skirt and a multicolored sequined top that seemed more appropriate for a New Year's Eve party than a family dinner on Christmas. Because she had the body of an eight-year-old child, the total effect was that of a little girl playing dress-up.

"My father has been telling us all about you, Serena," she said extending her hand, "but he didn't tell us you were engaged."

Serena shook the little hand, delivering what she hoped was a friendly smile. The two diminutive women made her feel like Gulliver entering the Land of the Lilliputians.

"Actually, we've been engaged for less than twelve hours, Phyllis," she said, handing her a large round tin wrapped in gold foil and tied with a red ribbon. "These are Christmas cookies. I bake them every year, and my friends seem to like them. I hope you will, too."

"Oh, no, not more *Christmas cookies!* I hope they don't have nuts in them! Mother and I are allergic to nuts."

"Some of them contain nuts, but not all of them," said Serena, her friendly smile starting to wilt at the corners.

"Too bad about you ladies! I'll eat all the ones with nuts," Stuart Rhodes offered. "Let's open them right now!"

He tried to grab the box but Phyllis held onto it, glaring at her stepfather.

"Mother, take this into the kitchen and give it to Cora. We're having plum pudding for dessert, but perhaps she can arrange these on a plate and put them on the table when we have our coffee."

"Thank God! I hate plum pudding," said Stuart, grinning at Serena.

When Margaret left the room, Serena focused on a small and incredibly ugly man sitting alone by the fireplace. He had not come forward to meet her, so she approached him with both hands outstretched.

"You must be Phyllis's husband."

"Yes, that's the toad," said Phyllis, laughing over her shoulder.

When he stood up to acknowledge her greeting, Serena understood the reason for the cruel nickname Phyllis had given him. He was shorter than his wife, and carried so much fat around his midsection that he appeared to be sitting in a circular kayak even when he was standing up. He was completely bald, and black eyes bulged behind thick glasses. Definitely a candidate for a makeover . . . or perhaps a kiss from a fairy-tale princess would have done the trick.

"You're very beautiful," he said, looking from her face to her hands clasping his, "and that's a magnificent engagement ring you're wearing."

"Oh, let me see!" cried Phyllis. Margaret, who had just returned from the kitchen, hastened across the room to join her. Heads together, they inspected the three-carat marquise-cut diamond flanked by baguettes and set in platinum. Their concentration was so intense, Serena half expected to see one of them produce a jeweler's loupe.

When Margaret stepped back, saying nothing, Serena inferred from her tight lips and reddening complexion that it was more ostentatious than either of her own engagement rings had been.

Phyllis said, "It's gorgeous, Serena. I guess you picked it out yourself."

"No, your dad bought it without my assistance, and surprised me with it last night."

"How does it compare to the engagement ring you got from your first marriage," asked Margaret, her face still flushed.

"I'm afraid I don't recall that ring well enough to compare them."

"Didn't you put them side by side and look?" asked Margaret.

"I can't do that. I returned Burton's rings when we got our divorce," Serena explained.

"You can't be serious!" Margaret turned to her ex-husband and said, "Ed, you allowed her to do this?"

"I advised her against it, but she did it anyway."

Margaret turned back to Serena.

"Why would you do such a foolish thing?"

"Because they were once a symbol of the love between us," said Serena. "When that love was gone, they meant no more to me than brass curtain rings."

"Hmmph," sniffed the former Mrs. Franklin.

She stared now at Serena's simple white wool jersey dress and gray suede pumps; then down at her own lollipop-green velvet pantsuit. A quick scowl at her image in the wall mirror reminded her to straighten her shoulders and suck in her stomach.

"May I pour you a glass of Chablis, dearest, or would you prefer something stronger?" asked Ed. He had already helped himself to a Scotch on the rocks. He was beaming, apparently under the impression that Serena's first meeting with his family had been flawlessly successful.

"Wine, please."

He poured the white wine into a stemmed glass and handed it to her. She tried a sip and smiled; it was excellent.

"Dinner is served," Vernon announced from the doorway.

"You can bring your drinks with you to the dining room," said Phyllis, taking charge again. "We're going to have our dinner now."

Moorestown, New Jersey

"Daddy, we've got something to tell you," said Lisa.

It was Christmas Day, and the three of them had just strolled into the great room after finishing a sumptuous holiday dinner. She set her wineglass down on the huge Lucite coffee table that lay like an ice rink between the two long white leather sofas.

"What is it?"

Lisa held out her left hand, and Steve stared at a sparkling solitaire set on a yellow gold band.

"What the hell is this?"

"It's an engagement ring, Daddy. Gary gave it to me for Hanukkah."

"You weren't wearing it last night!" Steve growled.

"We had planned to tell you about it last night, but when you told me about your fight with Cliff, I saw you were upset so I slipped it off and put it in my handbag."

Steve did not take his eyes from his daughter's face.

"What ever happened to Arnold Bernstein?" he asked. The blatant insensitivity was deliberate.

Her dark eyes blazed with anger.

"I stopped seeing him after I met Gary."

"This is what happens when a young girl moves out of her father's house and gets her own apartment . . ."

"*Dad*-dy!"

Gary stood up.

"I apologize, Mr. Kingsley, for not meeting you sooner, and for failing to ask you properly for Lisa's hand in marriage. I love her very much, and I will do everything in my power to make her happy."

Steve inclined his head toward the young man.

"You say you're from Israel, Gary. Did my daughter tell you she was brought up as a Catholic?"

"Yes, she did. She also told me that your son—who was brought up in our faith—married a Catholic girl. Did you object to that union?"

"No," Steve admitted, beginning to like this young man.

He could picture him cross-examining a witness in court. "As a matter of fact, I love Cheryl dearly."

"That's good to hear. Lisa has expressed a desire to convert to Judaism, and we've already spoken to my rabbi about instruction for her. How would you feel about that?"

A grudging smile began to spread across Steve's face.

"I just wish I had known some of these things before today," he said, his initial anger evaporating.

Gary raised his glass of wine. Slowly, Steve raised his own glass to touch Gary's.

Both men said in unison, *"L'chayim!"*

Lisa smiled at what she perceived as her father's consent to the marriage.

"Daddy, there's something else we need to talk about." she said.

"Something else? *Oy*, what now! You're going to spend your honeymoon at the South Pole?"

Lisa smiled, accustomed to her father's sense of humor.

"I took Gary to Tall Pines yesterday and introduced him to Mom."

Steve set down his wineglass so hard it almost tipped over on the coffee table.

"Dammit, Lisa, what's *wrong* with you? Did it ever occur to you that I might've wanted to be there when you did that? I mean, I know she's your mother, but she also happens to be my wife!"

"I'm sorry, Daddy—really I am! I never thought you'd be so upset. Don't you want to know what she said?"

"*So?* Tell me what she said. She recognized you?"

"Sure she did! She hugged me and she hugged Gary, and she wants to come to the wedding."

Steve's mouth opened, but no sound emerged.

"I told her *of course* we want her to come to our wedding, and walk up the aisle with you—and with us!"

Steve blinked several times. He was trying to make himself believe this dream could come true.

"Yesterday must've been one of her good days, kitten. What if your wedding day turns out *not* to be one of her good days?"

Lisa's eyes were shining.

"I'm sure God will help her, Daddy. *Please!* I want Mom to be at our wedding!"

CHAPTER 8

Cherry Hill, New Jersey: The Following June

The marriage of Lisa Kingsley and Gary Barnett took place at Temple Beth El, a Reform synagogue in Cherry Hill. Gary's parents and younger sister Rachel flew in from Tel Aviv for the joyous occasion. Steve had sent a dressmaker out to Tall Pines to take Anne Marie's measurements and let her choose the color and the fabric for her mother-of-the-bride ensemble. Today she was resplendent in a coral satin gown with a matching jacket. The color complemented her olive complexion and her dark-brown hair, which was starting to gray rather pleasingly at the temples. Steve was proud of her appearance, and prayed she would be able to get through the day without faltering.

As Jewish tradition dictated, both sets of parents accompanied the bridal couple as they walked down the aisle. Anne Marie smiled up at him as the procession began, and he could scarcely believe the lovely woman by his side was now living in a nursing home. He kissed her cheek and whispered, "I'm glad you're here with me today, honey."

When the procession ended, they seated themselves on the first row. Anne Marie turned around and announced to the people sitting behind them, "I'm the bride's mother, you know. Arnie Bernstein is such a handsome boy, and won't it be nice to have a dentist in the family?"

Most of their friends knew that Lisa had dated a dentist named Arnold Bernstein before she met Gary. The folks sitting behind them were friends from their old neighborhood in Cinnaminson, before they'd moved to Moorestown, and Steve wasn't sure whether they knew about the dentist.

He winked at them, and said to Anne Marie, "Sure, Arnie was a great kid, but she's marrying *Gary Barnett!* Having a lawyer in the family will be even better."

As the young couple stood under the *huppah* and began to repeat their vows, Anne Marie suddenly stood up and tried to squeeze past him. He pulled her down again as gently as he could. While Gary was saying, "Be sanctified to me with this ring in accordance with the law of Moses and Israel . . ." Anne Marie was saying in a shrill, piercing voice, "You better let me out, Steve! I have to pee, and I couldn't wear one of those diapers under this dress."

He saw Lisa, standing beside Gary under the *huppah,* put one hand over her mouth to stifle a sob.

As he escorted his wife up the aisle to a rest room at the rear of the temple, he spotted Cliff and Cheryl in the congregation. Head bowed, Cheryl was crying softly. As soon as he caught Cliff's eye, both men looked away. They had not spoken to each other for seven months.

When the ceremony was over, Steve drove Anne Marie back to Tall Pines, where the nurses were waiting to hear about the wedding.

When Rose, her favorite nurse, asked if she'd had a good time, she smiled and said, "Oh, it was a beautiful wedding. Such a handsome couple, but of course I didn't know them."

"Anne Marie, that was your *daughter's* wedding!" cried one of the younger nurses.

"Oh, now you're teasing me! I have a wonderful son . . . he's ten years old now . . . but I've always wanted to have a daughter." She patted her belly. "I'm pregnant, you know, so maybe the baby will be a little girl. I'm going to say a prayer tonight that God will send me a daughter."

Steve flung an agonized glance at the nurses. Without saying goodbye, he walked out of Anne Marie's room and out of the building as quickly as he could.

In the Tall Pines parking lot, he sat in his white Cadillac until all his tears had been shed. If he'd had a bottle of whiskey with him, he would have tossed back a shot. Maybe two. Instead, he mopped his eyes and headed his car south to the lavish reception already underway at the King's Feast.

New York City: The Same Day

"I still don't understand why you didn't have the wedding at my house in Cold Spring Harbor," said Phyllis peevishly. "Why didn't you?"

"We decided to make it very small and very private," Serena explained, and not for the first time. Phyllis had brought up this subject before. "Ed wanted just you and Chet, Margaret and Stuart, and a few of his closest friends from the firm."

"What about *your* family?"

"I don't have any family."

"None at all? Not even cousins?"

"I have two cousins, yes, but they live in California. I haven't seen them since we were all teenagers together in Brooklyn."

"I keep forgetting you're from Brooklyn," said Phyllis, wrinkling her pug nose, "because you don't seem like a typical person from Brooklyn."

Serena was tempted to ask what a typical person from

Brooklyn seemed like. It was her wedding day, so she resisted the temptation.

The waiter they'd hired for the occasion approached with a silver tray of hors d'oeuvres, and they both helped themselves.

"And why was the marriage performed by a justice of the peace," Phyllis persisted, "instead of a minister?"

"You could call it a compromise, I suppose," said Serena. "Ed is Presbyterian, and I'm Jewish."

"Jewish!" echoed Phyllis, choking on her egg roll. "Your name is Italian, so I assumed you were Catholic."

"My father was Italian . . . yes, and Catholic . . . but my mother was Jewish. I was brought up in her faith."

"Does my father know you're half-Jewish?"

Serena laughed. "Of course he does. I told him the same night he asked me to marry him."

Phyllis took a sip of champagne and popped another hors d'oeuvre, caviar on a toast point, into her mouth.

"Hmmm. Interesting. You're just full of surprises, aren't you?" she murmured after swallowing the mouthful.

"Oh, sure. International Woman of Mystery, that's me."

"Well, I have to admit one thing . . . you did a good job of transforming this apartment from a pigsty to a palace."

They both turned to look through the glass wall of the living room at the wraparound balcony, now featuring an umbrella table and an assortment of lemon-yellow and white patio furniture. In the living room, sunshine spotlighted the dark-green sectional couch on which they were sitting, the pale-green carpet, and the two matching lemon-yellow chairs that completed the conversational group. A large pale-green marble coffee table that stood in the center of the rectangle held a green-and-yellow bowl of hand-blown fluted glass. Inside the bowl, three baby gardenias floated on water.

Instead of the blue-and-white-checked gingham café curtains she'd jokingly threatened to put up, white vertical blinds hung above the massive floor-to-ceiling glass doors that led out to the balcony. The blinds were pulled aside, making today's cloudless blue sky over Manhattan island a part of the décor.

"This place was never a pigsty," Serena ventured in mild disagreement. "Ed called it Spartan."

"Whatever." Phyllis seemed to feel that enough had been said on that subject. "The lunch buffet was quite delicious. What caterer did you use?"

Serena chuckled. "The International Woman of Mystery."

"The International . . ." Phyllis echoed, then stopped herself. "Are you telling me *you* prepared all that food yourself?"

Serena giggled. "Why not? I love to cook."

"Who taught you how to cook?"

"My mother. My parents had a little neighborhood restaurant in Brooklyn, and my mother did all the cooking. When I was growing up, I used to help out on weekends with the cooking and serving. That's what gave me the idea to buy a little restaurant and fix it up after my divorce."

"You had a restaurant, too? Like your parents did?"

"Yes."

"In Brooklyn?"

"Yes."

After learning about Serena's restaurant, Phyllis evidently made a decision to stop just short of Twenty Questions.

"I hope that's the end of the surprises," said Phyllis.

She stood up without excusing herself and hurried outside where her mother and stepfather were gazing at Manhattan from the wraparound balcony. No doubt she would deliver a full report about the unsuitable woman her daddy had married.

Serena decided to go looking for Chet. She found him sitting alone in Ed's study, reading a law book.

"Chet! What are you doing in here all by yourself?" she chided him gently. "We want all of our guests to have a good time today."

He peered up at her through his thick glasses.

"Don't worry about me, Serena," he told her. "I *am* having a good time."

"Would you like me to bring you something to eat or drink?"

"No, I'm fine."

She walked into her bedroom and sat down on the blue satin chaise lounge. Looking across the room at her reflection in the mirrored wall behind the king-sized bed that dominated the room, she realized she didn't look as happy on her wedding day as she thought she would.

What was wrong?

She loved Eddie, but she couldn't help feeling a little hurt that he had never mentioned her restaurant to his daughter. And she was hurt—maybe astounded was a better word—that he had never told Phyllis about her mother being Jewish.

She believed Eddie loved her. Was it possible to love someone and, at the same time, be ashamed of the work they did . . . or the blood that flowed through their veins?

He and Margaret Whittaker had met in college; she was Presbyterian, from a fine old Long Island family. They'd had all those lovely privileges in common, yet their marriage had failed.

Serena, despite her lack of social status, evidently provided a quality that Eddie craved. He had given her his social status in return for that quality.

She would not need to get up in the early morning ever again to buy and cook the food for Serena's Kitchen. She had sold her little business, in operation for less than two years, and realized a comfortable profit—now invested in certificates of deposit at a bank in Brooklyn. She would probably never need to touch them, because she was now the wife of a wealthy man.

She thought of Mimi and Angela. They had not been invited to the wedding because, as Ed had pointed out, only family and close friends were invited.

"My secretary, Penny Sawyer, was not invited. Why would you invite your waitresses?"

The three of them had worked together so comfortably at Serena's Kitchen. She knew she was going to miss them. At the closing, she'd recommended to the new owner that he re-hire them when he reopened the restaurant.

What would she do all day, while Ed was at work? What had she done before, when she was married to Burton Epstein? Of course she'd had a son then, who needed her advice and attention. And love . . .

In the future, her daytime social life would depend largely on women. She and Ed would need to invite couples over for dinner so that she could make some women friends.

She looked down at her brand-new wedding band—a circlet of diamonds—and the ruby-and-diamond watch he had given to her last year on her fifty-fourth birthday. This morning when she'd finished dressing for the wedding, he had fastened a ruby-and-diamond necklace around her neck.

It looked magnificent above the scooped neckline of her shell-pink satin gown. Triangular panels of deep crimson lace flared below the gown's hipline, two in front and two in back. The dress had cost more than two thousand dollars, and when Ed told her, "It's yours," she'd felt like Cinderella.

Tomorrow she and Ed would leave on a ten-day cruise to Alaska (her choice) for their honeymoon. She'd always wanted to visit that ruggedly beautiful state, and June was the ideal month in which to do it.

What was wrong with her wedding day, she realized, was Ed's family. They did not like her, and she had to admit she did not like them, either. She hoped their future contact would be limited to a few times a year.

Later, as she showered and slipped into the sheer blue negligee she'd bought for her wedding night, she wondered if any of the guests at today's festivities would believe that she'd been sleeping alone in the king-sized bed since moving into this apartment. Ed had been sleeping on a studio couch he'd bought and set up in his library.

She wondered if he was grievously shy, undersexed, or was it a Presbyterian thing?

She was sitting at her dressing table brushing her hair when there was a knock at the bedroom door. She stifled a chuckle before calling out, "Come in, Ed."

He came up behind her, wearing new white silk pajamas and a matching robe. He was smiling.

"You look lovely, dearest," he said, gazing at her reflection.

She handed him the brush.

"Why don't you brush my hair for me?" she suggested, her eyes meeting his in the mirror.

He blinked several times and began to brush her hair, now drifting down her back like a silver waterfall.

"You have the most beautiful hair I've ever seen," he said, brushing it with feather-like strokes.

"You can brush it a little harder than that," she said. "Don't worry, it won't fall out."

He laughed out loud and brushed harder.

She untied the pale-blue ribbon that held her negligee closed, and let it fall from her shoulders. When both her breasts were exposed, Ed's hand dropped the brush.

"Oh my God! I knew your breasts would be beautiful, too," he whispered.

He knelt beside her blue satin bench, and she turned to face him. Feeling almost maternal, she took his face between her hands and pressed it against her breasts. His whole body began to shake violently.

He took one nipple into his mouth and began to suck. He made a whimpering sound like a puppy, and his arms went around her.

At last he lifted his head and looked into her face.

"Don't ever leave me, dearest," he begged.

She stood up, letting the negligee drop to the floor.

"I'll be with you always . . . if you give me what I want."

She moved slowly across the room and reclined on the bed with a teasing smile.

"Everything I have is yours," he gasped, still on his knees. *"Just tell me what you want!"*

"Come over here, darling, and let me show you . . ."

With a hoarse cry, Ed staggered to his feet and flung himself on the bed beside her.

When he entered her, Serena closed her eyes and moaned with pleasure. She didn't know why Ed had sexual hang-ups, but she was very glad she had figured out how to resolve the problem.

CHAPTER 9

New York City: Seven Years Later

Serena walked into her bedroom, kicked off the jade-green lizard pumps that matched her cashmere suit, and sank gratefully onto the powder-blue chaise lounge. She put her head back and closed her eyes with a contented sigh.

The luncheon at Chantelle that she had planned and organized had been successful beyond all expectations. The food had been superb, and the women who attended today had been generous. They had exceeded their one-hundred-thousand-dollar goal for AIDS research.

It was hard now to remember that she had wondered how she would fill her days while Ed was busy practicing law. As the wife of a wealthy Manhattan attorney, she was sought after by women's clubs and charitable groups—especially when they learned of her reputation as a diligent worker and competent manager.

Ed's colleague, Bradley Bellinger, and his wife, Carla, had become their closest friends. Carla had introduced Serena to the friends and acquaintances she had grown up with, and a new world had opened up for her—a world of women who used their money and privileged status to help those less fortunate than themselves: disabled veterans, battered wives, exploited children, and abused animals. Then there were the environmental groups like Greenpeace, Ed's special favorite. She'd often heard him say that if we fail to protect the health of our planet, eventually all plant and animal life will become extinct.

She opened her eyes and glanced at her watch. Ed should be home in another hour. She was anxious to hear about his visit to Dr. Patterson earlier this afternoon. She had become concerned about his persistent cough and shortness of breath. She had also suggested he stop smoking cigarettes, but Ed had replied, "I've been smoking since I was twelve years old. I don't think I could stop."

When he saw the look on her face, he added, "I'll try to cut down, dearest."

She had wondered aloud why Ed's parents had allowed him to smoke at such an early age, and he explained that he had learned to smoke at boarding school. His parents never knew the full extent of the curriculum their money had paid for.

When she heard Ed's key in the lock just before five-thirty, she dashed out of the kitchen to greet him. One look told her that he wasn't smiling.

"What happened at the doctor's office, darling?" she asked.

"He seems to think I might have emphysema. He took a battery of tests, but we won't know the results until next week."

Dismayed, she said, "I've heard of emphysema, but I've never known anyone who had it. What is it, exactly?"

"The way Bob explained it to me, everybody's lungs are like a bunch of little balloons. Do you know what happens to a bunch of balloons when they're inflated too much?"

She swallowed.

"They burst?"

He chuckled. A small one.

"No, not exactly. Did you ever see a rubber band that won't stretch anymore?"

Her eyes still fixed on his face, she nodded.

"Well, when your lungs are over-inflated, they get weak, like that rubber band. They lose their elasticity."

"And what does that do to you?"

"Makes it hard for you to breathe properly. Gives you a chronic cough. And since your heart depends on the oxygen from your lungs to function the way it's supposed to . . . it can affect your heart, too."

"What's he going to do for you, if the tests show that you really do have emphysema?"

He grimaced.

"Bob told me to give up smoking."

She clasped her hands together beneath her chin.

"And you're going to do it, aren't you?"

"He says I *have* to do it."

"Good for you! I'll help you. I've seen all kinds of advertisements on television about things you can do to help yourself stop smoking—lozenges, skin patches."

He hugged her.

"We'll beat this thing, dearest. I want to wipe that worried look off your face."

"Let's take all the cigarettes in this apartment and throw them down the trash chute right now!" she cried.

He laughed.

"I love your enthusiasm, but let's wait until we know for sure whether I actually have emphysema," he said soothingly. "Next week, when the tests come back. . . ."

Still looking into his face, she remembered he had told her he'd been smoking since he was twelve years old. He was now sixty-four. She knew he had to give up the habit, but she knew it was not going to be easy. For either of them.

* * * * *

Dr. Patterson called the following week. His diagnosis had been confirmed by the tests. Ed's right lung had a sixty-percent capacity, his left lung slightly less. He would need to take medication on a daily basis. He would need a nebulizer to spray his throat when he had a coughing fit or couldn't catch his breath. Dr. Patterson wanted them to look into buying or renting oxygen equipment to keep in the apartment.

Most important of all: *Ed would have to stop smoking.*

Serena again insisted that they throw away all the packs of cigarettes in the apartment. Ed suggested that they give them instead to Patrick Noonan, the night security guard in the building's lobby, who was a heavy smoker. She agreed reluctantly. It seemed immoral, somehow, to encourage someone else's smoking habit, but Ed persuaded her by saying, "He's going to smoke anyway."

They played the game for a couple of weeks. Ed was wearing a patch, which was designed to diminish his desire for smoking. On the occasions when he craved a cigarette, despite the patch, Serena would unbutton her blouse, bare her breast, and remind him that Dr. Patterson had instructed him to combat nicotine fits by putting something else in his mouth instead of a cigarette.

This worked effectively at home, but she suspected he had a stash of cigarettes in his office. She talked to Penny on the phone, enlisting her help. Penny confirmed that she sometimes smelled smoke in his office, but if she asked him about it he always claimed that it had been from a client's cigarette.

Feeling like a police detective, Serena questioned him. He stoutly denied that he was smoking at work, but in her heart she knew he was lying to her. And to himself.

One night she awakened shortly after midnight and found that he was not beside her in their bed. She searched the apartment, then the entire building, and eventually discovered him downstairs in the lobby—smoking one of the cigarettes he had given to Patrick Noonan.

When she led him back to their apartment, they were both crying.

Lawrenceville, New Jersey

It was the second Sunday in May, and Cliff and Cheryl arrived at Tall Pines with a box of Godiva chocolates and a bunch of red roses.

"Happy Mother's Day," they chorused, walking into the solarium where Anne Marie was sitting in a wheelchair. She looked puzzled until she saw the box of chocolates.

"Candy?" she asked hopefully. They nodded, and Cheryl handed her the box. She had trouble unwrapping it, and Cliff tried to help.

"It's *mine,*" she said angrily, slapping his hands away.

She gave the box to the nurse, who opened it for her.

"Aren't you glad your son and daughter-in-law came to visit you on Mother's Day?" prompted Rose.

Anne Marie stopped stuffing chocolates in her mouth long enough to scrutinize the visitors.

"That's not my son," she informed Rose, her words garbled by nuts, chocolate, and caramel, "and I haven't got a daughter."

"Daughter-*in-law,*" Rose corrected her. "Your son's *wife.* They brought you the candy, and lovely red roses, too."

Anne Marie studied them again, her forehead creased with the effort as she tried to concentrate.

At last she said, "This candy is good. I like candy."

Rose tried again. "Do you know who this young man is?"

"Don't try to tell me he's my son, because my son is only ten years old. His father never brings him to see me."

Rose looked at them sadly.

"I'm sorry. Sometimes she remembers. But not today."

Cheryl looked out the car window at the azaleas, pansies, and impatiens blooming in the center of the circular driveway as Cliff gunned the motor and drove away from Tall Pines.

Neither of them said a word. There was nothing to say.

New York City

After the taxi dropped them off in front of their building, Ed and Serena said good night to Patrick Noonan and stepped into the elevator.

"That was the nicest retirement party I ever attended," said Serena, keeping her voice light and bright.

"How many retirement parties have you attended?" asked Ed.

She grinned.

"This was the first."

They both laughed.

"They're keeping me on retainer, you know, as a consultant."

"Yes, Brad told me. I wasn't surprised, darling. They will still need your advice on difficult cases."

They got off the elevator and entered their apartment. Ed walked immediately to the bar in the corner of the living room and began to mix himself a drink.

She looked at the expression on his face and said

quickly, "Wasn't it nice that Phyllis and Chet were able to be there tonight?" She wondered if she should have crossed her fingers when she uttered those words.

"Yes, I was glad they were there. I had a long talk with them while you were having a drink with Brad and Carla."

"What about?"

"They want us to sell the co-op and move out to Cold Spring Harbor," Ed told her.

"What!" she exclaimed before she was able to stop herself, amending it quickly with, "Ah . . . why?"

"They know I have emphysema, and now that I'm retired they think I should be near family."

"Where would we live?" asked Serena. Her heart was beating slowly, like a muffled drum: no-*no,* no-*no,* no-*no.*

"Phyllis is having the guest cottage remodeled."

"Guest cottage?"

"You've only been out there a few times, dearest, and it was winter . . . maybe you never noticed it. It's behind the main house. Gray stone. Cute little place! Living room, kitchen, bath, and two bedrooms."

Serena felt as if she was sinking in quicksand.

"What about your law books?"

"We could use the second bedroom as a library."

"Darling, we have so many friends here in Manhattan! And I'm involved in so many charities . . ."

"We'd only be moving to Long Island! Not the end of the world. An hour from Manhattan. We could still see our friends!"

"Do I get a vote on this idea?"

"You're my wife. *Of course* you get a vote!"

"Well, I vote *no.* We have everything we need here! Our apartment is perfect. We have a fabulous social life with people we like and enjoy! What more could we possibly want?"

Ed turned around with a glass of brandy in his hand, and said, "I feel time is running out for me. I want to live near my daughter."

CHAPTER 10

Lawrenceville, New Jersey: Three Years Later

It was the Monday before Thanksgiving and the day was bitterly cold. The sky above Tall Pines was heavy and gray, like an asbestos curtain. There were no flowers blooming in the center of the circular driveway when Steve and his daughter Lisa arrived to visit Anne Marie.

"Happy Thanksgiving, Mom," said Lisa, kissing her mother on the cheek.

As if a fly had buzzed near her head, Anne Marie moved it a little to the side and continued to stare out the window of the solarium. A few snow flurries, like plant spores, floated in the air.

"We brought you a pumpkin pie from the restaurant, honey," said Steve. "Anton baked it especially for you. He said to tell you hello."

Anne Marie scowled, her gaze intent on the pine trees swaying in the wind outside the glass walls. Lisa pushed a chair close to her mother's wheelchair and sat down.

"Mom, I have some great news. Would you like to hear what it is?"

Anne Marie turned her head and stared at her daughter. She looked puzzled.

"I'm pregnant, Mom! I'm going to have a baby! You're going to be a grandmother!"

Anne Marie nodded, as though she understood.

"I had a baby once," she said. "It was a boy. I haven't

seen him for a long time because his father never brings him to see me."

"Mom, you had *me,* too! I'm your daughter! I'm *Lisa!*"

Anne Marie leaned forward, looking closely at the white wool suit Lisa was wearing.

"You can't fool me; you're a *nurse!*" she shouted suddenly, pushing Lisa away from her wheelchair. "Why don't you get lost? Can't you see I want to be alone with this good-looking doctor?"

She smiled up at Steve.

Lisa rose from her chair, sobbing loudly.

"Daddy, she doesn't know who I am!"

Steve's face was grim.

"Wait for me downstairs, kitten. I'll join you in a few minutes."

After Lisa left the solarium, he sat down in the chair she had just vacated and gently touched his wife's face.

"I'm here, honey."

"You can kiss me if you want," said Anne Marie. "I thought that crying nurse would never leave."

Steve kissed her lips, then went downstairs to find his heartbroken daughter. It was almost Thanksgiving, and he wondered what he had to be thankful for. He and his son hadn't spoken to each other for almost ten years, and his wife didn't know who he was.

As soon as he saw Lisa's woebegone face, he knew what he had to be thankful for. He had a daughter and son-in-law who loved him, and a grandchild on the way.

CHAPTER 11

Cold Spring Harbor, Long Island

Serena and Ed sat in the breakfast nook that was built into the corner of their pine-paneled country kitchen. They were having a second cup of coffee with homemade cinnamon buns, and watching the antics of a few birds in the large feeder Ed had installed next to the window three years ago when they first moved into the Abbotts' guest cottage.

He could not have accomplished that task today. It was a supreme effort for him to walk from the bedroom to the kitchen. When they visited Phyllis and Chet in the main house, Serena had to push him in a wheelchair.

"Most of the . . . birds have already . . . gone south for the winter," he observed, often catching his breath and wheezing between phrases. A cannula inserted in his nostrils carried oxygen from a portable tank.

"Wouldn't you say that makes them smarter than we are?" Serena asked. He nodded and smiled. A faint, ghostly smile, like a child's watercolor picture left out in the rain.

She looked up at the murky sky. "Looks like it might snow today, darling."

Seeming dejected and lost in thought, he did not respond. She began to clear the table.

"Shall we go into the living room now and watch the *Today Show*?"

"Okay."

He tried to stand, but fell back onto the red and white

cushions that padded the breakfast nook. She hurried back from the sink and held out her hands.

"Come on, tiger. You can do it."

She helped him rise gradually from the cushions, slipped an arm around his waist, and together they walked slowly into the living room. Twenty-three steps. He was exhausted, perspiring and panting, when he lowered himself into the green mohair recliner in front of the TV set and picked up the remote.

She sensed that his blue eyes, paler now behind his rimless glasses, were following her as she bustled back to the kitchen to rinse the dishes and put them into the dishwasher. When she returned to the living room ten minutes later to watch television with him, he was asleep.

At eleven o'clock she helped him into the walk-in shower in their bathroom, where a shower chair supported him while she washed his face and body, and shampooed his hair. Getting dressed was too strenuous for him now, so she helped him put on clean pajamas and a blue velour robe; socks and slippers.

"I can't eat . . . Thanksgiving dinner . . . in my pajamas," he protested feebly.

"If anyone complains, I'll hit them with a drumstick," Serena told him. "Don't you realize that having you at the table on Thanksgiving Day is what we're most thankful for?"

He smiled and whispered, "Having you . . . next to me . . . *every* day is . . . what I'm most . . . thankful for."

"My one-person fan club," she said fondly.

She knew he was watching from his wheelchair as she dressed herself in gray flannel pants and a lavender sweater embroidered with violets. They had not been able to have sex for almost two years. Even touching her breast caused him to gasp for breath.

At two o'clock she put on her black suede coat with the ermine collar that he had given her for Christmas last year; she pulled a woolen hat onto his head and covered him from neck to toes with a thick wool afghan, tucking it around him for the brief trip from the guest cottage to the main house.

"Keep your mouth closed while we're outside," she cautioned before she wheeled him onto their front porch and down the ramp they'd had built next to the steps.

"Can I have . . . Scotch?" he asked Stuart, who had assumed bartender duties for the holiday. Stuart looked at Serena for approval.

"Don't look . . . at her," Ed complained. "Look . . . at me!"

"The doctor said one glass of red wine a day is okay," she told Stuart.

Ed made a face, but he accepted the goblet of Merlot that Stuart handed him. It grew quiet in the living room as the three of them sipped at their drinks.

In the hall outside the living room, they heard Margaret saying to Phyllis in a piercing whisper, "Thank God I don't have to take care of that sick old man!"

Cora's turkey was golden brown and tender, the stuffing was moist and savory. Serena worried because Ed was not eating.

"You didn't finish what was on your plate, darling," she chided while Darlene was clearing the table.

"Saving room . . . for dessert," he said with a grin.

But when the warm apple crumb pie was served, he scarcely touched it.

"This is your favorite pie, Daddy," said Phyllis reproachfully. "Why aren't you eating it?"

"Too much . . . turkey," he explained.

Exasperated, Serena shook her head and laughed.

"You've got *chutzpah!*" she said.

Five pairs of eyes looked at her blankly.

"It's a Yiddish word. Means 'colossal nerve,' " she explained. No one laughed.

Phyllis and Margaret exchanged glances.

Ed's contradictory comments had been a classic example of *chutzpah*. She wondered what, if anything, made these people laugh.

They returned to the cottage early, before six o'clock, because it had started to snow. She lighted a fire in the gray-stone fireplace that took up one wall of their living room, and put a college football game on television for Ed to watch. He watched it for fifteen minutes and fell asleep.

She switched to a cable channel and watched a movie.

At ten o'clock she helped him into the bedroom. When she slipped under the comforter next to him, he said, "Please hold me . . . dearest. I'm . . . so cold."

He seemed to be chilled through, and she wondered if the short trips to and from the main house had been too much for him. She put her arms around his frail body, and felt his shivering subside when her own body heat began to warm him.

She awakened later, feeling cold herself, and got out of bed to check the thermostat. The heat seemed to be functioning properly, and the thermostat showed the temperature in the cottage to be seventy-five degrees.

When she got back in bed, she discovered the source of the coldness. She touched Ed's body; it felt as if it had just come from a refrigerator. His breathing was labored. She jumped out of bed again and turned on the lamp.

The skin on Ed's face was waxen, and his expression was agonized. She shook him gently and said, "*Eddie, Eddie!* Talk to me!"

He drew another strangled breath that sounded more like a groan. She grabbed the phone on the night table and dialed 9-1-1.

Because of the heavy snow and high winds, the ambulance did not reach the cottage until after one o'clock. She was waiting by the door, fully dressed in a sweatshirt, jeans, and boots. A down jacket with a hood waited nearby.

While the paramedics were in the bedroom examining her husband, the front door burst open and Phyllis dashed in, wearing a mink coat over her nightgown.

"*What have you done to my father?*" she screamed.

Taken aback, Serena stammered, "He was h-having chills, and h-his breathing is . . ."

"He was *fine* when he was in *my* house!" snarled Phyllis.

"Excuse me, lady," said one of the paramedics. "We've gotta get this man to the hospital right away."

Both women stood aside to let the gurney pass by, and the paramedic said to Serena, "You're the wife, right? Are you coming with us to the hospital?"

"Yes." She put her arms into the Kelly-green jacket that she had laid on the chair beside the door.

"I'm his *daughter,* and I'm coming, too," Phyllis announced shrilly. She shoved Serena aside and climbed into the ambulance first.

"You'll be all right, Daddy," she trumpeted to the unconscious man, "*I'm* in charge now!"

Windshield wipers beating at the curtain of snow, the ambulance began to inch down the long, slippery driveway.

CHAPTER 12

Elmont, Long Island

The black limousine passed slowly under the wrought-iron arch that spelled out *Presbyterian Cemetery*, swung right, and picked up speed. In the middle seat, Serena pressed a handkerchief to her eyes and cried like a child.

Phyllis, in the rear seat, leaned over her left shoulder and drawled, "You can stop crying now, Serena. Nobody's watching."

She would have said more, but Chet pulled her back and muttered, "Leave her alone, Phyl."

Phyllis wrenched her arm out of his grasp and snapped, "Since when do *toads* give orders?"

After the reprimand he lapsed into silence and Serena continued to weep.

Margaret tapped Serena on the right shoulder and said, "In your family background, my dear, public displays of grief may be commonplace, but *our* family finds them somewhat distasteful. It's been a difficult day for all of us, and your lack of control is not making it easier."

She nudged her husband, who was dozing beside her, and said loudly, "Isn't that right, Stu?"

Stuart opened his eyes, blinked several times, and said, "Huh? Are we there already? I'm hungry."

Breathing unevenly, Serena tried to choke back the sobs Ed's family found so offensive. She turned her head and stared out the window at the lingering drifts of snow beside the road, and the naked trees genuflecting to the harsh wind of late November. The limousine's heavy tires hummed rhythmically over the tar strips on the highway, carrying her farther every minute from Ed's final resting place.

She could not, would not imagine her life without him.

"I want to teach you how to smile again," he'd told her on the night he'd proposed marriage, ten years ago. "You don't smile often enough, but when you do, you could light up Manhattan."

She'd done a lot of smiling during the first seven years of their marriage. But the smiles had dimmed three years ago when Ed was diagnosed with emphysema and Phyllis had insisted that they sell the co-op and move to Cold Spring Harbor. At first they'd both argued that they were content in their apartment, but Phyllis won the argument when she told Ed, "I just want to take care of my daddy—and the beautiful lady who's become my second mother."

Serena had continued to resist the move to Long Island. She was certain Phyllis did not like her, and this made her question the fulsome phrases she was hearing. Eddie had scoffed at her doubts, of course . . . and then her first glimpse of the newly renovated guest cottage made her clap her hands with delight and forget her qualms.

Almost.

No expense had been spared. From the gray-stone fireplace in the living room—to the cushioned breakfast nook in the country kitchen—to the old-fashioned four-poster bed in the bedroom, every detail of the place had been designed to please.

Even during the last year of Ed's life, when oxygen equipment had become part of the décor, the cottage was still their sanctuary. They seized each day and celebrated it as best they could. During the first two years, they'd made love in front of the fireplace in the living room. Every day they'd eaten breakfast in the kitchen while they watched the bird feeder he'd installed outside the window. And four days ago on Thanksgiving, when he was dying, she'd held him in her arms to keep him warm in the four-poster bed . . .

Today, as the black limousine turned onto Spring Road, Serena could scarcely wait to let the memories in the little cottage embrace her.

When the limo driver opened the door and helped her out, she turned to Phyllis and whispered, "I don't feel up to a reception right now. If you'll excuse me, I think I'll go straight to the cottage and lie down."

Phyllis had a funny little smile on her face as she looked up at the taller woman.

"I'm sorry, but you won't be living in the cottage any longer, Serena," she said, not sounding sorry at all.

When the words finally penetrated, Serena asked, "What . . . what do you mean?"

"Now that Daddy's gone, my mother and Stuart will be living there."

"But that's my *home!* All my personal belongings are there."

Against her will, her lower lip began to tremble. She caught it between her teeth.

"I'm sure you can understand that I'd rather have my own mother living there than my father's second wife. Oh, *come on!* I hope to Christ you're not going to start crying again! Pull yourself together and listen to me very carefully: while we were at the cemetery, Vernon moved all your clothes and knick-knacks from the cottage and put them into your new room."

Knick-knacks? What was she talking about?

Their wedding portrait. The mother-of-pearl music box where she kept the jewelry Eddie had given her. The needlepoint eyeglass case she'd made for his rimless glasses; it spelled out *The Eyes Have It*. The white leather album with all the photos they'd taken in Alaska on their honeymoon.

Knick-knacks?

Phyllis was still speaking. "Your new room is on the first floor of my house, behind the kitchen." *My house*. She never included Chet and said *our* house, although he'd bought the place for her. "It has its own bathroom."

Was she supposed to say thank you for the bathroom?

Instead, she murmured, "I'm afraid I don't understand all this."

"What part didn't you understand?" Phyllis inquired with exaggerated politeness. "Do you want me to repeat it?"

Phyllis's pug-nosed face always seemed to radiate animosity. Today, swathed in mink, she looked like a Pekingese with acid indigestion.

Serena watched her light a cigarette and glance down the driveway. Her perpetual scowl deepened as cars began to arrive for the reception. The message to Serena was clear: this conversation was over.

Serena had one more question.

"Do you think this is what your father would have wanted, Phyllis?"

"I have no way of knowing that, and neither do you. Let me just say this—I'm in charge now. He made me the executor of his estate."

"Of c-course he did—you're his only child," Serena stammered, "but I th-thought I'd be staying on in my home."

A cacophony of car doors were slamming all around them.

"Look, I'd love to stand here chit-chatting with you,

Serena, but I have guests to take care of," Phyllis said.

With the cigarette jutting from the corner of her mouth like a lollipop stick, she seized Serena's arm and marched her toward the house. As they reached the side door, Serena glanced fleetingly at the gray-stone guest cottage, gold-washed in the late-afternoon sunshine. She ordered her mind to shut it out, and concentrate instead on her step-daughter's instructions.

"I suggest that you go to your room now and get settled."

As Serena began to make her way slowly toward the kitchen, she heard Phyllis say to one of their neighbors, "My stepmother is exhausted, so I told her to go lie down. She won't be joining us for the buffet."

Her voice was so sweet and solicitous that Serena looked over her shoulder to make certain the woman who was speaking was the same person who had just asked her if she wanted to hear the eviction notice repeated.

"Will she be staying on in the guest cottage?" the neighbor wondered aloud, sounding concerned.

"No, of *course* not! She's getting on in years, you know, and now that Daddy's gone she wouldn't be able to take care of herself."

More guests were coming through the front door. The neighbor raised her voice.

"Where will she go?"

Phyllis spoke loudly enough to be heard above the prattle of voices.

"I'm bringing her into my home, Celia. Chet and I will take her under our wing here. It's what Daddy would have wanted."

Serena found her new room behind the kitchen. She knew Cora, the Abbott's cook, slept on the third floor near the other two servants, but it was obvious the architect had intended this room for the cook. A single bed, a night table, a bureau, and a closet left barely enough space to walk. Her "knick-knacks" had been dumped on the bed, along with sheets, a blanket, and a pillow. The minuscule lamp on the night table supported a forty-watt bulb that glimmered dispiritedly behind a yellow parchment lampshade.

Most of her clothes had been squeezed into the closet. Her sable coat was missing. There was no room for the violet silk dress and the black suede coat with the ermine collar that she had worn to the funeral, and she wondered where she was going to hang them.

The mother-of-pearl music box containing her jewelry was conspicuous by its absence from the "knick-knacks" heaped on the bed.

The adjacent bathroom was smaller than the clothes closet. It was nothing more than a powder room with an incredibly narrow stall shower. Her drug items and cosmetics had been placed on a shelf above the washbasin. Serena thought about the bathroom she and Ed had shared in the cottage: it had mirrored walls, and a walk-in shower of rose-colored marble.

She picked up the wedding portrait which lay among her "knick-knacks" and whispered, "Eddie, Eddie, what am I going to do?" His happy face smiled back at her.

The only sound in the dismal bedroom was a hum of subdued voices and low-pitched laughter from the funeral reception now underway—for the husband she had just lost.

CHAPTER 13

Bradley Bellinger sat behind his leather-topped desk, waiting for Edward Franklin's relatives to settle down. After five minutes, he tapped a gold pen against his monogrammed coffee mug and said, "Are we ready to begin?"

Serena, who knew she had not been one of those to whom the question was addressed, glanced at Phyllis. She and her mother had their heads together, talking animatedly. As the others in the room grew quiet, they realized they were the ones holding up the reading of the will. Both exchanged meaningful looks and leaned back in their chairs.

"Before we begin these proceedings," Bradley Bellinger intoned, "I'd like to make a little announcement: each of you will receive a copy of the will after this meeting, so please remember to pick up your copy when you leave."

He glanced down at his own copy and commenced to read aloud: "I, Edward Samuel Franklin, being of sound mind . . ."

Phyllis, in a black wool pantsuit and diamond earrings so heavy they warped her little earlobes, sprang to her feet. She raised her hand as if she was in a third-grade classroom instead of a lawyer's office.

"Excuse me! Bradley? Do we really have to listen to the whole thing? You've known all of us for years; you're like part of the family. Can't you cut to the chase and summarize it for us?"

Bradley Bellinger, who did not like interruptions, tried not to frown.

"As you wish, Phyllis," he replied. He laid the file aside on his desk and spoke extemporaneously.

"There are several small bequests to household servants—and a ten-thousand-dollar donation to Greenpeace . . ."

"*What?*" blurted Phyllis. "What the hell is that—*Green Peas?*"

"Greenpeace," Bradley corrected her mildly. "It's an environmental organization whose members are dedicated to saving our planet and all its natural resources."

"I don't get it. Why would Daddy want to leave money to a bunch of wackos?"

Margaret intervened. "Ed was a left-wing liberal when I first met him in college." As soon as she realized everyone was looking at her, she shrugged dismissively.

"I thought he'd gotten over that college-kid stuff, but I guess I was wrong."

Without turning her head, Serena's eyes cast a sidelong glance at her husband's former wife. *That's right, you were wrong, Margaret. Eddie loved the beauty of nature and wanted to help preserve it.*

"Later we'll see about challenging *that* half-assed bequest," snapped Phyllis. "But for now, can't you get to the part about the *family?*"

Looking directly at Phyllis, Bradley bowed his head and resumed speaking.

"Certainly, my dear. Summarized very simply, the remainder of Edward's estate is divided into thirds: a third to you, and a third to each of his wives."

"No! I don't believe that! I'll never believe it!" shrieked Phyllis, leaping from her chair. She stamped her very small boot-clad feet, first one and then the other. A sort of demented dance.

"Daddy wouldn't do that to me!"

"To what or to whom are you referring?" Bradley asked. His expression was bland, but Serena thought she detected a wicked twinkle lurking behind his eyes.

"A *third* to Serena? *A third?* Why, they were only married a couple of years!"

"Ten years," the attorney corrected her quietly. Serena, watching his face, began to suspect he was secretly enjoying his role as straight man in this skit.

"Serena's an old woman and she has no family!" Phyllis ranted on. "What happens to her third when she dies?"

Bradley winced visibly and glanced at Serena. She raised her eyebrows and smiled, as though apologizing for her stepdaughter's lack of sensitivity.

"Upon Serena's death, her portion of the estate will go to you."

Phyllis glared, first at him and then at Serena.

"That's assuming she hasn't got it all spent by then!"

"Phyl," Chet protested in a low voice. "Get a hold of yourself."

"Shut up, toad! This has nothing to do with you!"

Serena picked up her coat and purse and headed toward the door, but Phyllis's piercing voice pursued her.

"Just where do you think you're going, madam?"

"Home."

"Sit down. We're not ready to leave yet."

Vernon had driven them in the white SUV.

"I'm ready to leave now. I'll take a taxi."

Bradley did not try to stop her, but he stood up and waved a large green-and-white legal-sized envelope.

"Don't forget your copy of the will, Serena!"

"I don't want it," she called over her shoulder just before the door closed.

* * * * *

After the moment of awkward silence that followed Serena's exit, Margaret turned to her daughter and said, "I rather resent your calling Serena an *old woman.*"

"Why?"

"Because I happen to know she's only sixty-five—three years younger than I am."

"Oh, for chrissake, Mother, don't be so touchy! We're talking *money* here, not how old Serena *is* or *isn't!*"

Stuart spoke for the first time.

"I, for one, am amazed to learn that Serena is sixty-five. She looks wonderful. I'd always assumed she was *forty*-something."

Margaret turned her head to glare at him.

"Just because she's tall and has no wrinkles on her face . . . and struts around with her nose in the air like she thinks she's Grace Kelly!"

"Grace Kelly's dead," Phyllis reminded her in that same piercing monotone.

"All right—*like Grace Kelly would look today if she was still alive.*"

"Now that you've all mentioned it, I happen to agree," Bradley Bellinger remarked innocently, or perhaps mischievously. "She does look like a silver-haired Grace Kelly."

Phyllis leaned across her mother to pound her fist on Bradley's desk.

"I don't give a rat's ass who Serena looks like! Can we *please* get back to the business we came here to discuss? Bradley, can we break this will?"

"I would strongly advise against trying to do that," he told her.

"Why?"

"Because it would take a lot of time and money to contest it in court, and I think most judges would see it as a fair division of the estate."

"Do *you* see it as a fair division of the estate?" demanded Phyllis, in a tone that clearly condemned any definition of *fair* except her own.

Bradley lowered his chin to his chest and peered at her over his rimless glasses.

"Yes, Phyllis. I do."

She stuffed her copy of the will into her purse and stood up.

"Well, then—I guess we're going to have to find another lawyer."

Serena squeezed her dark-green pantsuit into the crowded closet and slipped her arms into a white cashmere robe trimmed with black satin piping. The full-length mirror on the closet door reflected a tall woman with silver hair that fell around her face in natural waves, all gathered into a classic bun on the nape of her neck. Although it bore a sad expression today, her face was as smooth and unlined as a much younger woman's.

Her appearance had changed very little since the first day she had walked into Edward Franklin's office and asked him to represent her in a divorce action against her first husband. On that day, she'd never imagined that she would eventually be married to Edward Franklin. And on the day she and Eddie had married ten years ago, she'd never imagined that he would die and leave her at the mercy of his vindictive wife and hateful daughter.

She was not sure how much her third of Eddie's estate was worth in dollars, but she knew she needed money to live on if she was going to move out of this drab, cheerless room—this wretchedly unhappy house.

She knew she couldn't remain here and continue to watch Stu and Margaret living in the lovely gray-stone cottage she and Eddie had made their refuge.

Where would she go? Her brother was dead. Her son Mark had been dead for more than twelve years. Burt had remarried, not that she would have wanted to resurrect a marriage that was also dead. She had two cousins in California that she hadn't seen since they were all teenagers in Brooklyn—and that was the extent of her family.

She gazed at her husband's beaming face in the wedding portrait, which now hung on the wall of her dreary bedroom.

Eddie, she pleaded in her mind, *I don't know what to do! Please, please help me!*

CHAPTER 14

One Week Later

"We have an emergency here, Serena," said Phyllis, strutting into her stepmother's room without knocking, "and you're going to have to help us out."

Serena finished buttoning her blouse before responding.

"Good morning, Phyllis. What's the emergency?"

"Cora—our cook—decided to quit her job. The bitch packed up and left this morning, without giving any notice. I told her not to expect me to give her a reference."

"Can't you hire another cook?" asked Serena.

Knowing Phyllis as she did, she surmised that her stepdaughter had browbeaten Cora once too often.

"Of *course* I can hire another cook," said Phyllis irritably, "and I will. That's not the problem. The problem is that it takes time to find someone properly qualified, and tomorrow night is the Christmas/Hanukkah party for the officers of the New York Pharmacological Society . . . and their wives, of course."

Serena was puzzled. "How can I help?" she asked.

"I'm talking to you, but evidently you're not listening to me. I promised Chet that the dinner would be at *my house* this year. He's the vice-president, you know."

Serena nodded. She was glad that her stepson-in-law had respect from his colleagues. He certainly received none from his wife.

"There will be twelve people, including my mother and

stepfather, Chet and myself. And Cora is no longer here! *Now* do you understand?"

"What is it you want me to do?" she asked, but she had a pretty good idea what it was.

"I want you to cook the dinner, of course! I know you're a highly qualified cook."

"I haven't done any real cooking for ten years, Phyllis. I hardly think I'm qualified to prepare the type of dinner you're talking about."

"Please correct me if I'm wrong," Phyllis interjected swiftly, "but didn't you prepare the food for your own wedding reception?"

"Yes, but . . ."

"And didn't you tell me you owned a restaurant in Brooklyn before you married Daddy?"

"But that was . . ."

"Did you or did you not own a restaurant? Yes or no?"

"Well, *yes,* but it was just . . ."

"Just *what?*"

"Just a little neighborhood restaurant. I bought it twelve years ago after I divorced my first husband."

"And since my father paid for it, don't you think you owe me something?"

Stunned by the question, Serena sat down on her bed. "*Your father did not pay for it!* I had an inheritance from my parents. I used that."

"Why did you buy a restaurant if you were planning to marry my father?"

"I didn't plan any such *thing,* Phyllis. Your dad and I became friends during my divorce but he was a very ethical man, as you should know better than I do. He had been divorced from Margaret for seven years at that time, but he did not invite me to go out with him socially until my divorce was granted. Even then, I had no idea that he would ask me to marry him."

"How much money did you get when you sold the restaurant?"

Serena felt that the conversation was getting out of hand.

"I lost most of my money on the sale because I owned the place for only two years," she lied, realizing she'd said too much already—provoked by her stepdaughter's assumption that Eddie had bought her the restaurant.

"Well, I guess that just proves you're a very poor business woman," Phyllis concluded, "but I would venture to say that your restaurant experience demonstrates that you are capable of cooking for a relatively small dinner party."

"I haven't been in the restaurant business for the past ten years, Phyllis! And the only cooking I've been doing was for myself and your dad."

"Well, tomorrow night you'll be cooking for the officers of the New York Pharmacological Society. Cora and I planned the menu: jellied consommé with lemon slices, Caesar salad, veal Cordon Bleu, asparagus Hollandaise, dinner rolls, and for dessert—chocolate soufflé. Vernon will take care of the drinks before and after dinner, but we'll need hors d'oeuvres and a relish tray before dinner is served."

"Please, Phyllis! Don't ask me to do this!"

"I'm not *asking* you to do it. *You will do it!* You're hardly in a position to argue. You're virtually penniless, and you have no family except for this one. You're lucky to have a roof over your head."

"But I'm not really a gourmet cook!"

"For chrissake, if you can *read,* you can be any kind of a cook you could name. The food is already bought. My mother will help you . . . I'll help you . . ."

Serena had an instant Technicolor vision of herself

trying to prepare a dinner for twelve with two little kitchen witches underfoot telling her what to do. A scene from a horror movie.

"*No!* If I'm going to do it, I don't want any help from you or Margaret. I'll do the cooking myself, and I assume Darlene will do the serving."

"Naturally." Phyllis turned to leave the room, a smug smile wrestling with her normal scowl. "I'm glad you finally saw the light."

Serena surprised herself. She prepared the veal Cordon Bleu a day ahead of time and refrigerated the individual servings, ready for the oven. The consommé was refrigerated to jell in plenty of time for the party. The lemons, and all the relish tray and salad vegetables were washed, sliced, and refrigerated in plastic bags. She made her own dressing for the Caesar salad, and instead of using the frozen dinner rolls Cora had purchased, she made croissants herself.

She discovered a tarnished silver sleigh on the top shelf in the pantry—evidently part of a long-ago holiday centerpiece. After polishing it until it gleamed, she filled it with holly and placed it in the center of the table, where the green leaves and red berries contrasted pleasingly with the white damask tablecloth and napkins, the silver candlesticks and napkin rings.

Cora had bought frozen hors d'oeuvres in a local gourmet shop, so all Serena had to do was brown them in the oven before serving. The vegetables on the relish tray surrounded a crystal bowl containing her own special dip—cream cheese whipped with red horseradish.

The cocktails and dinner progressed smoothly, and Serena began to relax. The guests had lavishly praised each course as it was served. The portly president of the Pharmacological Society threatened to steal Phyllis's "cook."

Disaster struck while the chocolate soufflé was baking. In the dining room Phyllis rang the little silver bell she kept by her place at the table. Darlene, rushing through the kitchen to answer the summons, slipped on a few drops of Hollandaise sauce, which had dripped unnoticed on the floor. She lost her footing momentarily, and as she stumbled she slammed against the oven door with her considerable weight.

Serena cried, "Darlene, are you all right?"

The maid nodded, smoothed her uniform, and hurried on to the dining room. Quickly, Serena peered through the oven's glass door and saw her worst fears realized. The chocolate soufflé had fallen, now looking like the crater of Mount St. Helens after an eruption.

She stared at the ruined dessert for a moment, then turned to Vernon and asked, "Do we have any ice cream?"

When the butler produced two gallons of vanilla, she breathed a sigh of relief.

"Chocolate cookies?" was her next question.

He found a large unopened box of plain chocolate wafers, all of which Serena proceeded to crush with a rolling pin. Each dessert bowl served to the guests fifteen minutes later contained one large ball of vanilla ice cream rolled in chocolate cookie crumbs and lightly drizzled with raspberry syrup.

She stood by the door of the dining room and listened to the exclamations of pleasure as the guests devoured her concoction.

"Delicious!"

"Heavenly!"

"What *is* this, Phyllis?"

With a sense of foreboding, she heard her stepdaughter's reply.

"I have no idea what it is, but it was *supposed* to be chocolate soufflé."

The pots and pans were scrubbed and the dishwasher was gently churning soapsuds and hot water over the Lenox china. Serena could hear the guests in the front hall saying good night as she sat down with a cup of herbal tea at the kitchen table. She was exhausted, but satisfied with the results of her efforts. Her first culinary project in ten years had been pretty nearly perfect.

She'd almost panicked when the soufflé fell, but the substitute dessert she'd created at the last minute had gotten rave reviews. The president had asked for a second helping, but his wife had vetoed the request. Serena smiled at the memory.

At that moment the door opened and Phyllis appeared, her child's body inappropriately gowned in full-length gold lamé. "Well, you're looking very satisfied with yourself, madam."

Not certain how she should take the comment, Serena replied cautiously, "I thought it went fairly well."

"Oh, you *did*, did you?"

Phyllis was smiling, but it was not a pleasant smile. She teetered precariously on her high-heeled gold sandals, and Serena wondered how much she'd had to drink.

"I'm glad you came in now, Phyllis, because I want to tell you what happened to the chocolate soufflé . . ."

"Are we talking about the chocolate soufflé that you were supposed to prepare for dessert?" Phyllis inquired. Her smile looked more like a gargoyle grimace.

"Yes. You see, there was a little accident . . ."

Serena's explanation was cut short by a stinging slap across her face, delivered by Phyllis's small hand.

"*You self-righteous bitch!* Sitting here smiling, so proud of yourself because you did a little cooking!"

Phyllis tried to slap her again, but this time Serena saw it coming and ducked. The little hand, overloaded with diamond rings, struck the cup of just-poured tea spilling its contents into Serena's lap.

Serena leaped to her feet, crying out in pain as the hot tea scalded her thighs. Phyllis seemed oblivious to what had just happened.

"Sit down, you big baboon. I'm not finished with you yet! Don't you realize you humiliated me in front of my guests? I had told them to expect chocolate soufflé for dessert—and then in walked Darlene with the sorriest excuse for a chocolate soufflé that I ever expect to see! It looked like something for a kindergarten birthday party. I know you're from Brooklyn, but I hadn't realized you were so ignorant that you didn't know what a chocolate soufflé is!"

The barrage of insults and epithets felt like poison darts. Serena stood very still, protecting the essence of herself sheltered within her body, where the vicious barbs could not reach.

Without another word, she turned and walked out of the kitchen, away from her drunken stepdaughter.

"Remember the homeless old women you used to see in Brooklyn?" Phyllis called after her. "Well, Miss High-and-Mighty, you could end up becoming one of them, if you don't watch your step!"

When Serena closed the bedroom door, Phyllis raised her voice several octaves, sounding like a barker at the circus.

"Yeah, I can just see you now, shuffling along with all

your worldly goods piled in an old rusty shopping cart . . ."

She seemed overjoyed with the scene she had just described, and paused to emit several short snorts of laughter.

Serena was thankful she couldn't hear that strident voice anymore when she entered the tiny bathroom to medicate the blisters on her thighs.

CHAPTER 15

The next afternoon while Phyllis and Margaret were attending a charity luncheon and auction to raise money for homeless women, Serena walked quietly into the little TV room off the library. She turned on a soap opera so that Vernon or Darlene, if they happened to pass by, would assume she was watching it. She dialed Brad Bellinger's office.

Bradley was in a meeting room with a new client, but when his secretary told him who was on the line he excused himself and returned to his office to take the call.

Serena began by apologizing for the intrusion.

"Tricia told me you were busy, so I'll try not to take up too much of your time."

"Take as much time as you need, Serena. May I assume you're not calling to tell me your life is running smoothly?"

She was not surprised by the question. At the reading of the will, she'd had no doubt that the lawyer understood her unenviable position in the family after Edward's death.

"You assume correctly," she replied, shifting slightly in the recliner so her jeans would not put pressure on the bandaged blisters. "As a matter of fact, things are going so badly that I would like to move out of this house as soon as possible and get a small apartment somewhere out of the area—*New Zealand,* perhaps."

A dry chuckle from Bradley.

"Still got that sense of humor, I see. Ed always loved that about you—among your many other lovable qualities. Please tell me how I can help."

"I'm going to need money to start a new life somewhere else, Brad. How soon can I reasonably expect to get my inheritance?"

She heard a sigh on the other end of the phone.

"I was afraid that was the reason you were calling. Your stepdaughter and her mother have hired another attorney. They're suing the estate because they don't think you should be getting a third."

"I was his *wife!* What do they think I should get?"

Thunder grumbled in the distance as she waited to hear Brad's answer. She was ready to say she would accept a lesser amount just to bring the conflict to an end. She needed to start her new life as quickly as she could arrange it.

"Apparently they don't think you should get anything, Serena." He heard her gasp. "I know! Their claim is preposterous—and they'll never win! I tried to tell them that—and Anne Levine, their new lawyer, told them the same thing."

He drew a deep breath.

"They refuse to believe it! It's as if they're hoping you'll just . . . disappear."

Disappear?

Serena felt a sudden chill, like a sharp icicle tracing a leisurely path down her spine.

"What will happen now?" she asked, staring at the glass doors that overlooked the patio and the gardens. A pattern of fat rain drops, looking like a paw print, splashed against the door, and then another—an invisible animal walking sideways across the glass.

"Ed's estate could be tied up for months—maybe even *years*—in the courts. Unless they decide to drop their suit."

How could she endure living in this house with Phyllis for months or years? Right now she wasn't sure she could stand it for another day. Her heart shriveled in her chest and she felt disoriented, dizzy with disappointment.

Bradley heard the tortured silence.

"I could let you have fifteen hundred, Serena."

"No, Brad. It wouldn't be ethical for you to lend me money . . . you were Ed's attorney."

"I was also his friend—and still yours, I hope. The fifteen hundred would be a gift, not a loan. How do you think it makes me feel, knowing that you're caught in this damnable trap?"

"Not great, I guess. You're very kind, but I really couldn't accept money from you, Brad. I'll just have to think of some other way . . ."

"You know, I've always been sweet on you, Serena. How would you like to be my mistress? Believe me, I'd take good care of you!"

She laughed. She knew he was just joking, trying to make her feel better.

"Maybe I'd say yes, Brad—if I weren't so fond of Carla."

Still smiling, she hung up the phone and sat staring at the down-pouring rain.

A half hour later shrill voices in the front hall proclaimed the arrival of Phyllis and Margaret. They had returned from the luncheon, angrily cursing the unpredicted thunderstorm.

"Vernon, please see that these packages are taken over to my cottage." Margaret's voice. She must have bought something at the auction, thought Serena.

"Where's what's-her-name?" Phyllis's voice.

"Excuse me, madam?"

"Oh—you know. *Serena.*"

"Mrs. Franklin is in the TV room, madam." Although

respectful in the extreme, Vernon's voice could have flash-frozen a side of beef.

Using the remote, Serena increased the volume for *General Hospital.* Rising quickly from the red-leather recliner next to the telephone, she moved herself to the black mohair couch.

Moments later, Phyllis and Margaret appeared in the doorway.

"Well! Just look at the lady of leisure, watching her favorite trash on television!" said Phyllis.

"How was the luncheon?" asked Serena, hoping to deflect attention from herself.

"What do you care how the luncheon was? It's got nothing to do with you."

When she saw the sneer on Phyllis's face, Serena remembered her own mother's advice to her many years ago, when she was a child: *Be careful when you make an ugly face at someone. If you do it too often, it could grow that way.*

Evidently Margaret had neglected to warn her daughter of this possibility when she was a child. *Had Phyllis ever been a child?* Somehow, Serena couldn't imagine her playing jump rope or hide-and-seek with other little girls. She could only picture her as she was now . . . a child-sized adult with a mean disposition.

"Why aren't you in the kitchen starting dinner?" asked Phyllis. She snatched the remote from Serena's hand and clicked off *General Hospital.*

Reluctant to look at her stepdaughter's face when she answered the question, Serena focused on the wind-driven rain cascading down the glass door.

"Last night you gave me the impression that you were dissatisfied with my cooking. I assumed you had made some other arrangement."

"Well, you assumed wrong. You *will* continue to do the cooking in my house until I decide to hire someone else."

The word *hire* triggered a new idea in Serena's mind.

"Will I be paid for my services?"

"Paid!" echoed Phyllis. "Why, you ungrateful bitch!"

She lifted her hand as though preparing to strike her stepmother as she sat before her on the couch.

Serena stood up, towering over her stepdaughter. She already had a mouse under her right eye from the blow her face had received last night, and didn't want a matching one beneath her other eye.

"I'm very sorry, Phyllis," she said politely, not raising her voice. "If you want me to work in this house as your cook, you will need to pay me a salary."

"You seem to have forgotten that you're a member of this family, living in comfort under this roof through my generosity. As a family member, you should be willing to pitch in and help out in an emergency."

"I can't believe you're calling me a 'family member.' I have not felt like a member of this family since your father passed away," Serena told her, seeing the taut skin on her stepdaughter's face turn as red as the reclining chair in the corner.

"Are you *actually saying* that you will not do the cooking unless you are *paid?*" shrilled Phyllis.

"Yes. That is exactly what I'm saying."

"How much do you want?" Margaret interjected.

"Fifteen hundred dollars a month, and I want it in advance and in cash."

"What are you, *crazy?*" shrieked Phyllis. "We don't keep that kind of cash in the house!"

"I'm sure you'll be able to take it out of your bank," Serena suggested.

"And what about dinner *tonight?*"

Serena saw what she believed to be a hint of apprehension in the woman's almost-blue eyes—or maybe it was just confusion. She'd probably never expected Serena to come back at her. "Coming back" at Phyllis felt pretty damn good.

"You and your mother had a big lunch today. You could make sandwiches."

"I could, but I won't. Our husbands wouldn't be satisfied with just a sandwich! We'll go to a restaurant tonight," Phyllis snapped, seizing her mother's arm and pushing her toward the door.

From the hallway, she called loudly, "You're not invited, of course. As you just pointed out, you no longer consider yourself a member of this family, and we don't really make a practice of eating with the help."

After the four family members had departed in Stu's Lincoln, Serena prepared a light supper, using the leftovers from the previous evening, then sat in the kitchen with Vernon and Darlene to enjoy it.

When she dished out the dessert, Vernon pretended amazement. "*What!* No chocolate soufflé?"

She looked at him quickly, and then at Darlene, realizing they must have seen or heard the ugly scene last night between Phyllis and herself.

She smiled and said, "You'll just have to settle for my concoction. I think I'm going to call them *chocolate snowballs.*"

They all laughed, and Darlene said, "I'm sorry I got you in so much trouble, Mrs. Franklin."

"Please don't apologize," she answered. "Accidents like that do happen sometimes even in five-star restaurants."

"But if I hadn't stumbled against the oven . . ."

"If it hadn't been the soufflé, she would've found something else to complain about," said Serena. "She'd had too much to drink anyway. Really, Darlene, you mustn't blame yourself."

Vernon cleared his throat.

"Mrs. Franklin, my wife and I have talked it over . . . and we would like to come and work for *you* after—ah—after Mr. Franklin's estate is cleared."

Serena felt tears stinging her eyelids.

"Why, thank you! How kind you are!"

"We're not being kind, we're looking out for our own future," said Darlene.

"After Mr. Franklin passed," added Vernon, "and we saw the way Mrs. Abbott treats you now . . . well . . . when you move out of this house, we'll come to you wherever you decide to live."

After a moment's reflection, she decided it would not be appropriate to tell Darlene and Vernon about the lawsuit that could deprive her of the inheritance Eddie had intended her to have.

"You've made me feel much better . . . you'll never know how much," she said, smiling warmly at them both.

CHAPTER 16

Asleep in her narrow bed in the room behind the kitchen, Serena dreamed about Ed. She tried to embrace him in her dream, but he resisted her, saying something that she could not quite grasp. She awakened with a start.

The grandfather's clock in the front hall struck one.

It took her a few seconds to realize where she was. Moments before, she'd felt Eddie's presence, but now he was gone. If there really was a hereafter, she wondered what he had been trying to tell her. Could it have been something about her conversation with his friend Brad Bellinger—or about his daughter's suit against the estate?

He'd always said his daughter was "very fond" of her. Had he been telling her a white lie, or had he really believed it? Phyllis's actions since his death had left no doubt that not only was his daughter *not* fond of her, but that she actually hated her and probably always had. Remembering the events of the last two days made her groan aloud. If only she could turn off her brain the way you turn off a television set, and thus prevent unwanted images from parading before her closed eyes!

She rolled over and stared at the clock on the tiny night table. One twenty-five. If only she had a book to read! A lovely poem or an interesting story would provide a temporary escape from the disagreeable aspects of her life. But all her books were still in the cottage, and she couldn't face the inevitable arguments she'd have to go through to retrieve them. More to the point, if she actually succeeded in retrieving them, where would she keep them? There were no bookshelves here, and no room for any.

Wait a minute! There was a library in this house, and surely nobody would know or care if she borrowed one of its books at one-thirty in the morning. She swung her bare feet onto the floor and stood up.

The library was on the other side of the front hall. Her bare feet made no sound on the thick gray carpet. She passed the grandfather's clock as it struck half-past one. In the library, she lifted her hand to turn on a lamp so she could choose a book—but stopped when she realized there was a light coming from the adjoining TV room.

Could someone have left the light on by mistake? She was heading toward the open door, intending to turn it off, when she became aware of voices, easily recognizable as belonging to Phyllis and Margaret. When she heard her own name mentioned, her soft footsteps faltered and she almost stopped breathing.

Margaret was saying, "But what will you do if Serena refuses to go? What if she sends Vernon or Darlene?"

"Oh, Mother, stop worrying! Vernon will be busy driving Stuart to the airport tomorrow morning in the Lincoln, and I'll put Darlene to work polishing the silver."

"The silver doesn't need polishing."

"For chrissake, Mother, *I'm* running this house! If I tell Darlene to polish the silver, she'll damn well polish the silver!"

"I just don't like the whole idea. This man you hired—what's his name? Rudy? What if he talks? Don't you realize if there's a police investigation afterward, you'll be a suspect?"

"I already told you, nobody will ever be able to connect me to her death! I'll give her a spectacular funeral . . . even though she doesn't deserve it, the bitch . . . and I've promised to give Rudy a thousand dollars a month for the rest of his life as payment for his continuing silence."

"*A thousand dollars a month!* That's twelve thousand dollars a year!"

Phyllis emitted one of her snorting laughs.

"Oh, Mother, you're so naïve! Who knows how long *the rest of his life* will turn out to be?"

"What are you saying?"

"Forget I said *anything*. The less you know, the better."

"But how can you be sure Serena will die?"

"I'm sending her to De Luxe Leather to return my white suede evening bag—you know, the one with the broken catch? Rudy will be waiting in his car somewhere nearby."

"Maybe he'll only cripple her, and we'll be stuck taking care of her for the rest of her life," Margaret predicted gloomily.

"He's a professional! He's going to walk by and shoot her in the head before she has a chance to get out of the car, while she's still sitting behind the wheel. She'll die instantly!"

"What if someone hears the shot?"

"Don't you ever watch television, Mother? He's going to use a *silencer* on the gun, so the shot won't be any louder than somebody popping open a beer can."

"But a man with a gun and a silencer on *East Gate Drive?* Surely somebody will notice him!" Margaret insisted.

"He'll be carrying a coat over his arm; the gun and the silencer will be hidden underneath it."

"I'm just so afraid she won't agree to go to the leather shop, Phyllis. She's been acting pretty cocky lately. Last night when we got back from the restaurant, she asked me if I knew where her mother-of-pearl music box was—you know, the one with all her jewelry in it."

Phyllis snickered. "What'd you tell her?"

"I told her I didn't know what she was talking about."

"Good one. She can never prove it existed," Phyllis declared. "Listen, Mother, she'll go to the leather shop, don't worry. I'm going to give her the fifteen hundred dollars in cash that she asked for."

"I heard you tell Serena you don't keep that much cash in the house."

"Serena doesn't need to know there's a safe in the library," Phyllis retorted impatiently.

"She wants the money, so she'll be only too glad to do a little favor for me . . ."—the snorting laugh again—". . . and I can promise you she won't be so *cocky* by this time tomorrow!"

"I wish you weren't going to do this, dear. It's too risky."

"Okay, *fine*. I'll call Rudy and tell him to forget the whole thing, and we'll just sit back and watch Serena enjoying Daddy's money. Is that what you want?"

Margaret sighed. "No, of course not. What happened to our suit against the estate?"

"Anne Levine says we don't have a prayer of cutting Serena out of the will, and I can't find any other lawyer who's willing to try. That's why we have to eliminate her."

"I'm just afraid something will go wrong."

"Have a little faith in me, Mother! I've planned it very carefully. This is the only way we can be sure."

"But she *is* a good cook, you know! When she's dead, who'll do the cooking?" Margaret asked.

"Where are you? Out in left field with a hockey stick?" Phyllis demanded. "Getting rid of Serena is our first priority, not finding a cook. I'll call an agency the day after tomorrow. Stop whining, will you?"

There was a moment of silence, then Phyllis yawned loudly. "What time is it, anyway?"

Serena felt light-headed and her body was quaking like a dry aspen leaf. She knew she must not do anything stupid like crying out or fainting. They'd be coming out of the TV room any minute now, and they must not find her here in the library.

She tried to run, but her legs were not functioning properly. Holding on to the book shelves with her left hand she wobbled back to the front hall, stifling a gasp with her other hand as the grandfather's clock struck two.

She heard Phyllis say, "Go on back to the cottage, Mother. Everything is going to turn out according to plan, you'll see."

Serena tried again to run, but her quivering legs simply refused to support her body. She opened the hall closet next to the clock and slipped inside.

In another moment, the two women were in the hall.

"Where did you put your coat, Mother?" asked Phyllis.

Oh, no! What a stupid hiding place she'd picked! Footsteps, then the knob turned on the closet door, opening it a few inches. Serena held her breath and shrank back between the coats. In two or three seconds they would open the door the rest of the way and find her hiding here. And then they'd know she had overheard their conversation. Her whole body throbbed with every kettledrum beat of her heart.

"I think I put it on a chair in the dining room," Margaret said.

The chandelier went on in the dining room, pooling light in front of the hall closet, and Margaret called, "Here it is. I knew I put it in here."

Minutes later the front door closed, and Serena heard Phyllis lock it and activate the burglar alarm system. Would she go into the kitchen for a snack before she went to bed? Would she peek into Serena's bedroom to make sure she was in there, sleeping soundly? At the thought, her knees gave way totally, collapsing beneath her. She sank, trembling, onto the floor of the closet among the boots. Her heart seemed to have moved from her chest and was pounding in her throat.

If she wanted to outwit Phyllis's plan, she had many tasks to accomplish before morning—but she knew she had to wait until she was certain Phyllis was upstairs before coming out of her hiding place. She knew also that she had to control her trembling before she could do anything at all.

She took several deep breaths and told herself, *They want me to disappear, and I will . . . but on my own terms, not theirs.*

In the silent house it seemed much longer, but it was probably only five minutes later that she heard a toilet flush upstairs. Still fearful, she began to nudge the closet door open, a fraction of an inch at a time. The front hall was dark and deserted, silent except for the rhythmic ticking of the grandfather's clock. Serena padded slowly, on feet that were numb, through the dining room, the pantry, and the kitchen.

A sharp intake of breath when she saw the door of her room standing open! Then she remembered she had left it open herself when she went to the library to borrow a book. Only forty-five minutes ago.

She closed the bedroom door, turned on the light, and dragged her suitcase out from under the bed.

CHAPTER 17

"Good morning, Serena."

Phyllis sauntered into the kitchen in a maroon velvet robe that did unkind things to her sallow complexion. Without her usual heavy mask of make-up, Serena thought her stepdaughter looked like a recently exhumed mummy.

"Good morning, Phyllis."

She watched the diminutive woman pull herself up to her full height in an apparent effort to appear authoritative. She reached into the pocket of the unbecoming robe and withdrew an envelope.

"I have something for you. Last night I consulted my husband about your request for wages . . ."

Of course you did, thought Serena, biting her lip to prevent a faint smile at the unlikely image of Phyllis asking for Chet's opinion about anything.

". . . and we've decided to hire you as our cook. *Temporarily,* of course, until I decide to hire someone else. So here's the fifteen hundred dollars you asked for—in cash. Do we have a deal?"

"We have a deal," Serena agreed, slipping the envelope into the back pocket of her jeans. She imagined Phyllis planned to recover the money from her small bedroom later that day.

"Mother will be here any minute for breakfast," Phyllis continued, sounding almost like someone trying to make friendly conversation.

"I'll make some waffle batter," Serena said. "Waffles are

her favorite." She plugged in the waffle iron, then poured a cup of coffee and handed it to her stepdaughter. "So tell me—would you like waffles for breakfast?"

"Oh, no, just half a grapefruit and a slice of toast." She patted her concave stomach lovingly. "How do you think I stay so slim?"

Serena busied herself popping bread into the toaster and cutting a golden grapefruit in half so she wouldn't have to answer that question.

Not waiting for an answer, Phyllis rambled on. "Oh—by the way—later this morning, I'd like you to do me a little favor."

Here it comes! First the carrot, then the stick.

Phyllis had set her coffee cup on the dining-room table and was standing in the kitchen doorway with her hands flat against the doorjamb, swaying back and forth like a metronome.

Even if Serena hadn't overheard the plan for today, she would have been suspicious of Phyllis's civil comments and nervous manner.

"What is it?" she asked with what she determined was the proper degree of disinterest.

"Do you remember the white suede evening bag I bought last month?"

"No, not really."

She wouldn't make it easy for Phyllis to bait the trap.

"The catch is encrusted with semi-precious jewels. Well—anyway—the catch broke the very first time I carried it. I've been meaning to take it back to De Luxe Leather and get my money back. It cost five hundred dollars."

"Five hundred?" Serena echoed, knowing she was expected to be awed by such a large sum for an evening bag. As usual, Phyllis conveniently forgot that Serena had been married to her father, and that he had enjoyed surprising his wife with expensive gifts.

"On sale!" Phyllis finished triumphantly.

"Do you still have the sales slip?"

"Yes, I'll give you the bag and the sales slip when you're ready to leave. I used a credit card, so you won't be getting back any cash."

Serena bobbed her head to indicate she understood.

"I thought you could go around eleven." Serena was getting dizzy watching Phyllis sway back and forth, back and forth, in the doorway. "I'll give you the keys for the Jaguar, okay?"

"Okay."

"Ordinarily, I would've asked Vernon to do it," Phyllis blundered on, "but you see, he's taking Stuart to Kennedy Airport this morning."

Serena said nothing, letting her stepdaughter continue to wade knee-deep into unasked-for explanations for the errand.

"He's going to a CPA convention in Boston, you know."

"Uh-huh." Smiling pleasantly, Serena approached the twitching figure in the doorway with the slice of toast and sectioned half-grapefruit she'd asked for.

"Why don't you sit down in the dining room, Phyllis . . . your breakfast is ready. And I better pour you another cup of coffee . . . the one I gave you before must be cold by now."

At five minutes before eleven, Phyllis entered the kitchen clutching a bronze-and-white-striped shopping bag imprinted with the De Luxe Leather logo. Darlene and Serena were seated at the kitchen table polishing the silver.

"Time for your errand, Serena," she caroled in a high-pitched voice totally unlike her normal rasp. Darlene looked up, the expression on her face clearly asking: *Did this woman have a vocal cord implant since yesterday?*

Serena rose from the table, accepted the package from Phyllis, and picked up her denim jacket and her shoulder bag from the peg-rack by the back door.

"I'll need the car keys," Serena reminded her.

"Oh, yes, of course. Here they are!"

Phyllis withdrew them from the pocket of the hideous maroon bathrobe, which she was still wearing.

"Want me to pick up something for dinner tonight?" Serena asked. *A nice touch,* she thought.

"No, we have plenty of food in the freezer. I'll take out something to defrost while you're gone."

"Sounds good. I should be back in a half hour or so," Serena called cheerfully.

"Drive safely!" Phyllis cautioned in her brand-new best-friend voice.

Darlene tossed a quick glance at Serena and rolled her eyes.

Serena drove past the De Luxe Leather store where she knew her assassin was waiting, and continued on for several blocks to the Long Island Railroad Station. A bizarre calm had overtaken her, and she wondered how long it would last. After parking her car in front of a nearby pizzeria, she opened the trunk and removed the suitcase she'd packed and placed there during the night, using the *duplicate set of keys* that Phyllis didn't know she had. She shuddered, remembering how terrified she'd been when she entered the garage from the kitchen, uncertain whether opening the adjoining door would activate the burglar alarm.

She locked the car, and pocketed both sets of keys. The evening bag and sales slip, in the bronze-and-white-striped shopping bag, still lay on the front seat.

A farewell look at her silver-gray Jaguar. It had been a gift from Eddie on their first Christmas together in the guest cottage, but Phyllis had confiscated the keys on the day of her father's funeral. Although the car was Serena's, today was the first day she had been allowed to drive it since then.

Of course she knew why the restriction had been waived today!

Inside the Cold Spring Harbor station, she bought a ticket from the vending machine and studied the schedule on the wall. Her watch told her it was now eleven-twenty; her heart plummeted when she realized she had just missed the train at eleven-ten. The next one would not arrive until twelve-ten.

Should she remain inside the station or sit outside on a bench? She opted to remain inside, where she and her suitcase would be less conspicuous.

She glanced again at her watch. Only three minutes had gone by.

The assassin would be waiting for a tall woman with silver-gray hair to pull up in front of (or near) the De Luxe Leather shop in a silver-gray Jaguar coupe. He would be looking for her right about *now,* she realized. If he found the car where she'd left it but couldn't find *her,* he might come looking for her in other shops along East Gate Drive.

And he just might come looking for her here in the Long Island Railroad Station! The bizarre calm she'd felt earlier began to stretch tight.

She needed to change her appearance.

Snapping open her suitcase, she removed her Kelly-green down jacket with the fur-trimmed hood. She folded the denim jacket, placed it in the suitcase and snapped it shut, fumbling a bit when her hands shook. She donned the much warmer jacket, and pulled the hood up over her head, hiding her hair completely. It was an unseasonably warm day for early December and her head began to perspire almost immediately, but she kept the hood fastened tightly at the neck. She retracted the handle on her suitcase and slid it beneath the bench. Hoping she didn't look so tall, sitting down, she slid down so she was sitting on the end of her spine. The bizarre calm had been replaced by uncontrollable trembling.

Just after noon, a man in a baggy camel's-hair sports jacket entered the station. Acne scars, like tiny potholes, covered his face. Although the day was clear and sunny, he carried a plaid raincoat over his left arm. He scrutinized her quickly, then studied the train schedule on the wall for several minutes. She'd never seen him before, and he did not look like a Cold Spring Harbor resident.

Fear surrounded Serena like an icy fog. Her scalp felt as if it had become too small for her skull. Her mouth was so dry she couldn't swallow. *Take deep breaths,* she told herself, *but make them quiet ones. We're the only two people in this station. If he's the guy, and he realizes I'm frightened—it will be all over but the funeral sprays.*

At last he said, "Nice day."

She nodded her head, feeling the bizarre calm descend on her again.

"Mmm-hmm."

"Aren't you kinda warm in that jacket?" he asked.

She replied in a quavering, old-lady voice, "I've been having chills all morning. I think I have the flu. I'm on my way to Jamaica to see my doctor."

She let loose with a wracking cough that went on for a

full minute, following it with a faint moan.

The man said, "Hope ya feel better soon," and stepped outside. Serena noticed he had not bought a ticket. After a few minutes she went to the window. and watched him walk down East Gate Drive and stop next to her car. At the same moment, she heard the unmistakable sound of an approaching train.

Oh, thank you, God!

Three women walked quickly into the station and bought tickets from the vending machine. Her eyes still focused on the window, she yanked her suitcase out from under the bench, pulled up the retractable handle. She decided to walk out of the station with the three women. Her final glimpse of the man with the raincoat showed him pushing open the door of the pizzeria. How long would he remain there if he didn't see her?

The train was in the station.

She trundled the suitcase outside behind the three women, who she imagined were bound for a shopping spree in Manhattan. She got on the nearest car with them, took off the down jacket and sank, exhausted and perspiring, into a seat by the window. The man with the plaid raincoat was nowhere to be seen. When the train began to move, she released a gusty sigh and closed her eyes, feeling like a marionette without strings.

When her heart rate slowed to a normal rhythm, she began to consider what her destination should be. *Brooklyn?* Her certificate of deposit was there; she could cash it in. She'd bought a ticket for Penn Station, but she could change trains at Jamaica and head for Brooklyn instead.

But Phyllis knew she'd been born and brought up there, and Serena had (foolishly) led her to believe that she might have a bank account there. That would be the first place she would send the creep to look for her. She didn't know if it was possible for an investigator to track her through bank accounts, but why take a chance?

No, Brooklyn was out. She knew her CDs were safe there; she could cash them in later.

Right now, it would be better to get out of New York altogether. The nearest large city was Philadelphia. The train she was on would end up in Penn Station, so she could buy a ticket right there and catch the next train to Philadelphia.

But wouldn't it be cheaper to take a bus? The only money she had with her was the cash Phyllis had given her earlier this morning, so she'd have to start learning to economize. She had no idea how long that fifteen hundred dollars would have to last.

It was almost one-fifteen when the train pulled into Penn Station. During both her marriages she had always traveled by air or automobile, so she'd never been in a train station before. She was bewildered at first by the trains arriving and departing on different levels, the mile-high escalators, the arrows pointing to Thirty-Fifth Street, Thirty-Fourth Street, or Thirty-Third Street. When she saw a kiosk that offered information, she stopped.

"Excuse me. How do I get to the bus terminal from here?" she asked a balding man about her own age.

"Where do you want to go?" he asked.

"Philadelphia."

"You traveling alone?"

Serena nodded.

"Well, sugar, I would advise you to take a taxi." He paused and pointed toward the other end of the station. "Tell the driver you want the Port Authority Bus Terminal.

It's between Fortieth and Forty-Second Streets, only a few blocks from here, so don't let him take you on a Cook's tour of Manhattan."

He winked.

CHAPTER 18

"What do you mean—*you couldn't find her?*" Phyllis screamed into the phone. "She left here a few minutes after eleven, with a package from De Luxe Leather. She was wearing jeans and a denim jacket, she was driving a silver-gray Jaguar! I even gave you the *license number,* for chrissake!"

"Yeah, yeah—I found the car okay. She wasn't in it, but the package was right there on the front seat. I figured she went someplace, but was coming right back."

"Didn't you *look* for her?" Phyllis shrilled.

"Chill out, lady. Better believe I looked. The car was parked in front of a pizzeria, and I looked in there. I figured maybe she went in for a slice."

"Where *else* did you look?"

"De Luxe Leather, drug store, supermarket, train station . . ."

"Train station." Phyllis's almost-blue eyes glittered. "Was anyone in the train station?"

"Just some old lady with the flu. She wasn't wearing no denim jacket."

"What *was* she wearing?"

"Green jacket, I think, with a hood."

"Was it a down jacket trimmed with white fur?"

"I . . . ? dunno? . . . ah? . . . maybe . . ."

"You fucking idiot! That was *her!*" Phyllis stamped her little feet, first one and then the other. "Well, you're not getting any more money from me until . . ."

She paused when she noticed Margaret tapping a frantic forefinger on her lips. Darlene had just become visible through the door of the TV room, dusting furniture in the library.

". . . until you fulfill your end of the agreement," she finished, lowering the volume of her voice before she hung up the phone and turned to Margaret.

"Come with me, Mother."

"Where are we going?"

"We're going to inspect Serena's room. I think she flew the coop."

Cherry Hill, New Jersey: Same Day

"Telephone call for you, Steve," called Juliette.

He emerged from the restaurant kitchen and walked briskly toward the front desk.

"Who is it?"

She shrugged her shoulders and handed him the phone.

"It's a man."

"Steven Kingsley speaking."

"Good afternoon, sir. This is Dr. Lazarus."

Dr. Lazarus was the geriatric specialist Dr. Wolf had recommended to him after Anne Marie had been diagnosed with Alzheimer's.

"Yes, doctor?" Steve ran a heavy hand over his brush-cut gray hair. "Is my wife all right?"

"Mrs. Kingsley has lapsed into a coma."

"A coma?" he echoed. He rubbed his head again.

Aware that the hostess was standing next to him listening intently, he murmured, "Excuse me for a moment," covered the mouthpiece and said, "It's almost lunch time, Juliette. Please go check the salad bar."

"I already did that."

He gestured. *"So go check it again!"*

She tossed her curly red hair and sauntered toward the salad bar, aware that he could not help but see and admire the sinuous swing of her hips.

One time—*and one time only*—had he broken his iron-clad rule about socializing with his employees. *Socializing?* Now there was a euphemism! He'd had sex with the woman last night, and now he bitterly regretted it. Today she was behaving as if she'd been promoted from *hostess* to *mistress.* Her suggestive glances and double-entendre remarks made it plain that she was available whenever he wanted to come back for seconds. He despised himself for having given in to temptation once, and he had no intention of letting it happen again.

He turned away from his view of Juliette's busy backside, and spoke again into the phone's mouthpiece.

"Sorry for the interruption. Let me give you my cell-phone number, Dr. Lazarus. I'd appreciate your using it in the future. Now—please tell me when she went into a coma."

"It was discovered this morning when the orderly brought in her breakfast tray. He and the nurses tried repeatedly to awaken her before calling me. Of course I got over to Tall Pines as soon as I could, and examined her."

"How long do you think this—this problem will continue?" asked Steve.

"A coma rarely lasts beyond two to four weeks, Mr. Kingsley, but you must be aware that a persistent vegetative state can last for years . . . or even decades."

Steve's mouth formed a silent *no,* rejecting that possibility.

"But your best guess is two to four weeks, right?"

"I cannot make any promises," the doctor replied firmly, "but *yes,* that would be my best guess at this time."

"What are you doing for her right now?"

"Trying to prevent infection."

"Infection? What sort of *infection* could occur, with a patient lying quietly in bed?" asked Steve. He wondered if the doctor was an alarmist, giving him all the worst-case scenarios.

"Bedsores are a very common problem with patients in a comatose state," Dr. Lazarus told him.

"But that's not too serious, is it?"

"On the contrary, they're painful and quite serious. Any open sore is an invitation to bacteria, particularly if the patient is in a weakened condition."

Steve rubbed his head again.

"Any other problems we have to worry about?" he asked, sounding almost hostile.

"Yes. The real villain is pneumonia."

A few moments later Steve replaced the receiver in its cradle and sighed as he saw Juliette approaching.

At sixty-five, Steve was a tall, good-looking man with brush-cut gray hair. His afternoon visits to Gold's Gym helped ensure a back that was strong and straight, and a body still powerful. His facial features were rough-hewn; strangers sometimes asked him if he had American Indian ancestors.

With his wife in a nursing home, few people would have blamed him if he had taken a mistress. It had not occurred to him to seek a substitute for the woman he had chosen to marry more than forty-five years before. His life was circumscribed by his responsibilities at his restaurant and his weekly visits to Anne Marie. Holidays were celebrated with his daughter and son-in-law. Soon there would be a grandson or granddaughter. A small but beautiful family . . . a successful business. He told himself every day that he still had much to be thankful for.

He'd been sure he could handle Juliette. When she was hired he'd made her aware of his rule about not socializing with his employees, but she chose to ignore that by inviting him several times to have a drink with her after work. He'd consistently declined her invitations, done nothing to encourage her further, but even without encouragement she continued to come on to him.

Last night, believing all the employees had left the building, he checked all the doors and windows as he always did before setting the burglar alarm. When he walked into the locker room, Juliette was waiting for him, wearing nothing except thigh-high black stockings and a pair of high-heeled black sandals. She slithered across the room and put her arms around his neck. He had tried to push her away, but his testosterone—combined with ten years of enforced celibacy—anesthetized his conscience. He'd taken what she was offering, right there on a bench in the locker room.

No love was involved. He didn't even like her very much. He'd always been attracted to gentle, soft-spoken women, but Juliette had a desirable body, and he was sorely in need of sexual release. His subsequent regret was greater than any pleasure he might have felt.

"Your wife is in a coma?" Juliette asked now, her face a portrait of sympathy. She slid a comforting hand up and down his arm. Well, he couldn't very well deny the coma, could he? She'd overheard him repeat the doctor's word when he first picked up the phone.

"Yes—but the doctor told me it will last no longer than two to four weeks."

Hoping none of the other employees had noticed her proprietary gesture, he removed her hand from his arm and headed back to the kitchen.

He knew he would have to do something about Juliette.

New York City

In the rest room of the Port Authority Bus Terminal, Serena put on the denim jacket again, folded the down jacket and replaced it in her suitcase. Feeling much more comfortable, she went to the Reindeer ticket counter and bought the last available seat on the 2:00 p.m. bus to Philadelphia. When she boarded the bus, the only seat remaining was the window seat directly behind the driver. Her seatmate, a thin, middle-aged man, stood up to let her pass. He told Serena that sitting beside the window made him queasy and said he hoped she didn't mind taking the window seat. She assured him she didn't mind. He wanted to chat some more, but Serena told him, apologetically, that she needed to take a nap because she hadn't slept well the night before.

The truth was she hadn't slept *at all*, and now the adrenaline that had fueled her body as she fled from Cold Spring Harbor had trickled down to *empty*. Almost as soon as the bus roared out of the terminal, Serena nodded off.

Again, she dreamed of Eddie, her joy at seeing him diminished by his unhappy face and unintelligible message. She strained to hear his words and comprehend them. *What was it that he was trying to tell her?*

* * *

An hour and a half later she opened her eyes and blinked in the mid-afternoon sunshine. She was just in time to see a dark-red sports utility vehicle filled with laughing teenagers moving south in the left-hand lane alongside the bus. Seconds later, she noticed a sign that said: *Next Exit - #4 - Camden*. The SUV began to pick up speed. The youngsters evidently wanted to turn off at Exit #4, but they should have been in the far *right*-hand lane to accomplish that feat. Their vehicle was in the far *left*-hand lane, blocked by the bus in the middle lane.

As she pressed her face against the window and watched in horror, the teenaged driver of the SUV gunned the motor, signaled right, and sped recklessly in front of the bus. As the rear end of the car disappeared from view, she had a fleeting glimpse of the license plate. The first three digits were SGD—which caught her eye because they happened to be her maiden initials. Serena Grace D'Agostino.

The next few minutes were like a scene from a disaster movie. In an effort not to hit the car full of teenagers, the bus driver pumped the brake and veered sharply to the right. The brake action jolted all the passengers and made a sound like hissing blasts of thunder. Despite the driver's frantic tug of war with the steering wheel, momentum carried them in slow motion down a short hill beside the highway. When it reached the bottom of the embankment, the bus rolled over onto its roof.

CHAPTER 19

Terrified screams and cries of pain followed the bus's impact with the ground, as, in an effort to reach an exit, uninjured passengers began to scramble over those who were injured.

The bus driver shouted above the pandemonium, *"Quiet please! Help will be here very soon."* Surprisingly, the din subsided. His voice was loud and authoritative.

He tried repeatedly to enable the exit doors but they refused to open; apparently the collision had damaged the mechanism that controlled them. The driver forced open the window beside his seat and crawled out onto the ground. On the Turnpike, other vehicles had stopped and good Samaritans were climbing down the grassy hill to help. Those strangers and the driver began helping the passengers who were able to exit through the driver's window. All the other windows could not be opened.

The middle-aged man who'd been sitting beside Serena had a panic attack and kept gasping, "Please help me, I can't breathe." Serena tried to calm him down by promising to assist him. She could see he was a highly nervous person.

She half-pushed, half-dragged him to the window and called to the group of helpers, "Can someone please give a hand here? This man is very upset!"

A few minutes later the man was eased through the window with the aid of two brawny truck drivers. Weeping with relief, he sat down on the grass near other passengers who had managed to get out. The driver and the good Samaritans helped several more passengers to exit the bus, including a woman and her infant. Serena counted everyone in the group and informed the driver that seventeen passengers, counting herself, had got out through the window.

The driver nodded his thanks. He contacted the dispatcher's office on his walkie-talkie to report the accident and describe the bus's location. He concluded by repeating what Serena had just told him.

"Seventeen got out. The rest are injured. How serious? That I don't know yet. We'll need paramedics, ambulances. How many? Jeez, I was carrying fifty-two passengers. You do the math."

After ending the call, he told the group sitting on the grass, "Ambulances and cops will be here in a couple minutes. Did anybody besides me see what happened?"

Serena looked down at her hands, saying nothing, because she didn't want to call attention to herself. She was sure that newspaper and television people would follow along with the arrival of the ambulances and police vehicles. She didn't want Ed's family to see her picture on television or in the newspaper. Surely someone else had seen what happened!

Flashing lights and the wail of sirens heralded the arrival of New Jersey State Police, half a dozen ambulances, and a fire truck. Drivers of the first rescue vehicles paused to look down the embankment, then drove on for another mile, where the hill gradually leveled off. They made U-turns onto the grass, and doubled back to the accident scene.

Serena had heard about the "Jaws of Life," and now she watched in amazement as several rescue workers used the device to remove both of the bus's jammed exit doors. First they inserted the tips of the spreader arms into the crack of the door. Then they turned on a hydraulic motor to which the "jaws" were attached by a hose, and gradually spread the arms—like slowly opening a huge power-driven pair of scissors—until the door broke loose and dropped to the ground. The project was complicated by the fact that the bus was lying upside down. The workers had to stand on hastily erected platforms in order to reach the doors.

Once inside, the paramedics walked swiftly through the inverted bus, attaching different colored tags to each injured passenger. Serena deduced that they were using the color-coded tags to assign a priority to each passenger, ensuring that those who had suffered the most life-threatening injuries would be treated and transported to a hospital first.

She watched as a red-tagged woman, unconscious, with blood oozing from her ears, was lowered in a basket on ropes from the forcibly opened exit. Serena wondered aloud why she was strapped to a board. The man who had been her seatmate, now recovered from his panic attack, explained that her obvious head injury could involve the neck and spine; the board would keep any affected vertebrae from shifting and possibly causing further damage to her nervous system.

"How do you know all this?" she asked.

"I read a lot," was his answer.

The basket was loaded into one of the waiting ambulances, and together they watched it roll south on the grass until the terrain leveled off enough to allow access onto the right-hand lane of the Turnpike. The ambulance picked up speed, and the siren began its keening cry.

Working swiftly and efficiently, the paramedics provided emergency treatment to the remaining passengers, and carried or assisted them from the bus. As the last slanting rays of the sun cast an ocher-yellow glow on the scene, ambulances were departing and more were arriving every few minutes. Except for the TV cameramen and newspaper photographers, Serena imagined a battlefield might look a lot like what she was seeing.

While the rescue operations were in progress, police officers began to interview the seventeen passengers who were ambulatory. All seventeen had declined a trip to the hospital.

Serena's interviewer, Hector Rodriguez, was a young State Trooper who seemed very nervous. She suspected it was the first time he had interviewed victims of a major accident. It was the first time she had been a victim of a major accident—so she guessed they were evenly matched.

She knew she would be asked to identify herself, and she had already decided what name she would use. The same one she'd used to purchase her bus ticket.

"Grace D'Agostino," she told him.

"Did you think the driver of the bus was going too fast?"

"No."

"Did you see what caused the accident?"

Guiltily, she thought of the dark-red SUV filled with teenagers, recklessly pushing their luck as they zoomed in front of the bus. She noticed the bus driver standing nearby and suspected he was listening to the interview.

"I was asleep," she lied, looking again at her hands.

"What do you remember about the accident?"

"I remember a terribly loud noise when the driver was pumping the brake," Serena answered, "and I smelled burning rubber."

"You saw him pumping the brake?"

"Yes, I was sitting right in back of him."

"But you didn't see what caused the accident?"

"No."

"Do you think the driver handled the situation well?"

"Yes, I do," Serena said eagerly. She didn't want to get the driver in trouble—but she didn't want to tell this nice young man that she had witnessed the cause of the accident, either.

"He went off the road as if—well, as if he was trying to avoid hitting something."

The young policeman was looking at her quizzically.

"Like what?"

"I don't know. It was just a feeling I had. What reason would he have had to swerve off the road except to avoid hitting something?"

Maybe she'd said too much.

"Here's my card. If you think of anything else, let me know. Okay?"

"Okay."

Hector Rodriguez went on to the next ambulatory passenger. She was a tough-looking blonde. The heavy black eyeliner around her eyes made her look like a raccoon wearing a straw hat. She said her name was Gloria Gazelle.

"Did you think the driver of the bus was going too fast?" asked the officer.

"Yeah, he was going *way* too fast," Gloria said. "He was changing lanes, taking all kinds of chances . . ."

Serena couldn't restrain herself.

"He was not!" she exclaimed. "You know that's not true. Why are you saying these things?"

"Aw—I had a gig tonight, singing in a little club in South Philly," Gloria told her in a sandpaper voice. "I'll never get there in time now, with all this shit going down."

Serena wondered what sort of songs she sang, with that rough voice.

"It's too bad about your job, but that's no reason to try to get the bus driver in trouble!" she said reproachfully.

"Do you want to change your story, Miss Gazelle?" asked Hector Rodriguez politely, his pencil poised above his notebook.

"Yeah, okay. I guess he didn't do nothing wrong. I was just pissed about missing my gig."

After accepting a card from the State Trooper, she glanced at Serena and jerked her head toward the driver, who was still standing nearby listening to the interviews.

"What're you—his mother or something?"

"No, just a passenger, like you."

After Gloria flounced away, the bus driver stepped forward and said, "I'd like to thank you for what you just did. That was very kind of you."

Serena smiled and shrugged her shoulders. The bus driver sat down beside her on the grass.

"I was cut off by a bunch of slap-happy kids driving an SUV," he said miserably. "I had to swerve off the road to avoid hitting them."

He added bitterly, "They got off at exit number four and kept right on going."

"I know," Serena said without thinking.

The driver turned his head and gave her a searching look.

"I thought you said you were asleep."

"Oh, yeah, I was. What I meant was . . . I know the accident couldn't have been your fault."

They sat for a few minutes in silence, watching another ambulance take off. This one was carrying three patients, with injuries of less severity. Serena suddenly thought about her suitcase.

"When will we be able to get our luggage?"

"Not today, that's for sure," said the bus driver. "Everything has to stay like it is until the guys from NTSB come here and inspect everything."

"NTSB . . . ?" she echoed.

"National Transportation Safety Board."

"Oh, of course. When will they come?"

"Later tonight probably—or tomorrow morning at the latest."

"Will they send another bus to take us on to Philadelphia?" she asked glancing at Gloria Gazelle, who was gesturing and talking animatedly to the middle-aged man with whom she'd shared her seat on the bus.

"Sure, sooner or later," said the bus driver. "You got someone waiting for you in Philly?"

She shook her head.

"No, I don't even know anyone there." Noting his surprised expression, she added, "My husband died a few weeks ago. I was just going there to start a new life."

"You got no kids?"

"I had one son, but he was killed in a car accident twelve years ago."

Was there some reason she was telling this stranger her whole life story?

She thought he must be wondering why she was traveling to Philadelphia to start her new life. *What was wrong with New York?* He was looking at her and frowning as if puzzled. Aware that she was not a good liar, she thought he might suspect she'd been telling a lie about not seeing what caused the accident.

He appeared to be studying her hair, her face. It was hard to guess what he was thinking, but his next question surprised her.

"You Italian? I heard you give your name to that cop—Grace D'Agostino?"

"My father was Italian. My mother was Jewish."

He clapped a hand to his head.

"Hey! No wonder I felt like I knew you from somewhere. You're not gonna believe this—my *mother* is Italian, and my *father* is Jewish. How d'ya like that?"

She nodded and smiled. Very small ones. "A coincidence," she said.

She studied *his* face now, and saw a nice-looking man, very dark curly hair just starting to turn a little gray at the temples, probably in his late thirties or early forties. He appeared to be a little older than her son Mark would have been. With his dark hair and dark-brown eyes, he could almost have been her son.

"You know my name, but I don't know yours," she said.

"It was posted in the front of the bus, but you probably didn't notice. My name is Clifford Kingsley."

CHAPTER 20

Another State Trooper approached them. This man obviously knew the bus driver.

"Cliff? We'll need to have you come to the station now. We want to hear your story again—and I guess you know you'll have to take a blood test."

"I got no problem with that, Hank. Everybody off the bus now, right?"

"Right. Let's go, old buddy."

"Gimme one minute? I need to call Cheryl. This lady's got no place to go and she doesn't know the area. She's going to stay at my house until she gets her luggage."

Serena's eyes blinked in astonishment, but she said nothing.

"Another bus is on its way to pick up seventeen people and take them to Philadelphia; maybe she'd rather wait for that," the police officer said, directing his statement to both of them.

"I know, but this lady's a friend of my family," said Cliff. "My wife would never forgive me if I let her go on to Philadelphia by herself."

He winked at Serena.

The State Trooper looked at her and frowned.

"This okay by you, lady?"

She nodded. Somehow she was sure that this man was meant to play a role in her new life. She knew she trusted him.

"Make it fast," said the police officer named Hank, looking at his watch.

Cliff pulled a cell phone out of his pocket and placed the call. Just before he hung up, he said, "And give Dad a call and let him know I'm okay, honey."

After pocketing his cell phone, he handed Serena a Reindeer Bus Company card; he'd printed his name and address on the back of it.

"Cheryl will be expecting you."

He addressed one last question to the officer. "You guys'll see she gets there, won't you?"

"Don't worry, we'll take care of it."

Feeling certain somehow that she had made the right decision, she watched him get into a State Police vehicle with several officers. She lifted a hand to wave goodbye, and turned around to see a TV camera man behind her. Had he been filming them as they talked to the State Trooper?

"Did you take my picture?" she asked anxiously.

He grinned. "Yeah. Ever seen yourself on TV?"

"Is my picture going to be on TV?" she asked, her heart starting to pound again.

"Watch Channel Ten tonight . . ."

Before she could say another word, he was lost in the crowd of curiosity seekers, passengers still remaining, policemen, media people, and rescue workers getting ready to leave.

It was after seven o'clock when another police car picked up Serena and drove her to the address Cliff Kingsley had given her. Night had descended like a dark drop cloth on the South Jersey area; nature had turned on no moon or stars to illuminate the quiet streets. A mournful gray mist shrouded the streetlights.

For the first time since the accident, Serena thought about the happy-go-lucky kids in the dark-red SUV who had caused the disaster. They were probably at a party somewhere in the area, dancing and drinking beer.

Recalling the red-tagged woman with blood oozing from her ears, she gave in to a moment of rage. Of course those young people hadn't meant to harm anyone, but if that woman died, and if Clifford Kingsley lost his job—the driver of that SUV, and no one else, would be responsible.

Cheryl Kingsley was waiting for her when the cop car pulled up in front of a red-brick bungalow; she dashed down the sidewalk and greeted Serena with a hug.

"Oh, I've been so worried! Such a terrible accident! I've been sitting here watching it over and over again on television—it's on every channel."

She paused for breath, and added, "In fact, I recognized you as soon as you got out of the car because a half hour ago I saw my husband talking to you on TV! Can you believe that?"

Serena nodded and frowned. This was not good news.

Cheryl looked back at the police car. "Where's your luggage?"

One of the State Troopers answered that question. "She can't get it until after the guys from NTSB have been there."

Serena smiled at the officers who had driven her to Delran. "Thanks, guys! You've been very kind."

The Troopers smiled back and gave her an informal salute.

"Good luck," they called, as the cruiser pulled away from the curb.

Inside the house, she said to Cheryl, "I can't believe you and your husband are letting a complete stranger stay at your house. Does he do things like this all the time?"

Cheryl laughed.

"No, this is a first. He told me on the phone that he just couldn't let you go on to Philadelphia alone after the accident. He said you don't even know anyone there. Is that true?"

Serena nodded.

"By the way, my name is . . ."

She paused. Her ticket had been bought under the name of Grace D'Agostino, and that was the name she'd given the bus driver.

". . . Grace."

"And I'm Cheryl."

Serena sniffed. "Mmm! What do I smell?"

"Beef vegetable soup. It's been cooking all day in the crockpot while I was at work," said Cheryl.

"Where do you work?"

"I'm a hairdresser. I work at a local shop in Delran."

"That's convenient."

Serena glanced admiringly at the younger woman's sleek blond haircut.

"Could you eat a little something, or are you still too upset?" asked Cheryl.

At that moment Serena realized she hadn't eaten anything since breakfast, and that had been a scanty meal because she'd been too nervous to eat more than a few mouthfuls.

"I'm hungry," she admitted, "and that soup smells marvelous."

After a bowl of Cheryl's soup with several slices of rye bread and butter, Serena felt warm and safe—at least for tonight. She and Cheryl were having a cup of coffee with a wedge of Mrs. Smith's cherry pie when Cliff walked in, looking pale and haggard. He kissed his wife and waved to Serena.

"Jeez, what a day!"

He washed his hands at the kitchen sink, and sat down to enjoy the vegetable soup.

After his second cup of coffee, and a double wedge of the warm cherry pie, he leaned back, still looking exhausted, but the color had returned to his face.

"The blood test went fine," he told them.

"Why did you have to have a blood test?" asked Serena.

"It's standard operating procedure, to make sure I hadn't been drinking booze or doing drugs," he explained. "Of course I'm clean. But they still can't seem to swallow my story about the dark-red SUV that cut me off. Right now they're listing the cause of the accident as *Driver Error.* I wish to hell somebody else had seen it."

"I saw it," said Serena quietly. "I was sitting right behind you."

"You know, I had a feeling you saw it!" He stood up and started pacing around the kitchen. "So why did you tell that cop you were asleep when he asked you about it?"

"I *had* been asleep, but I woke up just before the accident."

"You sure you're not saying you saw it because I invited you to come here to my house, and you just want to help me out?"

"No! *I did see it.* And I saw the first three digits of the license plate on that SUV full of teenagers."

"Omigod!" Impulsively, he leaned over Serena's chair and kissed her cheek. "How the hell did you manage that?"

"They looked familiar, they jumped out at me, because they were the initials of my maiden name: SGD."

"And *I* noticed the year and the make of that car—it was a 2002 Ford Explorer!" exclaimed Cliff, looking jubilant. "With the first three digits of the license plate, I bet the cops'll be able to find that damn car. Let me make a call right now and tell Hank I have a witness!"

"*Wait!*" Serena's normally soft voice was like a pistol shot, stopping his arm as it reached for the wall phone.

"Why?"

"I can't talk to the police."

"Why not?" asked Cliff, his hand still hovering over the phone.

"Sit down, hon. Let her explain," said Cheryl.

Serena had been in the house for only a couple of hours, but Cheryl already felt . . . protective of her.

"It's—it's a long story. I don't want to involve you in my problems."

"Maybe you hadn't noticed, Grace, but *you're* already involved in *my* problems," Cliff reminded her, smiling through his frown.

"Let's go in the other room," suggested Cheryl, "and you can tell us your story."

After they settled on the blue corduroy sectional couch in the living room, Serena began to relate the sequence of events that had followed the death of her husband a few weeks before.

It was like a slide show, as she watched their facial expressions change from event to event. *Click. Click.* Curiosity—interest—sympathy—anger—shock—and finally horror, as her story concluded. When Serena stopped speaking, she saw tears in Cheryl's eyes and fury in Cliff's.

"You should've stayed in New York and fought those bastards in court," he declared, punching his right fist into his left hand. "You were his *wife!* That money belongs to *you!*"

"I don't want the money, and I don't want to fight anybody. I just want to get away. I was on my way to Philadelphia to start a new life."

"But what are you planning to live on?" asked Cheryl.

"I have a little cash—the money my stepdaughter paid me in advance for being their 'cook.' That should tide me over until I find a place to live and get a job."

"What kind of job will you be looking for?" asked Cheryl.

"Restaurant work. That's all I know how to do. I used to own a little restaurant before I married Ed. I'm a pretty good cook, and I know how to wait tables, manage employees, order food and supplies . . ."

She saw Cliff and Cheryl exchange glances.

"*What?*" she said, looking from one new friend to the other.

"If you're willing to stay here in New Jersey, we may be able to help you," said Cliff slowly. "My . . . ah . . . my dad owns a really nice restaurant in Cherry Hill."

She started to smile, but then the enormity of Cliff's dilemma hit her full force.

"What about the question of my talking to the police?" she asked.

"Simple," said Cliff. "I'll just tell the cops I remembered the first three digits of the license plate."

"And what reason will you give for *not* remembering it before?" asked Serena.

"I'll just say it must've been the shock of the accident."

Cold Spring Harbor, Long Island: The Same Night

Phyllis, Chet, and Margaret were in the little TV room off the library, watching the eleven o'clock news. When the scene of the bus accident on the New Jersey Turnpike flashed on the screen, Phyllis lit a cigarette and remarked,

"Oh, I'm so sick of looking at that goddam accident. Why don't they hurry up and give the weather report so we can all go to bed?"

"Hey!" said Margaret, jumping up from the couch and pointing at the television screen. "Look at that woman! Doesn't she look like Serena?"

Phyllis turned her head and squinted at the screen, but the picture had already shifted to a spokesman from the Reindeer Bus Company making a formal statement about the accident.

Margaret went back to the couch and sat down next to her son-in-law.

"It was her, I'm sure it was her. If she got out of here on the Long Island Railroad, like we're pretty sure she did, where would she go from Cold Spring Harbor? Jamaica? Manhattan?"

"*Brooklyn*. Back to her roots," said Phyllis in her raspy voice. "Like a rat going back to its hole."

"She knows that's where we'd look for her first," Margaret insisted. "That bus was on its way to Philadelphia. I'd be willing to bet that's where she was going."

"I still think she went to Brooklyn. But I'll get in touch with Rudy in the morning, and let him follow it up."

"Who's Rudy?" asked Chet.

"A private investigator I've hired to find Serena," replied Phyllis without blinking an eye or missing a beat.

"Why do we have to find her?" Chet wanted to know. "I don't think she wants the money."

"Don't be so naïve. Of *course* she wants the money." Phyllis regarded him with open contempt. "Besides, don't you realize the estate can't be settled until all the terms of the will are satisfied? *One way or another . . .*"

She exchanged a meaningful glance with her mother. Rudy

would find her all right—and make sure she never got one cent of Edward's money. A dead woman doesn't need money.

Besides, she'll be better off dead. No husband . . . no children. No one will even miss her.

"She sure was a good cook," Chet mused wistfully. "That Chinese food we ordered in tonight was the pits."

"I'll start interviewing cooks tomorrow," Phyllis said irritably. "What are *you* complaining about, anyway? All of a sudden you're a gourmet?"

Delran, New Jersey: Later That Night

"Hi, Dad. I told Cheryl to call you."

He cleared his throat. His voice sounded hoarse to his own ears. It was the first time he'd talked to his father for almost ten years.

"Yeah, she called the restaurant. God, Cliff, it's good to hear your voice! You all in one piece?"

"Yep. Guess it wasn't my time."

Steve decided not to tell him about his mother's coma. He'd been through enough for one day.

"You in trouble with Reindeer? Cheryl told me you had to go for a blood test."

"Just routine. The blood test was clean, of course, but the preliminary report is saying the accident was due to driver error."

"And you disagree?"

"Goddam right I do," said Cliff.

"Want to talk about it? I got all night."

Cliff gave his father a detailed report of the afternoon's disaster, and when he finished, Steve said, "Nobody saw that SUV but you, son?"

"We-ell, actually there was a witness—but I'm not going to let her talk to the cops."

"Why not?"

Cliff chuckled briefly. "You said you got all night?"

"I do, yeah, but your ass must be dragging."

"I think I'll sleep better if I get the rest of the story off my chest. You see, there was this woman on the bus. She was sitting directly behind me . . ."

Cliff tried not to disturb his wife when he slipped quietly into bed just after one o'clock, but Cheryl had been dozing fitfully.

"Did you call your dad?" she murmured.

"Yeah." He snuggled against her sleep-warm back.

"What'd he say about the accident?"

"He said if they fire me I can come back to work at the restaurant."

She turned to face him. "I knew he'd say that. Would you consider it?"

"Nah. It didn't work before, it wouldn't work now. We're too much alike."

A long silence, then Cheryl asked, "Did you tell him about Grace?"

"I told him the whole story. He'll give her a waitress job if she wants it."

"A *waitress* job!" Cheryl sat up in bed, now fully awake and indignant. "How about the *hostess* job? When I talked to him, he told me he was getting rid of Juliette!"

"I asked him about that, and he said he had a long talk with her. He says it's all straightened out. She promised she won't come on to him anymore."

"Hmmm."

Long after Cliff's steady breathing told her he was

asleep, Cheryl lay awake thinking about the problems faced by her husband, her father-in-law, and her new friend Grace D'Agostino.

CHAPTER 21

The next day, the following story appeared in the *Camden County Courier-Post*:

DRIVER CITED IN BUS CRASH ON NJ TURNPIKE

A preliminary hearing indicates that the Reindeer motor coach accident yesterday on the New Jersey Turnpike was due to driver error. Clifford Kingsley, 45, employed for almost 10 years by Reindeer, states that the bus bound for Philadelphia was cut off just prior to Exit #4 by the teenaged driver of a dark-red Ford Explorer, forcing the bus to swerve, plunge down an embankment and roll over. The accident killed one woman, and injured 33 other passengers, some critically. Seventeen passengers sustained no injuries. The driver was unhurt.

The mishap occurred in mid-afternoon in sunny weather, but none of the passengers questioned saw the dark-red SUV alleged by Kingsley to have caused the accident.

In a formal statement last night Farrell Smith, president of the Reindeer Line, extended condolences to the family of Violet Hathaway, the accident's only fatality; then said of the driver, "Clifford Kingsley has been with the company for ten years, and has never had an accident until today. His attitude, attendance, and driving record have been exemplary."

This reporter learned that Mr. Kingsley willingly submitted to a blood test to determine whether drugs or alcohol may have played a role in the disaster. A New Jersey State Police spokesperson stated that Mr. Kingsley's blood was free of drugs or alcohol.

The National Transportation Safety Board is still on the crash scene, inspecting the tire marks left by the bus as it swerved off the roadway, as well as the mechanical condition of the vehicle and its safety features. Investigation to determine the cause of the tragedy will continue. The driver is on suspension pending the outcome of the investigation.

Next to the story was a picture of the grief-stricken husband and daughter of Violet Hathaway, photographed as they were leaving Riverview Hospital. Both declined to be interviewed.

"Good morning. Are you Mr. Kingsley?"

"Yes."

He looked up from the invoice for liquor he was checking against the purchase order before signing the check to pay for it, and glanced without interest at a gray-haired woman in a blue dress standing in the doorway.

"What can I do for you?"

She smiled, and he took a second look. The woman had a dazzling smile. Her eyes were sort of silver, and—incredibly—her hair was the same color. Too bad about the bun on the back of her neck that made her look like a small-town librarian.

"Your son sent me. My name is Grace D'Agostino."

"Oh, yeah. You're here about the waitress job."

He got up from behind his desk and crossed the office to

shake her hand. He felt a strange sensation pass through his body as their hands touched.

"Static electricity," he said quickly, glancing down at the thick royal-blue carpet beneath their feet. "Did you feel it, too?"

She nodded, and they both smiled.

Funny, he didn't remember experiencing a jolt like that before. He'd swear he had actually seen a spark.

"Your restaurant is magnificent, Mr. Kingsley."

She was a tall woman, but she had to look up when she addressed him, and those lovely silver eyes looked straight into his. For a few seconds he couldn't remember the next question he'd wanted to ask.

"I—ah—have you had waitress experience?"

That beautiful smile again. "Mr. Kingsley, I can cook, I can waitress, and I can order supplies. I used to own my own place . . . nothing like *this,* of course! Just a little neighborhood restaurant."

Even her voice was silvery.

Remembering the story Cliff had told him last night, he wondered what reason anyone could have to dislike—no, to *hate*—this gentle, soft-spoken woman enough to want her dead. Then he answered his own question: *money,* of course. The Green Demon.

He couldn't seem to look away from her face. Especially when she smiled, as she was doing now. He was a Jew, brought up in that faith, but as an adult he'd sometimes attended Midnight Mass on Christmas Eve with his Catholic wife. Something about this woman's face brought to his mind the statue of Mary, mother of Jesus, in the manger scene set up outdoors every Christmas in St. Andrew's churchyard.

"How soon can you start?" he heard himself saying in a perfectly normal voice.

"If you need me right away, I can start right away."

He picked up the phone on his desk and pressed an intercom button.

"Juliette, I just hired a new waitress to replace Eleanor. She's gonna start today. I want you to take her into the locker room and see if you can find a uniform to fit her."

"You'll never know how much I appreciate this, Mr. Kingsley," Serena told him, extending her hand again. Steve was shaking it, and they were smiling at each other as Juliette flung open the door of his office.

"Well, just look at this! Holding hands already!" she exclaimed, giving Serena a keen once-over inspection. "What size are you, sugar—about a fourteen?"

"Usually, I'm a twelve," Serena replied carefully. She had a feeling that this redheaded woman had taken an instant dislike to her, but she couldn't imagine why.

Steve performed the introductions and sent them on their way. Just before the door closed, he called, "Welcome aboard, Grace."

"Well, you certainly made a hit with the boss."

Juliette was walking so fast that Serena had trouble keeping up with her.

"I'm glad he liked me," Serena said as they entered the locker room. "I need the job."

"Just watch your step, that's all."

This woman's warning made her think of Phyllis Abbott, who had told her if she didn't watch her step, she would end up as a bag lady.

"What do you mean?"

"What I mean," said Juliette ominously, "is that his wife is in a nursing home. In a coma. *Don't you get it?*"

"How sad."

When Serena looked puzzled, Juliette continued, "He's always horny as hell. He'll try to get into your pants, if you let him."

"Thanks for the warning," said Serena coolly.

She wasn't sure whether or not to believe what this ultra-glamorous hostess had just told her. It didn't match her first impression of Steven Kingsley, but she would remain vigilant. Just in case it was true.

Cold Spring Harbor, Long Island

"Nobody by the name of Serena Franklin bought a ticket from New York to *anywhere* on *any* bus line on the day she disappeared," said Rudy, consulting the dog-eared notebook in his hand.

He sat on the edge of the black mohair sofa in the little TV room and regarded Mrs. Franklin and her mother belligerently. He still found it hard to believe what they had told him . . . that the old broad with the flu had really been the woman he was looking for. If it was true, she ought to get an Oscar.

"She didn't *disappear,* Rudy," Phyllis corrected him in the same rub-your-nose-in-it tone she used when talking to her husband. "You saw her and talked to her. The old lady outsmarted you, that's all."

Phyllis had wracked her brain, but still couldn't figure out how Serena had known—*or guessed*—that this man had been hired to kill her.

"So whaddya want me to do now?"

"*Find her,* of course. And fulfill our contract. Or you don't get another dime from me."

"I need more information," he whined. "I need a piksher

of her. And I need to know what her name was before she married your old man."

"Serena *Epstein.*" Phyllis gestured to her mother. "Get a picture of Serena for him. Pull one out of their wedding album. She left it in her room."

Margaret hurried away in search of the picture.

"*Epstein* . . . that her maiden name?"

"No, that was her first husband's name. My father handled the divorce."

"Should I check out this guy Epstein?"

Phyllis shook her head.

"No, it wasn't a friendly divorce—and he remarried before she did."

"Her maiden name sounded Italian," Margaret chimed in eagerly. She'd come back with a wedding picture of Serena. "Do you recall it, Phyllis? Was it *Donatello?*"

"No, that wasn't it—but it did start with a *D*, I think," Phyllis conceded. "Maybe the toad would remember."

"The toad?" echoed Rudy.

Margaret frowned at her daughter's use of the nasty nickname in front of a stranger, but Phyllis laughed.

"Oh—that's what I call my husband."

Rudy left with the photograph a few minutes later, congratulating himself on having remained a bachelor.

Cherry Hill, New Jersey

Steven Kingsley stepped out of his office just in time to witness an incident involving his new waitress and an elderly couple seated by the window.

The woman had gone to the ladies' room, and the busboy, believing she had finished her dessert, removed the plate. When she returned to the table, she complained that her dessert had been taken away before she finished eating it. Her husband (who obviously hadn't noticed the removal of the dish) called the waitress over and berated her loudly, in language unbecoming a gentleman.

Serena turned one of her razzle-dazzle smiles on both of them.

"I'm terribly sorry that this happened," she said. "Please let me bring you another dessert."

"No, I'm too upset to eat it now," the woman told her, dabbing at her eyes with her napkin.

(Amused, Steve thought she must have led a rather sheltered life if missing a few bites of dessert reduced her to tears.)

Serena, still holding that smile, addressed the woman's husband.

"There will be no charge for your wife's dinner, sir," she said.

The man blinked several times.

"Well—hey, that's really nice of you."

"We want all of our customers to go home happy from the King's Feast," said Serena.

"You won't get in any trouble with the boss about this, will you?" he asked.

"Certainly not," Serena assured him. "Mr. Kingsley often says *good food and good service make good customers.*"

The pair left the table in fine spirits. After paying the bill, the man returned to the table and handed Serena a twenty-dollar tip. Then he asked for her name.

"Next time we come here, Grace, we want you to wait on us," he said.

As soon as he saw the valet bring their car to the front entrance, Steve strolled over to Serena and growled,

"Grace, when did you ever hear me say *good food and good service make good customers?*"

He was surprised to see her blush. He didn't think women blushed anymore.

"I'm sorry, Mr. Kingsley. Actually, it's something I used to say myself when I had my own little restaurant. I didn't mean to put words in your mouth . . ."

He grinned.

"Hey, I wish I *had* said it. It's true! And furthermore, I want to compliment you on your handling of that little mishap."

"I'll pay for that woman's dinner. They left me a very generous tip."

"Keep it. We can afford a free dinner now and then in order to keep a customer happy. You have good business instincts, Grace."

Another waitress tapped his arm.

"Mr. Kingsley, Juliette needs you at the cash register. A problem with a credit card."

They both turned around. Juliette, in a mint-green jersey dress that clung tenaciously to every part of her body, was waving both arms.

"Thank you, Beverly. Excuse me, Grace." He strode quickly toward the front of the restaurant.

Beverly said to Serena in a low voice, "Watch out for Juliette."

"Why?"

"She thinks the boss likes you, and she's jealous."

Serena made a you-must-be-kidding face. "I'm not interested in him."

"Maybe not—but she thinks he's interested in *you.* They had something going for a short time, I think, but he ended it and now she's on the warpath."

"Juliette warned me about him," Serena confided. "She implied that he's oversexed."

Beverly scowled. "Don't listen to her. He's a great boss . . . he hasn't come on to any of the women who work here."

"Except Juliette," suggested Serena.

Beverly shook her head. "Wrong. She came on to him."

This story made more sense than the one she'd heard from Juliette. For some reason, she was pleased that her positive perception of Steven Kingsley had been confirmed by Beverly.

After two marriages she knew that the sexual needs of most men are more compelling than those of most women. She admired Steven Kingsley for his ability to keep his libido under control, but she understood his capitulation—however brief—to Juliette's wiles. The hostess was an unusually sexy woman who flaunted her physical assets, no doubt aware of their cumulative effect on a man who had not had a partner for some time. It must have required a lot of willpower on his part to terminate the exciting—and convenient—relationship.

New York City

Rudy's cell phone began to play the Seven Dwarfs' marching song, *Hi-ho, hi-ho, it's off to work we go . . .*

He took the phone out of his pocket.

"Yeah?"

"This is Phyllis Abbott. My stepmother's maiden name was Serena Grace D'Agostino."

Reading from the scrap of paper Chet had given her, she spelled the surname into the telephone.

Rudy couldn't resist asking, "Was it your husband who remembered it?"

"As a matter of fact, it was," said Phyllis, with a trace of annoyance. "All right, now you've got her picture, and the additional information you asked for. Let's see some results, for chrissake. So far you've been about as much help as tits on a bull."

On the other end of the line, Rudy made an obscene gesture to his cell phone.

"I'll do my best, Mrs. Abbott."

"I've seen your best. You'll have to do a lot better than that."

CHAPTER 22

Delran, New Jersey

Cheryl poured two mugs of coffee and brought them over to the kitchen table, spilling a few drops when she skidded slightly on the scatter rug in front of the sink.

"That's the second time I've seen you slip on that nasty little rug," observed Serena.

"You sound like Cliff," Cheryl laughed. "Look, I stand on a white tile floor all day at work, so when I'm home in my own kitchen I like to pamper my puppies a little bit."

"Okay. I can understand that—but I still wish you'd get rid of that hooked rug. How about a foam rubber mat?"

"I'm attached to this little rug. My mother hooked it herself and had it in *her* kitchen. Tell you what I'll do—I'll ask Cliff to put some two-sided tape underneath it, to anchor it to the floor. Just to make you both happy!"

When she seated herself at the table, she added sugar and began to stir her coffee.

"I know I should be glad for you that you found an apartment, but dammit, Grace, I'm gonna miss you! You're such great company . . . and of course it doesn't hurt that you're also a great cook!"

Serena smiled. She would miss Cliff's warm-hearted wife as well.

"Oh, don't worry—you're not getting rid of me so easily. I want to have you and Cliff over for dinner. It'll have to be on a Monday night, when the restaurant is closed—and when he's not working, of course."

Cheryl made a face.

"Cliff is still on suspension, pending the outcome of the investigation," she said, "so *any* Monday night will be okay with us."

Serena looked stricken. She'd been at the restaurant from late morning until late evening every day since she began her employment there, so she hadn't realized he wasn't working.

"Suspended on full pay?"

"Half-pay."

"Oh, Cheryl!" Serena bit her lip. "Didn't the police find the dark-red Ford Explorer with the license plate that began with SGD?"

"Yeah, they found it. And the owner has a fifteen-year-old son."

"*Oh!* I'm sure that was the one! And driving without a license, if he's only fifteen!"

"The kid swears by the Father, the Son, and the Holy Ghost that he would *never* drive his father's car, and the father swears that his son would *never* tell a lie."

Cheryl rolled her eyes and made a grimace that left no doubt about her opinion of both statements.

"I really believe the police—and the NTSB—are now convinced Cliff is telling the truth. But they can't prove that the fifteen-year-old boy is responsible for the accident."

"You mean to tell me he's going to get away with it?" Serena was incensed. "A woman *died,* and some of the other passengers are still in the hospital!"

"I know, I know. My reaction was the same as yours when Cliff told me, but apparently there's no case without enough facts to support it."

"That's true. The lawyers call it *probable cause,*" said Serena. "Do you think it would help if I talked to the police?"

Cheryl shook her head.

"Aside from putting your life in jeopardy, I'm not sure they would believe you anyway. Don't forget the police brought you here. They know you've been living at our house since the accident, and they might've found out that Cliff's father gave you a job. They'd just think it was *payback.*"

And they might also question why it took me so long to speak up, thought Serena.

"Hey, let's talk about something else," Cheryl interjected quickly. "I want to hear about your new apartment!"

"Well," said Serena, brightening a bit, "it's a garden apartment, a second-floor walk-up. One bedroom, one bath, an eat-in kitchen and a living room. The best thing about it is that it's only six blocks from the restaurant. On nice days I can walk to work."

"What about not-so-nice days?" Cheryl asked.

"There's a bus that stops on the corner." Serena paused to sip at her coffee. "Another waitress, Beverly, lives there, too. That's how I found out about the apartment."

"Sounds like a good friend."

"She is. She's helped me in more ways than you can imagine," Serena said. She didn't elaborate because she thought bringing up Juliette's name might sound like a complaint. Besides, she wasn't sure if anyone in Steve's family knew how consistently the hostess tried to seduce him. There was no such thing as a perfect job, she knew that, but for every villain like Juliette there was a champion like Beverly.

"She's a single mom, trying to bring up two small children by herself," she added. "Her husband took off after the birth of her second child, and hasn't been seen since."

Cheryl stared out the kitchen window at the cloudy morning.

"God isn't always fair, is He?"

Serena, already sorry she had mentioned Beverly's children, could guess what Cheryl was thinking. Several times she had talked to Serena about the deep sorrow she and Cliff felt about their inability to conceive a child. Now here was Serena, telling her about a couple who had been blessed with two healthy children, and the husband had belatedly decided he wasn't cut out to be a family man.

She blinked as Serena reached across the table and patted her hand.

"Have you and Cliff ever considered adopting a child?"

"*I've* considered it." A gusty sigh. "Cliff won't even discuss it."

An affectionate look passed between the two women. Then Cheryl left the table to carry their empty cups to the sink, and Serena reached for the morning newspaper.

"I thought I'd look in the paper today and check out the ads for used furniture . . . you know, people who're moving out of state and want to sell their stuff instead of paying to have it hauled thousands of miles . . ."

"Good idea," said Cheryl. "If you find some nice stuff, we'll get it delivered for you. Cliff has a lot of friends with vans and pickup trucks."

Serena rolled her eyes.

"I'm going to owe you and Cliff big time. You realize that, don't you?"

Cheryl leaned forward.

"You don't owe us a thing. My parents died when I was a teenager, and Cliff's mom . . . well, she was a terrific lady,

Grace, but . . . even though she's still alive, it's like we don't really *have* her anymore. First the Alzheimer's, and now the coma. You've become sort of—our *foster mom.*"

Serena looked down at her hands holding the newspaper, tears lurking behind her eyelids. She wanted to make a little joke about providing foster care, but she couldn't squeeze it past the lump in her throat.

New York City

After leaving the ticket counter in the Port Authority Bus Terminal, Rudy strolled outside on Forty-Second Street to make a call on his cell phone.

"Morning, Miz Abbott. A woman named Grace D'Agostino bought a ticket to Philadelphia on the same day your stepmother—ah—left town."

"Good, good. That's got to be her. What else?"

"That was the same bus that crashed in South Jersey, about thirty miles before it got to Philadelphia."

"Oh my God! I remember that! On television they said there was a woman who died in that crash," said Phyllis eagerly.

"Better curb your enthusiasm, Miz Abbott. It wasn't your stepmother. That woman's name was Violet Hathaway, and she had a husband and a twelve-year-old daughter."

"Oh . . ." Phyllis muttered. Then she added, "My mother thought she saw a woman who looked like Serena on a television news report of that accident."

"I found out the bus driver is on suspension until they get done investigating the accident," Rudy continued. "There's a chance he might remember the D'Agostino woman. How 'bout I look up the guy and talk to him?"

"How 'bout you do your own thinking? You're supposed to be the professional, remember? You want me to come down there and hold your hand?"

"No," said Rudy, sounding sullen. "Look, lady, I thought you wanted me to call in from time to time and let you know what's doing, give you some input. You don't want that? Okay by me! This is a long-distance call, for chrissake."

"You must have me confused with someone who cares whether you pay for a long-distance call," Phyllis rasped. "Just do what you're supposed to do, if you want the other five thousand."

"And the thousand a month!"

"Yes, yes. The thousand a month," she echoed.

"Okay, Miz Abbott, I'm outta here. The next call you get will be from New Jersey."

"Listen, Rudy, the next call I get better be to tell me that the job is done!"

Delran, New Jersey

Rudy knocked on the door of the red-brick bungalow, and Cliff opened it.

"You Clifford Kingsley?"

Cliff glanced over the man's shoulder at the brown Ford Fairlane parked in front of the house. He was quite sure the visitor was not from the NTSB.

"Yeah. Who're you?"

"Name's Rudy. I'm a private investigator."

"You got a last name, Rudy?"

"Last name's Hamer. You're the driver of the bus that

crashed a coupla weeks ago, right?"

Cliff frowned. "What do you want?"

"I'm looking for a woman by the name of Serena Grace D'Agostino. I understand she was on that bus."

Taken aback for a moment, Cliff recalled that Grace had said her maiden initials were SGD. Obviously, she did not use her first name.

"Yeah, Grace was on the bus. Who sent you here?"

Rudy grinned. "The cops. They remembered dropping her off at your house a few hours after the accident."

"Yeah, I felt sorry for her. She was traveling all alone and didn't know the area. I invited her to stay here with me and my wife."

Rudy's close-set eyes brightened.

"She still here?"

Cliff had anticipated the possibility of this visit, and he and Cheryl had discussed how they would handle it. They had agreed that the most effective way to tell a lie is to tell a partial truth. What he hadn't anticipated, however, was his accelerated heart rate when he was face-to-face with the acne-scarred man who was almost certainly Grace's would-be assassin.

He stood aside and gestured for Rudy to step inside the house. He wanted to make sure the man knew Grace was not hiding here. Rudy walked in, looking around furtively.

"She stayed with us until her luggage was released by the National Transportation Safety Board," Cliff explained. *A partial truth.* "Very nice woman. What do you want with her?"

"Her husband died and left her a third of his estate, but she disappeared before she got the money. It's quite a bundle, I understand."

"So why do you think she took off?" asked Cliff, pretending to look puzzled.

"How the hell do I know? Maybe she's senile."

"My wife and I didn't think she was senile," Cliff told him. He thought of his mother and scowled.

"Look. Mr. Franklin's daughter hired me to find her so the estate can be settled. Do you know where she went when she left here?"

"Sure. The Greyhound Bus Station in Mount Laurel. My wife Cheryl drove her there," Cliff lied. "She was on her way to Philadelphia when my bus crashed."

Rudy's grin was dissolving. "You're telling me she went on to Philadelphia?"

"I guess she did. That's where she told us she was going."

"How long ago did she leave here?"

"Oh, I don't know . . . a week ago, maybe a little more."

"Have you or your wife heard from her since she left?"

"No. We wanted her to stay over for Christmas, but she insisted she wanted to go to Philadelphia."

"Does she have friends or relatives in Philadelphia?"

"That I don't know." Cliff sounded convincingly apologetic.

"Lemme know if she calls, okay?"

"Sure. How do we get in touch with you?" asked Cliff, hoping the man would give him a business card.

"You don't. I'll call you." Rudy hesitated, then asked, "Can I see the room she stayed in before I go?"

"Okay." Cliff led the way to the small bedroom Serena had slept in while she was their guest. Rudy looked around the room, opened the closet door and closed it again. He glanced quickly into the master bedroom, the bathroom and the kitchen on his way back to the living room.

"Well, thanks for your help, Mr. Kingsley."

"No problem. If you have any more questions, just give

us a call," Cliff said genially. "I hope you find the lady so she can get her inheritance."

"Yeah," said Rudy. *"Right."*

Cliff stood behind the vertical blinds in the living room, and watched the old brown car pull away from the curb and turn the corner. He pulled a handkerchief out of his pocket and wiped his face.

CHAPTER 23

The King's Feast was closed on Mondays, so the Monday before Christmas was the logical time for Cliff and Cheryl to come for dinner at Serena's new apartment. They arrived at the appointed time, bringing a housewarming gift. Serena tore off the flowered wrapping paper and found a pretty wooden tray. An artist had decorated it with a nostalgic scene of Atlantic City, New Jersey, in the early 1900s: striped umbrellas on the beach, bathers in modest black bathing suits, and people being pushed in wicker rolling chairs along the wooden Boardwalk. Surprised and deeply touched, Serena kissed them both before they sat down to eat the dinner she'd prepared.

They feasted on pot roast with golden egg noodles, a big tossed salad, and her chocolate snowballs for dessert. She had just poured a second cup of coffee for the three of them when the doorbell rang. Her hands began to shake as if they were palsied; she almost dropped the coffee pot.

"I'm not expecting anyone else." She sounded terrified.

"It could be someone selling magazines," Cliff said reassuringly. "Let me go see who it is."

A dozen possibilities were spinning through her mind like a videotape on fast forward. Who could have found out where she was living? Phyllis? Margaret? The assassin they'd hired? Her memory served up a never-to-be-forgotten picture of him: the acne-scarred face, the plaid raincoat over his arm that she knew hid the gun with a silencer. *Oh, dear God!* Had she put her new friends in danger?

"Cliff!" she called after him. She wanted to tell him not to open the door.

Then she heard him say, "*Dad!* What are you doing here?"

A moment later Steve Kingsley was in her little eat-in kitchen, his face the color of putty as he faced his son and daughter-in-law.

"It's Mom," he said. "She's got pneumonia." His mouth twitched, and he bit his lips together.

"How d'you know? The doctor called you?" asked Cliff.

Steve nodded. "Yeah. I'm on my way to St. Bartholomew's Medical Center. He had her moved there by ambulance this afternoon from Tall Pines."

"What are they doing for her?" asked Cheryl.

"Oxygen tent, and some kind of antibiotic. Intravenous. I guess it'd have to be intravenous."

He sat down in the fourth chair at the small glass-topped table, put his elbows on the surface and rested his forehead against his hands.

"I still can't believe it!"

"Mr. Kingsley, have you had any dinner?" asked Serena.

"No, but I don't think I could eat anything, Grace." He looked up at her. "I will take a cup of coffee, though, if you can spare one."

She poured him a cup, black, and he sipped it gratefully.

"Dr. Lazarus warned me this might happen, but I never thought it would. *I really didn't.* She's always been so healthy." Again, he looked at Serena. "Anne Marie's only sixty-five years old. She was just nineteen when Cliff was born. You wouldn't believe how pretty she was . . . like an angel . . ."

Cliff said, "Did you call Lisa?"

"No, I didn't want to upset her." He couldn't seem to keep his eyes from straying to Serena's face. "Did you know my daughter Lisa's going to have a baby?"

"That's wonderful," she said, "but don't you think your daughter will be more upset if you don't tell her about her mom and she finds out later?"

She pressed two fingers against her mouth, wondering what in the world had possessed her to give advice to her employer. Especially about a family matter.

But Cheryl was nodding. "She's right, Dad. Do you want *me* to call her?"

"No, it's better I should call." He jerked his thumb toward Cliff. "How 'bout you come with me, son? I can't drive and talk on the phone at the same time. Don't know how people do it! So you'll drive my car, and I'll sit next to you and call Lisa on my cell phone, okay?"

Still talking, he was already zipping up his black leather jacket. "By the way—thanks for the caffeine transfusion, Grace."

"How did you know where I live?" she couldn't help asking as the two men prepared to leave.

"You work for me, remember? Polly keeps cards in her Rolodex on all our employees. I knew Cliff and Cheryl were having dinner at your place tonight, so I dropped in at the restaurant and looked up your address."

Serena bit her tongue and nodded. She remembered now giving her new address and unlisted telephone number to his secretary the day after she was hired. Why did she always say the wrong thing to this man?

He didn't appear to have taken offense, and he even managed a little grin. "Maybe I just wanted to see if you know how to make coffee."

She felt herself blushing again.

★ ★ ★ ★ ★

Dr. Lazarus met Steve and Cliff at Anne Marie's bedside. His patient appeared to be on display in a glass case. She was half-sitting, half-reclining against her pillows within the transparent oxygen tent, unseeing eyes half-open. Her once-lustrous dark hair—now mostly gray and in need of combing—surrounded her face like dead weeds in winter.

"I'm not going to lie to you, Steve. This is what I feared most. Pneumonia is a common complication of chronically ill comatose patients. Anne Marie's immune system is not functioning well. In other words, her body is not responding to the antibiotic."

He pointed to the bag suspended above the bed, attached to her arm by a needle and a slender tube. When he saw the expression on Steve's face, he amended his statement.

"At least not yet."

"What are you saying?" asked Steve. "Is she going to die?"

His voice sounded hoarse and high-pitched to Cliff, who stood by his side staring down at Anne Marie and trying hard not to cry. Confronted by his mother's now-critical condition, he couldn't seem to find the right words to comfort his dad. Or even direct intelligent questions to the doctor.

On the way to the hospital they had talked about the dead-end status of the accident investigation, and Cliff had told his father about the man named Rudy who had come to his home looking for Grace. Steven had reprimanded him about that. *If he comes back again, I want to know about it right away. Not a week later.*

Dr. Lazarus put an arm around each of them. "If I knew who was going to live and who was going to die, I'd hang out my shingle as a clairvoyant instead of a physician," he said. "We're doing everything we know how to do. I've seen patients sicker than Anne Marie rally and recover from pneumonia. All I'm saying is that right at this moment I'm not optimistic about her chances. I hope I'm wrong."

Lisa, in blue jeans and a pleated cotton maternity top, arrived just in time to hear the doctor's gloomy pronouncement. She threw herself into her father's arms and sobbed. Her husband Gary who was right behind her looked worried, but his eyes were on Lisa, not Anne Marie.

His grim demeanor was not lost on Steve.

Patting his daughter's back, but looking at everyone in the room, he said, "Look, we came to see Mom, and now we've seen her. It's time to go home. Mom's in good hands here . . ."—he gestured toward Dr. Lazarus—". . . so the only thing we can do now is pray."

It was just before midnight when the phone rang on the night table beside Serena's bed. Fumbling for it, she knocked it to the floor and had to get out of bed to retrieve it. She sat on the edge of the mattress and held it to her ear.

"H'lo."

"I apologize for calling you so late, Grace. This is Steve Kingsley."

"Oh!" She turned on the lamp beside the bed. "How's your wife?"

"No better, no worse. But the doctor is not optimistic about her chances. The reason I'm calling . . . I won't be coming in to the restaurant tomorrow, and maybe the next day as well. Anne Marie and I have been married for more than forty-five years, and I want to spend some time with her while I still have her with me . . ."

"You don't need to say any more. I think it's wonderful that you feel this way about your wife," Serena said sincerely.

"So listen to me now. I'm putting you in charge of the King's Feast until I get back."

"No, no, *please* don't ask me to do this!" cried Serena. She could just imagine Juliette's reaction if she walked into the restaurant tomorrow and announced that the boss had put her in charge.

"But you're ideally qualified! Didn't you tell me you used to own a small restaurant?"

"Yes, that's true, but I've only been working for you for a couple of weeks! Some of your other employees with more seniority would be offended, I know they would."

Steve was reasonably sure he knew which one of the *employees with more seniority* she meant.

"Who would you suggest?" he asked.

"Well—*Juliette,* I think."

"Okay, then. I won't put you on the spot—even though I think you would do a better job. I'll give Juliette a call."

But he didn't call Juliette just then. He sat with the cell phone in his hand thinking about his family.

After dropping out of college, his son had worked in the restaurant for more than fifteen years as his assistant. They had disagreed about almost everything but when Cliff announced that he was quitting his job, his own disappointment had been like a physical blow. It had been bad enough that his son flunked out of college, and then that he had turned his back on the restaurant business—in order to drive a bus. The proportionate reduction in Cliff's income had forced him to sell his Porsche, and resurrected Cheryl's career as a hairdresser.

Lisa, his "baby," was a different story. She'd given him—and Anne Marie—nothing but pleasure since the day she was born. They'd spoiled her a little bit, mostly because she was such a sweet, pretty child. She graduated from Rider University with a degree in secretarial science, eventually becoming a competent legal secretary. After two years at Shapiro, DeMarco & Klein, she'd met Gary Barnett, a rising young attorney, and they'd fallen in love.

He winced, remembering the day of their marriage, and Anne Marie's unintentional mutilation of the ceremony. How sick with shame she would have been if she'd ever been able to remember it!

Memories. Tonight he seemed able to bring up only the bad ones. With a deep sigh, he folded his cell phone and headed up the stairs to his bedroom. He would call Juliette in the morning.

"Juliette, this is Steve Kingsley."

"You didn't think I'd know who it was?" Juliette's early-morning voice was dusky as a slice of dark toast and buttered with erotic suggestion.

"I'm calling to let you know that Anne Marie passed away during the night. The doctor just called me."

He was only glad that he, Cliff, Lisa, and Gary had all been there to see her last night. If Grace had not urged him to call Lisa, she and Gary might not have been there at all.

"Oh!" cried Juliette. "I wish you were here with me right now, Steve. I think you need one of my special hugs!"

He ignored her tasteless allusion to their one-time sexual encounter.

"I'm putting you in charge, Juliette, until I come back to work."

"And when will that be?"

"Not today. Not tomorrow. Thursday's the funeral. *Maybe Friday.* I'd like to be back by Friday."

"I'm coming to the funeral," she announced.

"You are *not* coming to the funeral. Only the family and close friends will be there. Didn't I just finish telling you I'm putting you in charge of managing the damn restaurant until I get back?"

"I'm surprised you didn't put Her Royal Highness in charge," she sneered, all pretense at seduction abandoned.

"And who might that be?"

Of course he knew.

"I'm talking about your latest girlfriend, Grace."

He exhaled through gritted teeth before responding.

"As a matter of fact, I asked her first, but she turned me down."

"Why?"

"She thought you would be upset. She suggested I ask you instead."

"So I have her to thank for this *great honor?*"

He felt the venom dripping through the phone, and was suddenly concerned for Grace's safety. How far would this woman go to protect what she perceived as her territorial rights? Why, oh why, hadn't he followed through on his original decision to fire this woman? He'd let her convince him that she had accepted their "just friends" status, but now she seemed to feel he owed her something, something more than a salary. She reminded him of a chicken hawk, and he felt like the chicken.

"Okay, forget it. I'll tell Grace you turned it down, and maybe then she'll agree to do it for me," he said. His tone was intentionally neutral.

"No, no, I'll do it. *Of course* I'll do it! But you really should close the restaurant on Thursday so the employees could attend the funeral."

"If I were you, Juliette, I wouldn't tell the boss what he should do."

CHAPTER 24

Serena knew the funeral took place on Thursday, and was astonished when Steve Kingsley called her at home that night.

"I'm so sorry about your wife, Mr. Kingsley," she said. "Is there anything I can do?"

He hastened to explain the reasons for his call.

"Thank you, Grace. No, I just wanted to know how things are going at the restaurant."

"Isn't Juliette giving you a daily report?" she asked.

"Yes, of course she is. I wanted to get your take on things."

"Everything's running smoothly. You needn't worry," she told him.

"Everyone treating you right, darling?"

She knew he meant Juliette. A little laugh before she answered, "Sure."

"I'd hoped to be back tomorrow, but I don't think I'm going to be able to do it," he said. "I haven't been sleeping well since Anne Marie . . . since she passed away, and the funeral today was—well, it was . . ."

"Mr. Kingsley, please don't try to explain! I do understand what you're going through."

"Yes, that's right, you really do. You lost your husband—when?"

"Five weeks ago."

The calendar said it was five weeks. Her heart and mind told her *years* had passed since Eddie's funeral. *Years* since she'd been Mrs. Edward Franklin, pampered matron of Cold Spring Harbor, Long Island.

There was a long moment of silence before Steve spoke again.

"Okay, darling, now listen to what I'm telling you: I just talked to Juliette, and she told me Anton went home sick today."

"Yes, I think he has the flu." She wished he'd stop calling her *darling.*

"We're closed on Saturday for Christmas, as you know, so tomorrow will be very busy. As I recall, we've got seven Christmas parties scheduled."

"Seven. That's right."

"I'd like you to take over Anton's duties."

"Tomorrow?"

"Yeah—tomorrow, and Sunday, and so on—until he comes back to work. Will you do it?"

Her heart began to thump. Anton was a pastry chef, trained in Paris. Could she actually replace him? She'd said no when Steve had asked her to manage the restaurant temporarily. She couldn't very well refuse to help him a second time.

"Don't worry, Mr. Kingsley. I can handle it," she told him with more bravado than confidence.

"I wish you'd stop calling me Mr. Kingsley. You can call me Steve, you know. Now, one more thing . . ."

She heard him hesitate.

"Last week I asked Cliff and Cheryl to invite you to come to my home for Christmas. You know I'm Jewish, but my wife was Catholic—and we always had Christmas at our house, the whole nine yards, for the kids."

"I'm half-Jewish, like your children," Serena blurted. "My father was Catholic but my mother was Jewish . . ."

"I didn't know that." Her name was D'Agostino. A dim memory, like a thorn, pricked at his mind.

". . . and we always celebrated Hanukkah and Christmas, both."

A Christmas tree in the corner and a Menorah in the window. He knew he'd seen that somewhere, a long time ago. When he was a kid. Or maybe it had been in an old movie?

"Quite a coincidence," he said at last. "Well, I just wanted to tell you . . ."

"You don't need to tell me anything," Serena interrupted him, certain he was not sure how to rescind the invitation without hurting her feelings. "I know you want to be alone with your family this Christmas, and you should be. I'm not in the least offended."

"*Hey!* Don't ever try to second-guess me, Grace! I was about to say we still want you to join us tomorrow night. And bring your toothbrush. You'll be staying over through Christmas Day."

"But I'm practically a stranger! I know your son and daughter-in-law, but I've never even met your daughter!"

"If your mother was Jewish, she must have told you that it's a Jewish tradition to invite a stranger to share the Sabbath meal."

Her mother's voice floated to the surface from her childhood.

"Yes, I do remember hearing her say that, but we're not talking about the Sabbath meal."

"Who says we're not? This year Christmas Eve falls on a Friday!"

Serena agonized over what to wear to the holiday celebration at the home of her boss. A dress or a pantsuit?

When she called Cheryl from the restaurant on Friday, Cheryl said, "The pantsuit will be fine. It's always casual—just the family."

"Okay, I'm glad that's settled. So what time are you picking me up?" she asked.

"What time do you get off work tonight?"

"Well, the restaurant closes at ten. I guess I'll be ready to leave by eleven." She paused. "Maybe we should say eleven-thirty, to be on the safe side, because we're so busy today. And I'll need to go home for a few minutes to change clothes and pick up something at the apartment."

After Steve's phone call the night before, she'd spent the rest of the evening baking Christmas cookies, which would have to serve as her gift to the entire Kingsley family. She had no decorative tin in which to box them, so she'd arranged them on the hand-painted tray Cheryl and Cliff had given her as a housewarming gift when they came for dinner on Monday night. She'd covered the tray full of goodies with plastic wrap. It was on the kitchen table at her apartment, waiting to be transported to Moorestown.

"That's no problem," Cheryl assured her. "We're looking forward to seeing you."

"It's been a terrible week for your family," said Serena. "I'm still not sure I should be there at all."

"Cliff and I think the world of you, Grace. So does Dad." Cheryl's affection crept through the phone, warming Serena's heart. "See you tonight."

She'd planned to be outside waiting for them at eleven-thirty, but Juliette found several extra tasks for her to do. She had just finished cleaning the salad bar area when she looked up and saw Cliff and Cheryl standing outside the employees' entrance gesturing to her: *Come on!*

It was only then that she realized it was snowing outside. It must've started in the last hour. Her first thought was sentimental: *A white Christmas, just like the ones I used to know*. Her second thought was practical: *We need to get to Moorestown while the roads are still passable.*

She held up her forefinger to indicate she would be there in a minute, then dashed into the locker room to get her coat and purse. As she struggled into her down jacket, Juliette strolled into the locker room.

"In a hurry, are we? You must have a hot date," she said with a sly grin.

"Not likely." Serena zipped up the jacket, grabbed her purse, and said, "Well, Merry Christmas, Juliette! See you Sunday."

As she hurried through the darkened restaurant toward the employees' entrance, she didn't notice the locker-room door crack open a half-inch behind her.

Steven Kingsley paced the floor of the great room, in front of the fieldstone fireplace where a cheery fire was blazing. He admitted to himself that he was apprehensive about the imminent meeting between Grace and his daughter. Lisa knew, of course, about the "woman from New York" who had stayed briefly with her brother and Cheryl—and then had begun working at her father's restaurant. But what would she say about that woman's arrival at the Moorestown house on Christmas Eve? He realized now he should have told her ahead of time.

What reason could he give, in case she asked for one? That he felt sorry for anyone who was alone at holiday time? (That happened to be the truth.) Or should he try the story he'd given to Grace, about the Jewish tradition of inviting a stranger to share the Sabbath meal?

What a coincidence that Grace D'Agostino turned out to be half-Jewish, like his own children! Again, the annoying memory scratched at his mind.

A Christmas tree in the corner and a Menorah in the window. He could see the scene in his mind. What was the name of that movie?

How ironic, he reflected now, that Cliff had married a girl from a Catholic background—just as he had done—and that Lisa, brought up as a Catholic, had converted to Judaism in order to marry Gary. Their child would be brought up in the Jewish faith.

The sound of Lisa's voice in the front hall ended his reflections.

"Hi, Daddy!" In a red velvet skirt and a white linen maternity top embroidered with green leaves and red berries, she walked into the great room . . . preceded by her expectant belly and followed by her attentive husband.

She hugged him and said, "Cliff and Cheryl not here yet? They're coming, aren't they?"

"Of course they're coming, and they're bringing that woman I told you about—Grace D'Agostino."

Lisa stared at him blankly. *"Who?"*

"You know, the woman who stayed with them for a few days after the bus accident," Steve said impatiently. "She works for me now at the restaurant."

"Why are they bringing *her?*"

"Because I asked them to invite her to spend Christmas with us. Her husband just died five or six weeks ago. She's new to this area, and she would've been alone otherwise."

He thought his ad-lib explanation had gone rather well.

Lisa and Gary seated themselves across from Steve on one of the twin white leather couches. One of the logs in the fireplace snapped, sounding like a pistol shot, and sparks flew up the chimney like bits of confetti. The silence lengthened.

Finally Lisa asked, "Are you *interested* in this woman?"

"I can't believe you're asking me a question like that," Steve said heatedly, "one day after we buried your mother!"

"And I can't believe you invited another woman to spend Christmas with us in your home," Lisa retorted just as heatedly, "one day after we buried my mother!"

"What the hell are you talking about—*another woman?*" growled Steve. "She's a nice person, she's one of my employees, but I'm not *interested* in her, whatever that's supposed to mean!"

"Is she gonna stay here overnight?"

"No, of course not! I'll make her stand outside in the snow to wait for Santa Claus!" He was shouting now.

"You never invited one of your employees here for Christmas while *Mom* was alive!" Lisa shouted back. Her face had flushed a deep red.

Gary stood up, his dark eyes smoldering.

"If you don't calm down in the next ten seconds, I'm taking you home," he told his wife. His voice was like tempered steel.

Voices and laughter in the front hall terminated the argument. Moments later Serena walked into the great room, flanked by Cliff and Cheryl. She was wearing her dark-green pantsuit with a sprig of holly pinned to the collar, and carrying her tray full of Christmas cookies.

"Happy Hanukkah and Merry Christmas, everyone!" She lowered the cookies to the Lucite coffee table that lay between the two white leather couches, where a punch bowl filled with eggnog waited. She straightened up, smiling the beatific smile that Steve so admired.

Cheryl did the introductions. “Grace, this is Cliff’s sister Lisa, and her husband Gary.”

Gary stood up to shake her hand. Lisa remained seated and offered her hand; Serena took it, bent over and kissed her cheek.

“No wonder your dad is so proud of you,” she said, still smiling. “You’re lovely.”

“I look like my mother,” said Lisa.

Serena glanced at the portrait of a pretty, dark-haired woman that hung on one side of the fireplace. A portrait of Steve hung on the other side.

“Yes, you do! I can see the resemblance,” Serena agreed. “Lisa, I’m so happy to meet you—and so sorry that I never got to meet your mother.”

Lisa bobbed her head.

Cliff pointed to the tray on the coffee table.

“Serena made the cookies . . . they’re a gift for everyone,” he announced.

She removed the plastic wrap and said, “Please, help yourselves.”

Lisa, sipping at a cup of eggnog, declined the offer the first time the tray went around but after hearing the exclamations of delight from the others, she finally tried a pfeffernuesse snowman (rolled in powdered sugar); then sampled a chocolate peanut butter Christmas tree decorated with multi-colored M&Ms.

The cookies were delicious; Steve got Lisa to admit that much. But when he noticed that she kept glancing back and forth from Serena to him, like a spectator at a tennis match, he decided to stop looking at Serena.

He hadn’t realized just how challenging that would be.

* * * * *

When it was time to go to bed, his two children occupied their "old" rooms with their spouses. Serena slept in a guest room that had its own adjoining bath.

Steve, in the master bedroom, lay in the king-sized bed he had shared with Anne Marie for most of his adult life. He was not sleeping because every nerve and muscle in his body was acutely aware of Grace being here, under his roof, in a room just down the hall. Had Hilda, his housekeeper, given her an extra blanket earlier today when she made up the bed in the guest room? Was Grace wearing pajamas or a nightgown?

Or . . . ?

He listened to the tree branches outside his window, creaking under their unaccustomed burden—the staccato sounds muffled by the steadily falling snow. At last he whispered a prayer for Anne Marie and closed his eyes.

CHAPTER 25

Sunday: The Day After Christmas

"So how was your holiday?" asked Juliette in the mocking drawl that always sounded to Serena like a re-run of the old television show *I Love Lucy.*

"Quiet," she answered.

"Do anything special?" Juliette persisted, tilting her head to the side like an interested friend. Serena's alarm system beeped. She knew Juliette was not her friend.

"I don't have a family, remember?"

"How about the *boss's* family?"

"What about them?"

"Oh, cut the crap! I know you spent Christmas with the Kingsleys."

"Who told you that?"

"Nobody had to tell me. I saw you get into the car with Cliff and Cheryl when you left here Friday night." She was still smiling, but it was no longer an interested-friend smile.

"When I asked you if you had a hot date, you played it cute and said *not likely.*" Her scornful imitation of Serena's voice sounded like a combination of Betty Boop and Wilma Flintstone. "But it was more than likely, wasn't it?"

"If you know all the answers, why are you asking so many questions?" Serena snapped.

"Oh, what's this? The Virgin Mary has a temper? I don't believe it!"

Without attempting further comment, Serena donned

the chef's hat that covered her hair. Everyone who worked in the kitchen at the King's Feast was required to wear one, and Anton was still out with the flu. When she walked out of the locker room, Juliette's laughter followed her like the whine of an out-of-season mosquito.

Later the Same Night

When Steve called at ten o'clock just before he left the restaurant and asked Cliff to meet him at the Moorestown house, they'd both been curious.

"Maybe he wants to retire and let you manage his restaurant," Cheryl had suggested.

"I don't know what he's got up his sleeve, but I'm sure that's not it," Cliff had replied. His father was too young, too healthy, and too *ornery* to retire.

Now it was almost eleven-thirty, and Cliff hadn't called or returned from his father's house. She tried not to worry, but ever since the bus accident she couldn't seem to help it. Her hand was hovering over the kitchen phone when it rang.

Certain that it was Cliff, Cheryl picked it up and said hello after the first ring. A man's voice with a New York accent said, "Clifford Kingsley there?"

"I expect him in a few minutes. Who's calling?"

"Name's Rudy. Is this Mrs. Kingsley?"

She knew immediately who was on the other end of the line. Cliff had told her about the visit from the man named Rudy Hamer who claimed to be a private investigator.

"Yes, I'm Cliff's wife. Is there something I can help you with?"

"Maybe. I'm trying to locate a woman named Serena Grace D'Agostino."

"Oh, yes! My husband told me you're looking for her so she can claim her inheritance. Is that right?"

"Yeah. Have you heard from her recently?"

"No, I'm sorry. We haven't heard from her since the day I drove her to the bus station in Mount Laurel."

"But you're pretty sure she bought a ticket to Philadelphia."

"Well, maybe . . . maybe not," said Cheryl deliberately. She and Cliff had disagreed about what they should say if the "investigator" called or came again. She'd suggested they try to mislead him, and Cliff had said, "Not a good idea. You're a lousy liar." But Cliff wasn't here, and she still thought it was a great plan.

"Whaddya mean, maybe *not?*" Rudy asked.

"While Grace was staying with us, she mentioned a couple of times that she has two cousins who live in California."

"Where in California?"

"Modesto."

Cheryl had never been to California and hadn't the slightest idea where Grace's cousins lived, but she had a girlhood friend who had moved to Modesto. In her mind, she had selected that city as home for the California cousins.

"Do you have their names?"

"I never asked. She only mentioned them once or twice."

She smiled when she heard him mutter something that sounded a lot like an obscenity. As she hung up the phone, the smile grew wider. Who said she was a lousy liar?

May he spend the next month roaming the streets of Modesto looking for a woman with silver hair worn in a bun!

Like a comic-strip character with a lightbulb above her

head, a bright idea suddenly illuminated her thoughts. She picked up the phone and dialed Grace's apartment.

"It's Cheryl. Hope I'm not calling too late."

"Are you kidding? I'm just getting home from the restaurant."

"I just had the most wonderful idea. You know I'm a hairdresser."

"Yes . . . ?"

"Would you let me cut and style your hair?"

"Cut my hair?" Grace sounded astonished. "Why would you want to do that? I've worn it this way for—for years!"

"I believe that's exactly the point I was trying to make. You're such a lovely-looking woman, and it's time to bring your hair style into the twenty-first century, along with the rest of you."

"Well, I—I don't know," Serena stammered. "Let me think about it."

"Okay, think about it. But you might just as well say yes right now because I'm going to keep on bugging you until you do."

They both laughed, and Cheryl began to visualize the hairstyle she would create for the older friend she had come to love so dearly.

Just after midnight Cliff walked into the bedroom where Cheryl was watching Jay Leno. She switched off the television set and said, "What'd your dad have to say?"

"He was concerned about me hanging around indefinitely on half-pay. He's bought another restaurant in downtown Philadelphia. It's actually a boat, anchored in the harbor. He's gonna call it the King's Yacht."

Cliff was unable to hold back the grin. "He wants to know if I'd be willing to manage it."

"What about your job at Reindeer . . . what happens if they clear you when the investigation is over?"

"Dad says these investigations take a long time—a year, maybe even longer. He thinks I'll be a basket case by then. Listen, even if I'm cleared of any blame in the accident, they still might not let me drive again. They'd probably give me an inside job—a dispatcher, maybe."

Not knowing whether he'd decided to accept his father's offer, Cheryl decided to walk the line.

"Do you think you'd like being a dispatcher?"

He laughed out loud.

"Honey, I'd rather manage a restaurant."

She squealed, jumped out of bed and hugged him. She was so happy, in fact, that she completely forgot to mention the phone call from Rudy.

Cut, Color, and Curl was closed on Mondays, but since that was Serena's only day off, Cheryl opened the shop for a short time during the afternoon of the following day. A nasty mixture of snow and freezing rain was assaulting the large front window as she and Serena hurried inside.

"Ready for your makeover?" she teased as she draped Serena with a flowered cape.

"Actually, I'm a little nervous."

Serena stared down at the floor as heaps of wavy silver-gray hair began to accumulate around the chair—but when she worked up enough courage to look in the mirror, she gasped. A silver cap of soft curls framed her face; her silver-gray eyes looked huge and her high cheekbones were perfectly defined. Cheryl dropped the scissors and clapped her hands.

"My God, Grace, am I good or what? You look like a model for *Vogue* magazine!"

On their honeymoon at Montauk Point, Long Island, Cliff had bought her an alabaster lamp in the shape of a lighthouse that she'd used ever since as a night-light in their bedroom; its golden-peach beam glowing softly from within through the translucent marble-like surface. As she looked at Grace's face reflected now in the mirror, she thought it had a similar glow.

She wondered if anyone else had noticed the way her father-in-law looked—and then tried not to look—at Grace on Christmas Eve. At that time it had been right after her mother-in-law's life had ended, but the day-to-day, husband-wife relationship had ended ten years before when he committed her to Tall Pines. Her mother-in-law had become a stranger living in Anne Marie's body, and Steve had become a sad visitor whose memories of his wife—like old, outdated garments—no longer fit the new persona.

What would he say when he saw Serena without the matronly bun?

Cheryl hugged her friend as they prepared to leave the shop, and Serena said, "Hey, I feel like I'm on my way to the junior prom!"

Camden, New Jersey

Rudy finished the last slice of cold pizza from the night before and called it breakfast. A mixture of snow and sleet sounded like some asshole throwing gravel against the window of his room. He was getting sick and tired of this shitty rooming house where he'd been staying to save money. As a matter of fact, he was getting sick and tired of this shitty job.

He was afraid to call Mrs. Abbott. He didn't want to

hear her sarcastic comments when he told her he hadn't found her stepmother. He made himself a cup of instant coffee, using lukewarm tap water from the washbasin in his room, and reflected on his telephone conversation with Cliff Kingsley's wife the night before. He had a hunch the woman he was looking for had not gone to Modesto, California. In fact, he had a hunch that Mrs. Kingsley knew where the old lady was hiding . . . and that the story about Modesto had been a red herring intended to send him on a wild-goose chase. Mrs. Kingsley was a lousy liar.

With a deep sigh, he picked up his cell phone and dialed Cold Spring Harbor, New York.

"Abbott residence."

"Miz Abbott, please," he said.

"And who might I say is calling?" This woman had an Irish brogue.

"Tell her it's Rudy."

When Phyllis came on the line, he said, "Did you get yourself a new housekeeper?"

"She's the new cook, and I ask the questions, Rudy, not you. It's been so long since I've heard from you that I thought perhaps you had lost my telephone number."

"Nah. I've been busy working on—you know."

"Yes, I *do* know. And I expect to hear the answer I've been waiting for."

When he didn't respond, she asked, "Rudy, do you own a computer?"

He laughed. "I don't need no computer in my line of work!"

Phyllis did not laugh. "This is the computer age. You can find a missing person on a computer, did you know that?"

"I can't learn all that shit at my age," he bleated.

"Then I guess I'll just have to look for someone who can," she snapped.

"Who's gonna pay for a computer, Miz Abbott?"

"Consider it an investment in your future," she replied, and hung up the phone.

CHAPTER 26

Cherry Hill, New Jersey

When Serena arrived at the restaurant the next morning, she found that Anton was back at work. He thanked her—a trifle stiffly—for filling in while he was sick. He said everyone had informed him what a wonderful job she had done.

"I only did the easy desserts, Anton," she told him. "I never even tried those fancy ones you know how to make: English trifle, cherries jubilee . . ."

He began to smile. "I teach you, I weel teach you so you know how to make zem next time."

"Stay well, Anton," she said. "Being a dessert chef is hard work."

A Gallic shrug. "Ees not so hard. You are good lady, good chef."

He was kissing her on both cheeks just as Steve walked through the kitchen door.

"What's going on here?" he demanded.

Serena laughed. "Anton was just thanking me for pinch-hitting for him while he had the flu."

Steve stepped closer and stared at Serena.

"What happened to your hair?"

She laughed again.

"Do you like it?"

He walked around her, studying it from every angle.

"Ask me next week. I'll have to get used to it."

He seemed unaware that everyone in the kitchen was watching them.

"Let me guess. My daughter-in-law attacked you with a pair of scissors."

"*Attacked* is not the word I would have used. I think I'd have to call it a joint venture."

"Grace, you look like a goddam teenager," he growled.

Serena couldn't seem to stop giggling.

"When was the last time you saw a teenager with gray hair?" she asked.

"Your hair isn't gray," he declared. "It's silver . . . or maybe *platinum.* Whatever it is, it's the same color as your eyes."

"Well, *well!* I've heard of the merry widow," drawled a familiar voice, "but now I'm hearing the merry *widower!*"

Every head turned to see Juliette posed in the doorway like an advertisement for a gentlemen's late-night supper club. Beverly rolled her eyes at Serena and pushed past Juliette into the main dining room, where several customers were already seated and studying lunch menus.

"I'd like to see you in my office, Juliette," Steve said quietly. "Right now."

His face had not changed expression, but Serena saw a muscle twitch next to his left eye.

Camden, New Jersey

There was no way Rudy was going to buy a computer. Even a used one would cost a few hundred, and he didn't know how to use it anyway. He went downstairs and asked his landlady if she knew of someone who had one.

"Sure. Kevin Graham. He lives on the second floor,

right underneath you, sweetie. He's some kind of writer, I think."

That evening, Rudy paid a visit to Kevin Graham, and watched in amazement as one of the Internet's search engines located the woman named Serena Grace D'Agostino—also known as Epstein—also known as Franklin. Tracking her further, through her Social Security number, he learned that she was working at a restaurant known as the King's Feast, in Cherry Hill, New Jersey. The computer showed her last known address to be the home of Clifford Kingsley in Delran, but he was almost certain she was no longer living there.

He offered the man a few dollars, but Kevin waved it away.

"It was my pleasure, man. Glad I could help you out," he insisted, remembering to add, "And Happy New Year!"

"Same to you," replied Rudy.

As soon as he found the D'Agostino woman and did what he had to do, he'd have to come back here and take out Kevin Graham as well. It couldn't be helped, because he was one of those upright, uptight guys. When the story came out in the newspapers about the D'Agostino woman's unexplained death, he would consider it his civic duty to call the cops and tell them about the acne-scarred man who had asked him to locate the woman.

After putting a "silent" bullet in Kevin's head, he'd return to his room, collect his belongings, and leave this grubby rooming house in downtown Camden. He'd used the name Roland Hughes when he rented the room. He was paid up through the end of the week, so the landlady wouldn't miss him until then. By that time he'd be back in New York.

Cherry Hill, New Jersey

Steve pointed to a chair in front of his desk.

"Sit down, Juliette. I have a proposition for you," he said.

Ignoring his order, she seated herself on the side of his desk, facing him, and crossed her long nylon-clad legs. The slit skirt of her black satin dress parted to reveal a tantalizing bit of thigh.

"Will I like it?" she asked, slowly moistening her lips with the tip of her tongue.

"I don't know. Remember the little talk we had, I guess it was about a month ago? When I told you I would never think of you as anything but a friend, and you promised to stop coming on to me?"

"Of course I remember, Steve, but things have changed since then," Juliette asserted, re-crossing her legs with a swish of nylon on satin. "Your wife passed away."

"My wife's passing has no bearing on my feelings about you. Again I'm telling you, I will never think of you as anything but a nice friend."

"A month ago, you didn't seem to mind *screwing* your nice friend," Juliette reminded him, the seductive drawl beginning to ferment into a vintage whine.

"It was a delightful few moments that I will not soon forget," Steve told her politely, choosing not to remind her of the circumstances, "but it will not happen again. Are you ready now to listen to my very fine offer, or do you want to continue to sulk?"

She slid off his desk, smoothing down the black satin gown.

"Let's hear what you consider a very fine offer."

"I've bought another restaurant—actually a boat in Philadelphia harbor. I'm calling it the King's Yacht. It will be different from the King's Feast, in that it will have music and dancing. More like a night club."

"Who's gonna manage it?"

Juliette was trying her best to sound cool, but he had her full attention. Her eyes were narrowed, gleaming.

"My son Cliff will be the manager. I'm offering you the hostess job at double your present salary."

"If you want to get rid of me that bad, how come you don't just fire me?" she snarled.

"Because you're a good hostess, and I think you'd be a natural for a night club operation."

"And who's gonna be the hostess at the King's Feast?" she asked. Her pretty face was contorted with hatred. "No, don't tell me. Let me guess."

"I'm making you a damn good offer, Juliette. You're a fool to turn it down."

"Who says I'm turning it down?" she retorted. "You're the boss! You can hire and fire and screw anybody you want!"

Steve stood up behind his desk, moving his hand sideways in a throat-cutting gesture.

"I've had it up to *here* with you, Juliette. This offer will be on the table for ten more seconds."

"Okay, *okay*. I'll take it."

Cherry Hill, New Jersey: New Year's Eve

Along with Valentine's Day, Mother's Day, and Thanksgiving, New Year's Eve was probably one of the busiest nights of the year at the King's Feast.

Juliette was still the hostess. Her new position would

begin after extensive renovations had been completed at the new restaurant. The waitresses and busboys had heard about the King's Yacht, of course, and everyone was counting the days until Juliette would leave to take over her new job. Serena had accepted the position of hostess at the King's Feast when that job became available.

Just before midnight, Serena loaded a tray with twelve dessert plates and a birthday cake for a customer whose eightieth birthday would occur on January first. He, his children, grandchildren, and great-grandchildren were all at the restaurant tonight, waiting to sing happy birthday to him as soon as Serena arrived with the cake. Normally she would not have lighted the eight large candles until she was ready to put the cake in front of him, but his table was next to the kitchen. As midnight approached, pandemonium reigned in the restaurant: customers shouting and laughing, waitresses and busboys racing to and fro. Just this once, she decided to light the candles in the kitchen.

As she walked purposefully toward the kitchen door with her tray, she did not see the foot that tripped her. She sprawled headlong onto the blazing cake, screaming when the front of her uniform caught fire.

CHAPTER 27

Serena lay on the floor screaming with pain and terror.

Beverly, who had just re-entered the kitchen, knelt and rolled Serena onto her back, pulled her apron up and smothered the flames. Anton, who had made the birthday cake, shouted, "I see Juliette! Eet was Juliette who make her fall!"

Less than a minute later Steve dashed through the kitchen door.

"Carlos told me—omigod! *Grace!* What happened? What the hell happened here?"

Serena, still sitting on the floor with her apron and the front of her uniform scorched and smoking, shook her head. She was in shock and for the moment unable to speak.

Anton tugged on the sleeve of Steve's dinner jacket and shouted, "Eet was Juliette! Juliette make her fall!"

"I'll deal with her later. Somebody get Grace's jacket! *Hurry up!*"

Carlos, the busboy who had reported the incident, dashed into the locker room and reappeared with Serena's down jacket and handbag. When Steve tried to lift her from the floor, she waved him away. She'd found her voice.

"Please, Steve—I'm okay."

But Steve insisted on helping her as she stood up, wobbling a bit.

"I'm taking you to the hospital," he growled, his arm around her shoulders.

"But—but what about Mr. Teitelbaum's birthday cake?

It's almost midnight, and the whole family is sitting out there . . ."

Anton was already busy frosting another cake. Beverly gave Serena a gentle push.

"Listen to the boss! You have to let a doctor examine you, Grace. We'll take care of the old guy's birthday, don't worry about it."

Other waitresses nodded, murmuring agreement. Looking around the kitchen at all the concerned, caring faces, Serena's eyes filled with tears.

"They're like my family," she whispered to Steve as he escorted her out the back door.

He had never seen Grace cry before. So why did those tear-filled eyes suddenly look more familiar? He shook his head, helped her into the passenger seat of his car, and closed the door.

As Steve Kingsley's emerald-green Cadillac exited the parking lot, it passed a brown Ford Fairlane entering through the opposite lane. Rudy gave the keys to the valet, and strolled through the dramatic entrance to the restaurant, which had been designed to resemble a medieval castle. Customers entered by crossing a drawbridge, which spanned a moat. In spring and summer, ducks swam in it—but now, on the last night of December, there were no ducks. The moat was frozen beneath a grimy quilt of snow.

Inside, it was bedlam. At one minute after midnight, the restaurant lights were flashing on and off, everyone was screaming Happy New Year, and a few people were singing, "Should auld acquaintance be forgot . . ."

He was greeted by a stunning redhead in a green satin dress that left nothing to the imagination. He saw her glance at his old plaid raincoat and scuffed shoes before she said, half-shouting above the din, "Good evening, sir, and Happy New Year. Do you have a reservation?"

"I'm not here for fun," he told her. "I'm a private investigator, and I'm trying to locate a woman named Serena Grace D'Agostino. I understand she works here."

"What do you want with her?" asked the redhead, motioning him into Steve's vacant office so they could hear each other.

"She's the widow of a man by the name of Edward Franklin. He left her a third of his estate, and nobody knows what happened to her. I guess she was, you know, *grieving* after her husband died. She just up and left New York—and his family wants her to come back and claim her share of the estate."

He watched the green eyes narrow.

"How much would she stand to get?"

"I dunno exactly, but I'd say somewheres in the neighborhood of three, maybe three and a half million."

A strange little smile curved the woman's mouth.

"Now, isn't that a shame! Grace *used* to work here but she got burned in a kitchen fire. She's not working here any longer."

"Got her home address?" asked Rudy, pulling a dog-eared notebook from the pocket of his raincoat.

"No, I'm so sorry, I don't. She moved away and left no forwarding address."

Rudy tilted his head and frowned; he studied the woman for a moment. Was she telling the truth?

"Wasn't there a Workers' Compensation claim?"

"No. The restaurant paid all her medical expenses, plus a separation bonus."

"You're the owner here?"

She smiled graciously.

"I'm the owner's wife."

Rudy opened his notebook.

"Mind giving me yer name?"

"Of course not. It's Juliette Kingsley."

"You were very, very lucky," the young emergency-room doctor told Serena, who was sitting bare-chested on the examination table. He pointed to the patches of reddened skin and a dozen or more blisters on her breasts.

"It was a lot more than luck," said Serena. "When my uniform caught fire from the candles, another waitress pulled my apron up and put out the flames."

"You were on the floor, face down?"

Serena nodded. "She rolled me over on my back and extinguished the fire."

"Quick thinking. But in the future, wait until you get to the table to light the candles on a birthday cake!"

"Normally, that's what we always do. But tonight we were so busy, I decided to light them in the kitchen. The old gentleman's table was just outside the kitchen door, and I wanted to make a grand entrance with eight candles blazing."

"You almost made a grand exit instead," the doctor remarked dryly. "Ah, here's the nurse. She's going to put some antibiotic cream on those blisters to prevent infection, and then we'll give you a prescription for the cream. Just keep applying it three or four times a day until the burned areas and blisters are healed. Keep them covered, but don't make the bandages air-tight."

When the nurse finished applying the cream and bandaging her breasts, Serena slipped her arms back into her scorched uniform and reached for her jacket.

"Your husband is still outside in the waiting room," said the nurse.

Serena chuckled. "That's not my husband. That's my boss."

"Well, *that's* hard to believe. He's been sitting out there crying."

"Crying?" echoed Serena.

"That's what I said."

"Oh, I think I know why. He lost his wife just before Christmas. Being in a hospital again must have brought back bad memories."

The nurse raised both eyebrows and shrugged.

Rudy was beyond frustrated. He stopped at a twenty-four-hour fast-food drive-in and then returned to his rooming house. His landlady asked, "Did you get the information you needed from Kevin?"

"Yeah."

She grinned, giving gums and teeth equal space.

"Happy New Year, Mr. Hughes."

"Same to you."

Sitting in his grungy room munching on a soggy cheeseburger and lukewarm French fries, he reviewed the events of the evening.

The redheaded woman identifying herself as the owner's wife had given her name as Kingsley. Same last name as *Clifford* Kingsley. Experience had taught Rudy to distrust coincidences. He'd thought at first that all the members of the Kingsley family were trying to protect the woman he was after, but something about the redhead's demeanor caused him to reassess the situation. He suspected she'd made up the story about Serena Grace D'Agostino not working there anymore.

He knew she'd believed his story, but he'd gotten the feeling she wasn't trying to protect the woman. He had a hunch she just didn't want her to get the inheritance he'd been stupid enough to mention. Of course, the woman who'd hired him didn't want her to claim it either.

Ha-ha! He decided he would visit the restaurant again and talk to the husband.

A hook shot sent his beer can into the wastebasket, and he popped open another one. A long swallow, as he glanced at the grainy picture of a mob of revelers welcoming the new year in Chicago, on the small black-and-white TV set in his room . . .

Jeez! What a way to spend New Year's Eve!

Over her vehement protests, Steve took Serena to her apartment and refused to leave until he saw her tucked in bed. He kissed her on the forehead and said in his gravelly voice, "You're not to come back to work until those burns and blisters are healed!"

When she started to say something, he barked, "Grace, that's an order!"

Seeing the look on her face, he added in a softer voice, "Whaddya think we have sick pay for? Anton was out for a week . . . don't you think he got paid? Stop worrying!"

It was one-thirty when he walked through the back entrance into the kitchen of the King's Feast. Everyone crowded around him, asking how Grace was doing.

"She's gonna be okay. From the hospital I took her to her apartment, and she argued with me all the way . . . she wanted to come back and finish out the night here." He laughed. "I told her she must've hit her head when she fell."

He glanced around the kitchen.

"Where's Juliette?"

Silence. Cooks, waitresses, and busboys exchanged glances.

Finally Beverly said, "She's out by the cash register."

He said, "Did anyone besides Anton see her trip Grace?"

"Me. I see her," said Carlos.

"You saw her stick her foot out and trip Grace?"

"Si." The busboy nodded vehemently.

Steve touched Beverly's shoulder. "I want you to act as hostess until closing."

She looked down at her clothes. "In my waitress uniform?"

"Why not?" He took her arm. "Everybody's here already. Do you think they're gonna care how the person that takes their money is dressed?"

They walked through the restaurant together. When they reached the register, Steve said, "Juliette, Beverly is going to relieve you now."

Juliette gave them both an outraged glare. "Why?"

"Because I'm going to walk you to the locker room to pick up your things."

Juliette paled visibly, but she lifted her chin and managed to convey a measure of indignation.

"Everyone thinks I tripped Grace, but I *didn't!* I wasn't even in the kitchen when it happened! If she says I did it, she's lying!"

Steve gripped her arm and marched her out of the dining area.

"Grace didn't see who tripped her—but other people did."

"They're lying! Those bitches all hate me because I'm beautiful and they're not!"

"Save your breath, *beautiful.* The people who saw you were male. You're fired."

"What about my pay?"

"You'll get your last check in the mail," he told her, shoving her through the locker-room door. "Now pick up your stuff and get out."

CHAPTER 28

When she heard the door click shut after Steve left the apartment, Serena got up and slid the chain bolt in place. She returned to bed and lay quietly with her eyes closed. It was the beginning of a new year, and she wanted to summon a picture of the husband who had left her six weeks before. She frowned, and her jaw clenched as she willed Eddie's image to appear, but the only face her efforts produced was the face of Steve Kingsley.

Steve was taller than Eddie, and had the body of a former fullback. His hair was brush-cut gray, and his black eyes had the proud look of an eagle. His looks seemed to reflect his name. A *king,* accustomed to giving orders and having them obeyed. A powerful enemy, she thought now, but an intensely loyal friend. And Steve Kingsley had made it clear from the beginning that he was her friend.

When they met, she'd had an odd feeling about Steve. That feeling was probably due to the spark of static electricity that passed between them the first time their hands touched. That static electricity thing had never happened again, and she'd almost forgotten about it. Until tonight.

At the hospital, the nurse had told her he was sitting in the waiting room crying until he learned that her burns were superficial, and would heal within a week. And he had tucked her into bed and kissed her on the forehead before he returned to the restaurant. She reached up and touched her forehead. His lips had been firm, but gentle.

When he'd invited her to spend Christmas with him and

his children, she'd thought he just felt sorry for a recent widow alone at Christmas. But tonight he had behaved like a man who liked her. Maybe even—loved her? She asked herself: was it possible?

He was a good-looking man, anyone with eyes could see that. He was the sort of man that women of any age would turn around to look at on the street. He radiated energy, confidence, and success. He was the sort of man who could have any woman he wanted—and didn't men his age want *young* women? She was the same age as Steve! What would he want with a sixty-five-year-old woman when he could have one in her thirties or forties? Reason overruled romance! Lying there in bed, she laughed at herself—*you silly old woman*—before she felt the tears on her cheeks.

Steve Kingsley's feelings for her were compassionate . . .

Not passionate.

She got out of bed again and took one of the sleeping pills they had given her at the hospital, so she could tune out her foolish thoughts and go to sleep.

Another woman lay sleepless on black satin sheets in her Pennsauken apartment, but her thoughts were quite different from Serena's.

How many years had she wasted on Steve Kingsley? How long had she stifled her envy of Anne Marie—waiting for an opportunity to step in and take her rightful place by his side? Juliette Kingsley! How many times had she tried that name on her tongue—and it tasted sweet! She had foreseen her future clearly, as the beautiful, red-haired wife of a wealthy restaurateur, mingling with society people, dressed in clothes that came from Bloomingdale's instead of Wal-Mart's.

She'd live in the big white-brick house in Moorestown

that she'd driven past a thousand times, picturing herself and Steve strolling in the garden, hand in hand.

She'd learn to swim and play tennis so she could use the pool and tennis court on his property. She'd have her hair and nails done every week. She'd have her own little sports car—a Jaguar, maybe, or a Porsche. She'd have servants to hire and fire and order around. And best of all, she'd never have to work again!

Occasionally, she'd eat dinner at the King's Feast, seated with Steve in his special alcove, and she'd beckon to Beverly and say, "I asked for medium-well-done. This filet mignon is medium-*rare*."

And Beverly would have to bow her head and say, "I'm so sorry, Mrs. Kingsley. I'll ask the chef to broil another steak for you . . ."

She'd baited her hook with a cleverly timed and executed roll in the hay (or more accurately, on the locker-room bench) that she knew Steve had been powerless to resist. After all, she knew how to tease a man—please a man—and leave him begging for more.

Everything had been moving along according to plan until that smug, smirking Grace came into the picture, with her silver hair and saintly smile. She, Juliette, had always thought she knew men better than they knew themselves, and she still couldn't figure out what a sexy animal like Steve Kingsley saw in that over-age Girl Scout.

After Anne Marie had conveniently died, there would have been nothing to keep Juliette from claiming the prize she'd worked so long and hard to get—if Grace D'Agostino had not come to work at the King's Feast.

And now look what had happened! She'd lost the promised hostess job at the new Philadelphia restaurant as well as the job she'd held for ten years at the Cherry Hill restaurant, and Steve had told her before she left that "in good conscience" he could not give her a reference—verbal or written—if she applied elsewhere for a hostess job. The bastard had even told her she was lucky Grace had refused to press assault charges against her. Her greatest regret was that Grace had not burned her face and broken her neck when she fell on the birthday cake.

Cherry Hill, New Jersey

The glamorous redhead was not on duty when Rudy arrived at the restaurant on New Year's Day. A brown-haired woman wearing a beige suit greeted him and—like the redhead—asked if he had a reservation.

"I need to speak with Mr. Kingsley," he told her.

"May I tell him what it's about?" she asked politely.

"It's a confidential matter about one of your employees," he said.

A few minutes later the hostess ushered him into the spacious office. A big, handsome gray-haired man strode around a massive mahogany desk to shake his hand.

"Steven Kingsley. And you are . . . ?"

"Rudy Hamer. I'm a private investigator. I've been trying to locate a woman named D'Agostino, and I understand she used to work here."

"Who told you she used to work here?" he asked, with no inflection on the words *used to.*

"Your wife. I was here last night around midnight."

"My wife, eh?"

"Yes, sir. You're a lucky man . . . she's a looker."

The expression on Mr. Kingsley's face gave Rudy the distinct feeling that he had said something he shouldn't have.

"Sit down, Mr. Hamer. Why do you want to locate Grace D'Agostino?"

Rudy seated himself on a red velvet chair. He glanced over his shoulder at Mr. Kingsley, who was pacing in back of him.

"She's—ah—the widow of Edward Franklin, a very wealthy attorney from Long Island, New York," he explained, looking over his other shoulder. Kingsley was really making him uneasy, walking around behind his back.

"Go on. I'm listening."

"She inherited one-third of Mr. Franklin's estate, like around three, three and a half million dollars, but she up and left town—disappeared, actually—before she could claim her inheritance."

"Why do you think she left town, Mr. Hamer?"

Rudy shrugged. "Beats me. Mr. Franklin's daughter hired me to find her and bring her home."

"Dead or alive?"

Rudy blinked. "What the hell does that mean?"

"I think you know *exactly* what it means," said Steve, seating himself behind the desk and leaning back in his chair. "How much is Mrs. Abbott paying you?"

Rudy blinked again. "How d'you know her name?"

"I have private investigators too, my man. I repeat, how much is she paying you?"

"Twenty-five big ones," Rudy lied without blinking.

"I'll double that if you end your search right now and go back to New York."

Already sorry he had not said fifty, Rudy began to whine.

"She'll just hire somebody else if I come back empty-handed."

"Who says you're going back empty-handed?" asked Steve. "You'll be going back with a death certificate."

"A death certificate?" echoed Rudy, peering across the gleaming desk.

"Yeah. A death certificate showing the cause of death as a gunshot wound to the head."

Rudy's scalp prickled with cold sweat. Obviously, he had underestimated this guy. "*You're* gonna do the job?"

Steve smiled, a cold smile, and his eyes flashed jet black.

"Come back tomorrow, Mr. Hamer. A copy of the death certificate will be waiting for you."

Rudy stood up. "Hey, listen, I still got a coupla questions . . ."

"No questions. See you tomorrow, Mr. Hamer."

Five minutes later Steve dialed a number on his cell phone.

"Hey, Steve," said a voice on the other end. "It's been a long time!"

"Yeah. Where does the time go? How's the family, Sal?"

"Good, real good. Every time I watch my boy play soccer, I think: *Bobby would still be wearing that lousy brace on his foot if it wasn't for my friend Steve.* Bobby's like a different kid now: a million friends—no more problems in school—since he had that operation! And I swear I'm gonna pay you back every penny someday!"

"I told you then and I'm telling you now—I don't want your money," Steve growled. "Just knowing that Bobby has no more club foot, that's enough for me! But *today*—today I got a little job for you. You still in the same business?"

"Sure, I still got the print shop. Whaddya need?"

CHAPTER 29

Camden, New Jersey

Juliette strolled out of the unemployment office with the air of a newspaper reporter who'd been sent on an investigative assignment to get the facts on what makes people unemployable. A teenaged boy in the parking lot whistled at her, and she said, "Fuck off, junior." He gave her the finger.

She exited that parking lot as fast as her car could move. Dammit, she was *not* like those disgusting sub-human creatures on line in there, smelling of chewing gum, sweat, and baby vomit. She had signed up to receive checks while she was unemployed, but she hoped she'd never have to see the inside of that place again.

Knowing she could not count on a reference from Steve Kingsley shot a hole in her chances of nailing a hostess job in a fine restaurant. Unless . . .

A new scheme began to take shape in her mind.

She saw the elegant sign for Le Chateau, only two blocks from the King's Feast, and drove into their parking lot on impulse. She knew Steve was always in his restaurant between eleven and eleven-thirty every morning, and she hoped the proprietor of Le Chateau had similar habits.

It was eleven-twenty when she looked through the big picture window near the entrance and saw a portly gentlemen seated behind a desk in a tastefully appointed office. She unbuttoned her jacket so that her low-cut sweater would make a statement about her assets, licked her lips, and tapped on the window. When he looked up, she gave him her most beguiling smile.

As she knew he would, he came immediately to unlock the front door and admit her.

"Good morning," she purred. "My name is Juliette Black. Are you the owner of this gorgeous restaurant?"

"I am. My name is Pierre Chandelle. May I help you, Mademoiselle Black!"

"Oh, I hope so! I'm looking for a hostess job, but I would consider only a five-star establishment."

"Le Chateau is a five-star restaurant, mademoiselle," he said proudly, telling her what she already knew. "Would you like to step into my office?"

She let him help her off with her jacket and hold a chair so that she could sit in front of his desk.

"Do you have any hostess experience?" he asked. He had a very slight accent, and she wondered if he was really French.

"Yes, I worked at Henri's for many years, but I left there four years ago in order to care for my invalid mother," she told him in her best Florence Nightingale voice.

"Ah! Henri retired last year," Mr. Chandelle said. (She had, of course, known that—and chosen the restaurant for that very reason.)

"Oh, I knew it had closed, but I didn't know why," she replied.

"Your mother," Mr. Chandelle prompted, "did she . . . ?"

"Passed away just before Christmas." She produced an embroidered handkerchief and dabbed at her eyes, taking care not to smear her eye make-up. "I miss her terribly, but I need a job now. All Mom left me was the little condo in Pennsauken where the two of us have been living these past years."

She let her handkerchief drop to the floor and bent forward to retrieve it, giving Mr. Chandelle a front-row view of her cleavage. When she picked up the hankie and snuggled it between her splendid breasts, she was gratified to see perspiration blooming on Mr. Chandelle's bald head.

"I already have a hostess who's been with me for twenty years," he told her, "but lately she's been making a few mistakes. I've been thinking about replacing her. Perhaps our Heavenly Father has sent you to me, mademoiselle! When could you start?"

Juliette glanced at a framed photograph of an elderly woman on his desk.

"Oh, is this your wife?" She tilted her head to one side and used her interested-friend voice.

"Yes, that's Marguerite. She passed away six months ago," he replied.

She tilted her head to the other side and smiled wistfully.

"It seems we've both lost someone we loved. I can start right away, Mr. Chandelle."

As she drove away in her old BMW, she was smiling. She had not lost her magic touch! She had secured a job without any reference from Steve Kingsley or anyone else. She'd asked for double the salary she'd been getting at the King's Feast, and the old goat had agreed.

Mr. Chandelle had told her she couldn't start right away, because of the old hostess who'd been with him for twenty years. He'd have to give her two weeks' notice.

She realized she'd have to sleep with him occasionally, not a pleasant thought. He was older than Steve, and not nearly as good-looking, but she believed he might have more money.

As she was leaving, she'd heard him wheeze when he

bent over and kissed her hand. If it turned out that he was unable to perform in bed, she would just let him play with her boobs. That would probably be enough to keep him happy, and the rewards would probably be worth it. He would want to give her gifts, of course. She tapped the steering wheel. *Hey, I could use a new car, Pierre, baby!*

She thought about her mother, retired on a small pension and living in Naples, Florida. Wouldn't she be amazed if she learned about her untimely death a few days before Christmas?

She laughed out loud. It was the first good laugh she'd had since she watched Grace fall on the birthday cake.

The thought reminded her that she had one more task to accomplish before starting her new job at Le Chateau. She had to make certain that Steve Kingsley never had a chance to marry Grace D'Agostino.

Rudy sat on the red velvet chair and scrutinized the death certificate. He held it up to the light to see the water mark, and examined it under a magnifying glass he'd brought along in his shabby briefcase, a briefcase which now held fifty thousand dollars in cash.

"Looks genuine, Mr. Kingsley."

"That's because it *is* genuine, Mr. Hamer."

Rudy smiled, revealing a mouthful of crooked yellow teeth.

"Hey, I gotta hand it to you. You're a real pro. You really knocked off the old broad, huh?"

Steve Kingsley sprang from the chair behind his desk and with both hands, grabbed the lapels of Rudy's plaid raincoat, lifting him bodily from the red velvet chair. When Rudy's face was on a level with his own, his black eyes stared directly into the smaller man's pale-blue ones.

"Are you a praying man, Rudy?"

"S-s-sometimes."

"When you leave here you better go to church and say a prayer that Grace D'Agostino lives a very long life. Got that?"

"Got it," Rudy croaked.

"Now, two things you gotta remember. First, Grace D'Agostino is not a broad, she's a lady, something you know nothing about. Second, if she should die *for any reason* during my lifetime, I will find you and take appropriate action."

He let go of the plaid raincoat, dropping Rudy back onto the red velvet chair, then contorted his own right hand to look like a gun and pressed his forefinger against the acne-scarred forehead.

"Do you catch my meaning?"

Rudy seemed to have a little difficulty replying audibly to the question, but he nodded his head twice.

"Good. Now get the hell out of my face."

CHAPTER 30

"Good morning, Miz Abbott. I have good news for you."

"Well, it's about time, Rudy, wouldn't you say? I hope you're telling me you *finally* fulfilled your contract!"

Rudy reflected that the passage of six weeks had not mellowed the woman who had hired him.

"Yeah, and I have a death certificate," he boasted, "which I will give you when you pay me the money you owe me."

"The sooner the better. How about today?"

"Suits me. I'll come to the house."

"No, *you will not!* We can't be too careful now, just in case there's an inquiry. There are servants here—family members—neighbors . . ."

"Didn't seem to worry you none before," Rudy observed.

"I passed you off as a private investigator before, looking for my beloved stepmother. Now that she's actually gone, we'll have to be more discreet. We'll meet at an out-of-the-way spot."

"Where?"

"Montauk Point."

"*Montauk Point!* Jesus Christ, lady! I'm not driving way the hell out to the end of Long Island!"

"You will if you want the rest of your money," she told him, "and the first thousand a month bonus I promised you."

He rapidly calculated his total take on this job—from

Steve Kingsley and this crazy broad—and decided to go for it. Sixty thousand in cash, and a thousand a month, like a goddam pension . . . hey, he could live like a gentleman, just take an occasional job to break the monotony. He'd buy some fancy clothes, maybe a new car . . .

"Okay. What time?"

"Five o'clock."

"Why so late? It'll be getting dark by then, and I'll have that long fucking drive back."

"Are you telling me you're afraid of the dark, Rudy? Or are you afraid of me?"

"I'm not afraid of nothing! Just tell me where to meet you."

"You know where the Montauk lighthouse is?" she asked.

"Yeah."

"Listen to me very carefully. You'll be on Montauk Highway, that's Route Twenty-Seven. A couple of miles before you get to the lighthouse, you'll see a rest stop on the right-hand side of the road, where motorists can park for a few minutes and take photos. Pull off there, and I'll be waiting."

"What kinda car will you be driving?"

"A silver-gray Jaguar. Does that sound familiar, Rudy?"

"Whaddya mean?"

"It should sound familiar! It was my stepmother's car. Do you remember now? She was driving it the first day of this ordeal—the day you let her get away."

Cherry Hill, New Jersey

"My God, Serena, you look like—like a queen," said Steve. "All you need is a crown."

It was just before five o'clock, and they were standing in the lobby area of the restaurant, near the cash register. He gestured for her to turn around, and she spun slowly before him. She had chosen a violet gown with a fitted top, long sleeves, and a V-neck. The skirt flared gracefully from her hips down to her high-heeled violet sandals. She wore no jewelry except for a pair of old-fashioned amethyst earrings. Her shining cap of silver hair curled softly around her face, and she had applied a modicum of make-up: blush, mascara, pink lipstick, and a hint of lavender shadow on her eyelids.

A woman always knows when she looks her best. Serena's sparkling eyes and the faint smile on her face proclaimed a shy self-esteem. She had almost forgotten how it felt to see her image reflected in the admiring eyes of a good-looking man.

"So you're satisfied with my selection," she said, the statement turning up at the end to become a question.

"Satisfied doesn't even begin to cut it. I wish I had a bigger vocabulary," he said, grinning broadly.

The first customers of the evening strolled through the entrance: three elderly couples who had been "regulars" for years. Serena greeted them graciously, and they followed her to a round table for six.

"Something new—a hostess with class," remarked one of the men.

"Your dress is lovely, my dear . . . is that silk chiffon?" asked his wife, touching the sleeve of Serena's new gown.

"Yes, I believe it is," she answered, smiling as she handed them their menus.

One of the other men said, "We'd like Grace to wait on us. She's the best waitress in the place."

She'd heard the old saying, *Clothes make the man*. Apparently, they make the woman, too. Serena remembered this customer very well. She had given his wife a free dinner when the busboy removed her dessert before she had finished eating it. She opened her mouth to identify herself, but before she could do so, Steve came up behind her and said, "Grace is no longer one of our waitresses. Beverly will take care of your table."

"What happened to Grace?" asked the man.

"She accepted a better job," Steve said, winking at Serena.

"You were a fool to let her go." The man was scowling.

"What makes you think I let her go?" Steve slipped a proprietary arm around her shoulders. "I promoted her!"

They left the table together, amid congratulations and exclamations of amazement.

". . . should have recognized her!"

". . . looks like a million bucks in that dress."

". . . much better than that redheaded floozy . . ."

Montauk Point, Long Island

"Okay, let me see the death certificate," said Phyllis.

Her almost-blue eyes glittered as she slipped into the old Ford Fairlane next to Rudy. He'd made a move to get into the Jaguar, but she stopped him. She had reasons for wanting the transaction to take place in his grubby old station wagon.

He started to open his battered briefcase, and stopped. He'd picked up what he believed was a tail on his way to this meeting. He couldn't figure out why she would want to have him followed, but he'd managed to shake the pursuer before he hit Montauk Highway.

"Not so fast. Lemme see the money first."

She withdrew an envelope from her black alligator briefcase and showed him the cash inside.

"Five thousand dollars, plus another thousand for your first month's bonus," she intoned.

He grabbed the envelope and handed her the New Jersey death certificate.

Just as he had done, she fingered it, held it up to the light, put on her glasses and scrutinized it, probably comparing it to the New York death certificate she had recently received for her father.

"Good work, Rudy," she said at last, almost smiling.

His smile was a bit wider. Sixty-six thousand, *with more to come!* And since the D'Agostino woman was alive and well, he hadn't even had to knock off Kevin Graham, the guy in Camden who'd looked her up on his computer.

Phyllis removed a split of champagne from her sleek briefcase, and two plastic glasses: one pink, one white.

"Will you join me in a little drink to celebrate a job well done?"

Rudy would have rather had a beer, but he shrugged.

"Sure, why not?"

He watched her open the bottle and pour. They clicked glasses.

"Here's to success and prosperity!" she said.

"I'll drink to that," he agreed, and took a tiny sip.

She darted a furtive glance at him.

"Drink up!"

Rudy made a face. He'd never sampled champagne before, and thought it tasted like Alka-Seltzer. He held his breath and drained the glass.

"So tell me, Rudy," said Phyllis, "did Serena suffer much, or was it quick?"

"It was quick," he told her. "She never knew it happened."

Relaxed and smiling broadly now, Phyllis tilted her head back and chug-a-lugged her champagne. Instantly, the empty glass fell from her hand, and she clawed at her throat.

"Whatsa matter, Miz Abbott?" he asked. "Are you okay?"

A strangled screech came from her throat. She said something that sounded like "wrong glass." She gagged and slumped over the dashboard, retching violently. Bad-smelling foam oozed from her mouth and dripped onto the floor mat of Rudy's Ford Fairlane.

"Holy shit!" said Rudy. *She was gonna kill me, but she got the glasses mixed up!*

He got out of his car and looked around. The sun had disappeared below the horizon, and no cars were visible in either direction. He put on his gloves, picked up the tiny woman in his arms and carried her easily back to the silver-gray Jaguar that had once belonged to her stepdaughter. He propped her up behind the wheel, slobbering and moaning incoherently, then placed the champagne bottle and the glass she'd used on the passenger seat beside her.

The black alligator briefcase and the money were in his own car, and he put the death certificate and the plastic glass he'd used in the pocket of his raincoat.

He walked across the gravel rest stop, and climbed back into his brown Ford Fairlane. When he drove away in the deepening dusk, it was exactly half-past five.

Three days later the following story appeared in *Newsday*, the Long Island newspaper:

POLICE BAFFLED BY SOCIALITE SUICIDE

Mrs. Phyllis Abbott, wife of Dr. Chester Abbott, Vice-President of the New York Pharmacological Society, was found dead in her car today near the Montauk Point lighthouse. The woman, a longtime resident of Cold Spring Harbor, had been missing for two days. She had ingested most of a split of champagne, apparently laced with a powerful drain cleaner. There was no evidence of foul play, and police have ruled it a suicide.

Mrs. Abbott's father, eminent attorney Edward Franklin, died in November, leaving his considerable fortune to his daughter, and to his two wives, Mrs. Margaret Rhodes and Mrs. Serena Franklin. Several weeks after his death, Mrs. Franklin disappeared, and efforts to locate her have been unsuccessful.

The dead woman's mother, Mrs. Margaret Rhodes, who resides with her husband in a guest cottage on the Abbotts' estate, insists her daughter was not depressed, and that she left her home on Tuesday afternoon in good spirits to meet with the private investigator they'd hired to locate her missing stepmother. She told police the investigator's name was Rudy Hamer. Police want to talk with him, calling him a "person of interest" in the case.

As Cold Spring Harbor residents discussed the puzzling story in the newspaper, a well-dressed man with an acne-scarred face walked into the overseas terminal of Kennedy Airport. He was carrying a black alligator briefcase when he boarded a British Airways flight bound for London. The passport and airline ticket had been obtained under his real name, Rodney Haines.

CHAPTER 31

Cherry Hill, New Jersey

"My office, Grace."

Her brow puckered in a frown. He sounded very serious. Had she done something wrong? Two minutes later when she walked in, Steve closed the door and motioned for her to take one of the red velvet chairs in front of his desk.

"Steve, what is it?" she asked.

"I've had a guy in New York following up on Rudy—you know, that clown your stepdaughter hired to . . ."

"Yes, yes, I remember the name." How could she ever forget it? "What happened?"

He handed her a faxed copy of the *Newsday* article headlined *Police Baffled by Socialite Suicide.*

Wide-eyed and open-mouthed, she read the article twice before she looked back at Steve.

"That woman would never kill herself!" she exclaimed.

He nodded. "From what you've told me about her, I happen to agree with you."

"What do you think she was doing way out at Montauk Point?"

"Fred—my investigator—is an ex-cop. Retired on disability. He took a bullet in the right lung, but his mind is still sharp. Here's what he thinks happened: your stepdaughter set it up to meet Rudy at Montauk to get the death certificate . . ."

"Death certificate?"

Steve frowned. As usual, he had put off explaining his actions to someone he cared about.

"Yeah. I gave a death certificate to Rudy, to get rid of the bastard." He did not mention the additional fifty thousand dollars he had given him.

"A death certificate . . . for me?"

"Well—*yeah*. It was a phony, of course, but it was printed by a professional—a friend of mine who owed me a favor. It looked genuine."

"So Phyllis thought he had fulfilled his contract, and she was meeting him to pay him off."

"I think she had no intention of paying him off."

Serena gasped. "You think she was planning to kill him?"

"Yeah, that's what Fred thinks, and I'm inclined to think he's right. Does that make sense to you?"

Knowing Phyllis? "Yes, it does."

"Here's a fact that wasn't in the newspaper story: the lab found no trace of drain cleaner in the bottle of champagne. Only in the plastic cup she drank from."

Serena immediately grasped the implication; she leaned forward eagerly.

"There were *two* cups!"

"Sure. One for her and one for him. She must have got them mixed up."

"That doesn't sound like Phyllis!"

Steve raised one dark eyebrow, and a smile nudged at the corners of his mouth.

"Something, or *someone,* guided her hand. Maybe there really is a God."

She thought about that statement for several minutes. Then she said, "The article says the cops are looking for Rudy."

"Yeah, but they've got nothing to link him to that woman's death. If our theory's right, Fred figures he wiped his fingerprints, if any, from her car, took the clean cup with him—along with the payoff money she would've had to show him before he gave her the death certificate."

"And what happened to the death certificate?"

"The cops didn't find it, so he must've taken that, too. Probably burned it or flushed it down the toilet."

"Did your friend actually see him meet Phyllis?"

Steve rubbed his head and scowled.

"He was on Rudy's tail, but the bum managed to shake him. Fred says he was definitely headed east, going toward Suffolk County, when he lost him."

"Where do you think Rudy is now?"

"If you were in Rudy's shoes, would you hang around Long Island?"

"*No!* I'd go as far away as I could get. Maybe out of the country."

"Bingo."

He paused and sent her a searching look.

"These people can't hurt you anymore, Grace. Maybe you want to claim your inheritance now?"

"I don't want it. I think it's cursed."

Almost Two Weeks Later

When the phone rang next to her bed, it was after midnight and Serena was sleeping soundly. Sunday was always a busy day at the King's Feast, and this one had been no exception. She rolled over, groaning, and picked up the phone.

"Grace, it's Beverly."

Instantly awake, she sat up in bed. "What's wrong?"

"It's Teddy, my seven-year-old. He's in terrible pain, and I don't know what's wrong with him. I called nine-one-one and an ambulance will be here any minute. I think he's gonna have to go to the hospital."

"Do you want me to come over there and stay with Emily?"

"Oh, Grace—would you? I hate to bother Mrs. Dunn at this hour."

"Don't even think about it! I'll be there in two minutes."

It wasn't easy being a single mother, especially with the hours Beverly had to work. Mrs. Dunn, who watched the children whenever Beverly needed her, was an elderly woman who had arthritis. Taking care of two lively youngsters, aged seven and five, was not easy for her—but Beverly had no one else. Her husband had taken off right after Emily was born, and she thought it would be a waste of time and money to try to find a man who didn't want to be found.

Serena locked her door and dashed along the catwalk to the other end of the building. The ambulance was already in the parking lot, its red and white lights flashing their silent message to the stars that hovered above the small apartment building. She waited in Beverly's living room while the paramedics examined Teddy in the bedroom. When they lifted him onto the gurney, she heard him scream, "Mommy! Mommy!"

"It's okay, baby, I'm right here. I'm going with you," Beverly answered, struggling into her winter jacket as she followed the gurney into the living room. She paused long enough to hug Serena and whisper, "God bless you, my friend," before she ran out the door and down the steps to climb into the ambulance with her son. Moments later the ambulance moved out of the parking lot, lights still whirling, as it sped silently toward Riverview Hospital.

A small figure in pink sleepers peeked fearfully around the corner of the bedroom door. Serena smiled at her.

"Hi, Emily! Do you remember me? I'm your mommy's friend Grace."

The little girl nodded solemnly.

"Teddy has a really, *really* bad tummy ache." She rubbed her own tummy for emphasis. "My mommy has to take him to the hos-pit-al."

Serena took off her down jacket and sat down in the recliner. She discovered that it rocked, and she patted her lap invitingly.

"Let's wait here until Mommy gets back, shall we?"

"Will you read me a story?"

"Sure."

"Can I bring my blankie?"

Serena almost smiled.

As a toddler, Mark had loved his blanket, too.

Emily climbed into Serena's lap with a pink afghan and a Dr. Seuss book called *Horton Hatches the Egg.*

Serena read aloud, " 'I meant what I said, and I said what I meant, an elephant's faithful, one hundred percent.' " She chuckled because Emily was reciting the words along with her. She rocked gently to and fro as she read the heart-warming little story, and it was not long before both of them were asleep—warmed by each other and the soft pink afghan.

Serena was awakened by more flashing lights, but not silent ones this time. A siren was wailing, and a bass horn honked in short, sharp blasts. She looked down at Emily, who continued to sleep. Lifting her lightly, she carried the little girl back into the bedroom and tucked her into the lower bunk bed. The bedroom clock told her it was three-thirty.

She put on her down jacket and stepped out onto the catwalk in front of the apartment. Other residents were already out there, and she asked Beverly's next-door neighbor what was going on.

"Somebody threw a firebomb into one of the apartments at the other end of the building, and it's still burning. The apartments around it had some damage, too."

"Do you know which apartment it is? What number?"

"No, I don't." The woman looked over Serena's shoulder inside the apartment. "Where's Beverly?"

"She had to take Teddy to the hospital, and I'm watching Emily."

"What's wrong with Teddy?"

"The paramedics on the ambulance were pretty sure it was his appendix," Serena told her. She paused, then said, "Would you mind sitting in Beverly's apartment for a few minutes? I live at the other end, and I want to see if my apartment was damaged."

The woman readily agreed, and Serena sprinted along the catwalk as fast as she could. When she turned the corner of the building, she stopped short when she saw Steve Kingsley fighting with a fireman outside her apartment.

"You don't *understand!*" he was shouting. "I know the woman who lives here!" He gestured wildly at her door, number 217.

"You can't go in there, buddy, the fire isn't out yet!"

Another fireman had to help restrain Steve, and told him, "The good news is, we got the arsonist. Believe it or not, it's a woman!"

Steve wasn't listening to what had just been said. He shouted, "For chrissake, will someone please tell me whether the woman who lives here got out okay?"

Both firemen shook their heads.

"It was a gasoline bomb . . . the whole place was gutted. Nobody could've lived through that inferno."

"*No!*"

Again, both firemen battled to hold him back as he fought to get into the burning apartment. His body sagged as he gave up the struggle at last, tears rolling down his face and dripping from his chin.

"Steve!" Serena ran to his side and put her arms around him. "I'm *here,* I'm *okay!*"

He turned his head and stared at her.

"How the hell did you get out? Those firemen said . . ."

"I wasn't here, I was in *Beverly's* apartment! She had to take her son to the hospital around midnight, and I was baby-sitting her little girl."

Steven crushed her against his chest, and she felt the anvil-chorus thumps of his heart against her body.

"Thank you God, thank you God, thank you God," he kept repeating, over and over. He leaned down and kissed her lips; she tasted his tears. "I thought I'd lost you, Grace."

When she reached up to brush the tears from his cheeks, she realized her hand was shaking. If she'd been in her own apartment instead of Beverly's, she wouldn't be standing here right now.

"How did you find out about the fire?" she asked.

His arms still around her, he said, "I hired my friend Fred—you know, the ex-cop—to watch your place ever since I fired Juliette. I had a hunch she was going to pull something."

He stopped and took a deep, shaky breath.

"I never thought she'd actually try to kill you, though."

"You mean Juliette did this? She actually did it *herself?*" Serena was thinking of her stepdaughter, who had hired someone else to do her dirty work.

"Yeah, she did. Look, Fred's got her cuffed to the door handle of his car."

He pointed down at the parking lot. Serena looked down and could barely make out a female figure, black-clad like a cat burglar, glaring up at them.

"After he cuffed her, Fred called in the fire. Then he called the cops. Then me." He sighed. "I don't think he tried to rescue you. From all accounts, flames were shooting out of your bedroom window, and I guess he thought it was hopeless."

Serena wished her body would stop shaking. Her bedroom window overlooked the catwalk where they were standing, and apparently that was the window through which the bomb had been thrown. If she had still been in her bed, the bomb would have exploded right on top of her.

More sirens heralded the approach of two police cars, and Steve finally released her from his arms.

"Come on, honey, let's go down and talk to the cops. I wanna see that bitch go to jail, where she belongs."

"You go on down, Steve. I have to go back to Beverly's apartment and get the regular baby-sitter to come over and stay with Emily. I'll join you in a few minutes . . ."

CHAPTER 32

Three Months Later

When Steve's cell phone warbled at eleven-twenty, he and Serena had already enjoyed an exciting evening. Leaving Beverly in charge of the King's Feast, they had attended the Saturday night "grand opening" of the King's Yacht.

Wearing a raw silk evening skirt, charcoal gray, and a white silk organza blouse with balloon sleeves and a Chelsea collar, she had touched her flute to Steve's and Cheryl's in a series of champagne toasts to the success of Cliff's beautiful new restaurant. Cliff had joined them at their table for a few moments when he was able, as they dined on lobster and filet mignon, peach Melba and bananas Foster. When the band began to play at nine o'clock, Steve danced with her—and occasionally with his petite blond daughter-in-law as well.

It had been a memorable evening, overflowing with pride and joy, despite the absence of Lisa and Gary. The birth of Lisa's baby was imminent, and she'd had one episode of false labor. Gary did not want to take a chance on crossing the Delaware River into Pennsylvania. Everyone expressed disappointment, but understood the reason for the decision.

Serena admitted to a secret twinge of relief. Whenever they were together, Lisa always watched her intently, something between a glare and a stare, as though waiting for her to reveal cleverly hidden fangs and claws.

After dropping Cheryl off at home, Steve had driven

Serena to her new apartment (same building) and invited himself in to spend a few more minutes in her company. Serena's tiny apartment was welcoming, she realized, because of all the little homey touches that only a woman knows how to create. A bowl of fruit in the center of her kitchen table; fragrant herbs in tiny pots on the kitchen windowsill; a print of Renoir's *The Boating Party*, nicely framed, hanging on her living-room wall.

After everything in her former apartment had been destroyed in the fire, she'd decided to *rent* the furniture for this one because she couldn't afford otherwise to replace everything at once. Rafferty's Rentals had provided a navy-and-white-striped sofa, a dark-red leather easy chair with matching ottoman, brass lamps with pleated white linen shades. All rentals with an option to buy.

As always, the leather chair beckoned to Steve. He sank into it with a contented sigh and clicked on the television set that stood atop a low bookcase housing a few cookbooks, detective stories, and romance novels. When she heard him gasp, Serena stopped in the middle of the living room on her way to the closet to hang up their coats.

A familiar face filled the television screen. The news reporter was saying, "Juliette Black, the glamorous restaurant hostess who tried to kill her former co-worker by firebombing her apartment, has decided to plead guilty. Her attorney made the announcement this afternoon."

A close-up of the attorney appeared, and continued the commentary: "Ms. Black has signed a statement certifying that she understands she is admitting guilt, and that she made the decision voluntarily."

The eleven o'clock news anchorman asked why someone accused of attempted murder would voluntarily take such a drastic step, and the attorney replied, "We opted to enter a guilty plea because we hope for a dismissal of all charges, due to mitigating circumstances."

"What mitigating circumstances?" the news anchorman and Steve demanded in unison.

"Ms. Black was recently fired from a job she had held for more than ten years," the lawyer explained, "and at the time of the incident she was mentally unbalanced by her loss. Furthermore, she is gravely concerned about who would care for her invalid mother if she goes to prison."

"Horse shit!" bellowed Steve. "Her mom lives in Florida, and she's no more an invalid than I am!"

"Attempted murder with a deadly weapon is a class-two dangerous felony, for which the minimum prison term is twenty-one years," the anchorman reminded viewers. "Add to that the charge of aggravated felony arson, for which the minimum penalty is seven years . . . and you have some idea why Ms. Black and her attorney decided to take a chance on a guilty plea."

Then he asked if the intended victim had been injured in the fire.

"No, she's fine. She was visiting a neighbor at the time of the incident," the attorney answered glibly.

"Yeah, *right!*" roared Steve, getting to his feet and prowling around the living room like a Bengal tiger in search of prey. "She was over at Beverly's apartment having tea and crumpets at three-thirty in the morning!"

"Don't upset yourself this way, Steve," Serena begged him. "My late husband was an attorney, you know, and . . ."

"If they drop all charges against that bitch, I'll kill her myself!"

Serena tugged on his hand and made him sit down again in the easy chair; she perched on the ottoman facing him.

"Please listen to me, Steve darling, listen to what I'm

telling you," she pleaded. "That was Juliette's lawyer talking. Before the judge makes a decision, he—or she—will hear from the prosecuting attorney, and learn the *reason* Juliette was fired. Don't forget that whole incident with the birthday candles is on record at Riverview Hospital."

"And I'm gonna make damn sure the prosecutor knows that Juliette's mother is alive and well and living in Florida!"

Suddenly a look of amazement crossed his face, and the volume of his voice dropped to a near whisper. "You called me darling," he said, and a smile lifted his mouth like the morning sun peeping over the horizon.

"Well, yes, I . . ."

"You what? You *slipped,* is that what you were gonna say?"

He leaned forward, both powerful hands imprisoning her face as he brushed her lips with his own. It started out as a tender kiss, but rapidly accelerated as his tongue pushed into her mouth. When he felt her tongue respond, his breath quickened and he pulled her body closer. After a long moment, his mouth released hers and he said hoarsely, "Grace, I know I shouldn't say this. It's too soon, but . . . I can't help it. I'm in love with you."

She said nothing.

He stroked her cheek. "You know I'm speaking the truth, don't you, honey?"

Eyelids dropping swiftly to cover her eyes, she said, "I know you're speaking the truth when you say it's too soon."

She still could not believe that the kiss had actually happened. They'd been spending every Monday together since the night of the fire. She enjoyed cooking dinner for him, and he enjoyed eating it with her. The chocolate snowballs had become his favorite dessert. He liked to sit in her living room reading the evening newspaper while she loaded the dishwasher. Afterwards, they talked quietly, played cards, or watched television. It was as if he put off as long as possible the inevitable end of the evening, when he entered the white-brick house in Moorestown alone. He'd never made a move that could be construed as sexually aggressive.

They'd become close friends, and she'd told herself he just missed the *companionship* of being married, a comfort he hadn't enjoyed for ten years.

Now, as she allowed her gaze to rise and meet his, she understood that this man was sexually aroused, and her body told her that she was aroused as well. How could that be possible, when she still had dreams about Eddie? How could it be possible when he had just buried Anne Marie two days before Christmas—and it was now only April?

"How do you feel about me?" he asked huskily, refusing to relinquish that long look.

"You're my best friend," she murmured, but knew a telltale blush was heating her cheeks. He tightened his grasp on her upper arms and let his gravelly laugh fill the small living room.

"Don't ever try to play poker, honey. You'd lose your shirt."

She felt his fingers slide into her silky, silvery hair as he added, "I'm a lucky man. Luckier than most! I've only loved two women in my life. You're one of them. I'm just waiting for you to say you love me too. You do, don't you?"

Without waiting for her reply, he said, "We'll have a spectacular wedding. Anton will do the wedding cake."

Still unable to look away from his dark eyes, she wondered if another wedding was what she wanted. She'd tried marriage twice, and the score was one divorce and one death. At their age, wouldn't it be better, perhaps, just to remain good friends?

Besides—what would his children say?

Correction: what would *Lisa* say? She was pretty sure Cliff and Cheryl would be pleased.

"I know you love me. Please! I want to hear you say it," Steve urged.

She opened her mouth to tell him she believed they should just remain good friends.

That was the moment when his cell phone began to play the Toreador Song from *Carmen*.

CHAPTER 33

"Yeah, Gary." Steve turned the cell phone aside and informed her unnecessarily, "It's Gary."

Gary evidently asked whom he was talking to, and Steve replied. "Grace. I'm at her apartment. We just got back from the grand opening. You guys missed a great evening."

Then: "So what's happening there?"

An instant later he shouted, "A boy? *A boy!*"

Serena was still sitting on the ottoman facing him, and he leaned across the space between them and kissed her lips again.

"Seven pounds fifteen ounces!" he reported proudly, and Serena smiled and sighed. *Mark had been eight pounds three ounces.*

"How soon can we come to the hospital?" He glanced at his watch. "Oh, shit. I forgot. It's almost midnight. Yeah, of course she's tired. Morning okay? We'll meet you there about ten. Congratulations, *Dad!*"

A short silence while Gary supplied more information.

Steve replied, "What time is it in Israel? What'd they say?" He laughed loudly. "I know they're as happy as we are! See you tomorrow at ten."

He closed the phone and hugged her, rocking back and forth.

"I've got a grandson, honey!"

"Who's in Israel?" she wanted to know.

"Gary's parents."

"On vacation?"

"No, they live there. They're gonna book a flight in a few days. You'll like them, helluva nice couple."

He looked toward the kitchen. "Got any champagne in the fridge?"

She shook her head. "The three of us drank two bottles of it tonight, remember? You want a champagne hangover in the morning?"

"Hell, no. I've been there, done that." He hugged her again. "You sound just like a wife."

"You mean a wet blanket?"

"No, I mean a wife. *Practical.* Sometimes I need practical. When I'm happy or excited I have a tendency to get carried away."

She frowned, feigning surprise. "*Really?* I never would've guessed."

He chuckled. "Grace, I love you. I love your sense of humor. I love your sweetness. But most of all—I love your chocolate snowballs."

She burst out laughing.

"Steve, you're a little bit crazy but I—I love you, too!"

He stood up. "Okay, now we're engaged."

"Wait a minute!"

"Wait a minute *nothing!* Didn't you hear what I said before? Just wanted to hear you say you love me too!" He picked her up and walked into the bedroom, holding her in his arms.

"Please, darling! Listen to what I'm telling you! This is happening too fast! I think . . ."

"*Don't think.* Just let me make love to you." He deposited her on the bed and began to unbutton her silk organza blouse. "God, Grace, I've wanted you for such a long time!"

"Steve . . ."

His lips muffled her final, feeble protest.

When they were both naked, Steve gazed wonderingly at her body.

"There were no grandmothers that looked like this when I was a kid!"

"How many naked grandmothers did you see as a kid?"

"I'm giving you a compliment, and you're making jokes. I'm saying you don't look like a grandmother!"

"I'm *not* a grandmother."

"The hell you're not! You're gonna be my wife, you'll be that baby's *bubbe!*"

"Steve, let's not make any plans until after we talk to your children."

"Will you stop worrying already? The kids'll be ecstatic! Piece of cake!"

She thought about Eddie, who'd always insisted that his daughter was her biggest fan. She realized now that he'd wanted to believe it. Just as Steve wanted to believe both his kids would be "ecstatic" about their getting married. She knew better. She knew any marriage that involves existing children is rarely a *piece of cake.*

But rational discussion would have to wait. Steve was kissing her eyelids—touching his tongue to her earlobe—cradling her breasts with his hands. When his eager mouth began to suck on her nipples, she succumbed to the desire surging through her body like wild honey. She felt young and weightless, lithe and limber beneath his body. When he entered her, she rose to meet him, moaning with pleasure, and wrapped her legs around him. She tightened her legs, and they soon found a powerful rhythm that sent them soaring to the crest of an enormous wave. As he trembled on the brink of his climax, she cried out, "Steve! Take me with you!" As soon as his hand reached between her legs and caressed the tiny sensual bud there, the wave crashed around them both.

Wipeout!

Legs and arms entwined, they tumbled into the abyss and then lay exhausted, gasping. Serena felt his tears on her face, and realized she was crying, too.

Minutes passed as their respirations gradually slowed to normal. Their bodies had just connected in the most miraculous way two people can, and both seemed to sense that a spiritual connection had occurred as well.

Words were superfluous.

Bodies side by side, still touching, they floated into a deep, dreamless sleep on the magic cloud that was Serena's warm bed.

She made French toast with maple syrup and hot, fragrant coffee for breakfast. After his second cup of coffee, Steve leaned back in his chair and said, "I'd like to know a little more about the woman I'm going to marry. Did you live in Cold Spring Harbor all your life?"

Shaking her head, she poured a second cup of coffee for herself.

"No. Only the last three years before Eddie died. Before that we lived in Manhattan."

"So you were born in Manhattan . . ." he prompted.

"No, no, I was born in Brooklyn, and grew up there."

"Hey!" he exclaimed. "I was born in Brooklyn, too!"

Serena raised her eyebrows.

"I never knew that! I always assumed you grew up in New Jersey."

"I moved to New Jersey from Flatbush when I was fourteen."

A tingling sensation moved up Serena's arms.

"My first boyfriend moved from Flatbush to New Jersey just before my fourteenth birthday. His name was Steve, too."

Steve's coffee cup clattered when he put it back on the saucer.

"What was his last name?"

"Katz."

"Jesus Christ! I had a girlfriend before I moved, and her last name was D'Agostino, too, but her first name was Serena!"

"Steve, my maiden name was *Serena Grace* D'Agostino!"

They stared at each other across the table, trying to absorb the reality of what was happening.

"Why do you just use your middle name?"

"I was called Serena all my life, but I decided to use my middle name when I was running away from Cold Spring Harbor."

"And I changed my last name from Katz to Kingsley when I bought the restaurant! The Katz Feast would've sounded like canned food for kitties."

Serena began to cry.

"Oh, Steve! Is this really happening? Is it really you?"

She wiped her eyes on a paper napkin and added, "Hey! You promised to call me every Sunday, but you never called."

"My parents wouldn't let me, because it was a long-distance call."

Tears still glistening in her eyes, she laughed.

"I don't want to hear your flimsy excuses."

"Well, you promised to write to me, but you never wrote!" he countered.

"That's because you never called!"

Steve stood up and walked around the little table.

"Do you remember what you said to me just before I got into my parents' car?"

"Yes, I do." She could scarcely speak because her voice was shaking. "I said, 'I'm not gonna say goodbye, Steve, because I know we'll be together again someday.' "

He pulled her to her feet and his arms closed around her.

"Looks like *someday* finally came," he said.

His voice sounded gruff. She looked up at his face and saw a lone tear leaking from the corner of his left eye. She brushed it away with her fingertips.

"I remember your long dark-brown braid," he murmured, touching her silver hair. "How long has your hair been this color?"

"Since my son died," she answered.

On their way to the hospital they stopped at Wal-Mart's because Serena wanted to buy a gift for the baby. She chose a fuzzy white teddy bear with a music box concealed inside. When she wound it up, it played Brahms' Lullaby. Steve wanted to pay for it, but she insisted on using her own money. "This is from *me.* You can buy your own gift." Then she bought half a yard of blue satin ribbon and fashioned an extravagant bow around the bear's neck.

"My mother bought a bear like this for Mark when he was a baby," she reminisced softly, hugging the toy to her chest, "but that one played *The Teddy Bears' Picnic.*"

He reached out and touched her hand.

"It must've been awful for you, honey, losing your only child."

She nodded. "It was like an amputation."

"I know it happened a long time ago, Serena, but if you want to talk about it to someone who loves you, I'm a good listener."

She shook her head. "Maybe someday, but not today."

It had been almost thirteen years, but the memory of Mark's death still had the power to wring pain from her mind and heart.

Steve had an apologetic look on his face, as though he regretted trying to persuade her to talk about something that made her so sad. He stopped in the middle of Wal-Mart's and put his arms around her and the teddy bear.

"Well, now you'll have a beautiful little grandson to play with," he said, beaming proudly as if he had arranged it all for her as a special gift.

For a moment, she allowed herself to remember how it felt to hold an infant in her arms. The sweet little sounds. The new-baby fragrance. The tiny fingers and toes, and the look of wonder in those great big eyes . . .

She looked up at him, and her lips curved in one of her beatific smiles.

"When you smile like that, you look like Mary. You know . . . the mother of Jesus," Steve told her.

"I'm not letting you drink any more champagne, darling. I think those bubbles make you hallucinate the next day," Serena said as they walked out to the parking lot with the teddy bear.

When they arrived at the hospital, they detoured past the nursery to sneak a preview of Aaron Michael. According to Jewish tradition, he had been named for Anne Marie, his recently deceased biological grandmother.

Rapt, Steve and Serena stood before the nursery window and stared at the bassinet labeled *Barnett.* The baby had a thatch of dark hair and was crying lustily.

"Football for sure." Steve nodded wisely. "Look at him! See how he's trying to kick off the blanket?"

Serena rolled her eyes. "Just your typical demented grandfather!"

"It's a guy thing. You wouldn't understand."

They were still laughing when they walked into Lisa's room.

Lisa, wearing a pale-blue satin robe, was sitting on the bed holding hands with Gary. Her curly hair framed her face like a dark cloud.

"Hi, Daddy!" She was smiling, but her smile dimmed when she saw Serena and the teddy bear.

"Why is *she* here?"

Serena stopped halfway across the room. *Oh, God, why hadn't she listened to herself when she told Steve it was too soon?*

Steve said loudly, "She bought a present for the baby."

"My son has everything he needs."

Since Serena seemed to be glued to a spot in the middle of the room, Steve grabbed the teddy bear and wound it up. As the tinkling notes began to play, he laid it on the bed next to his daughter. She made no move to touch it.

"Cute, huh? Didya ever see anything like this before, Gary?"

"No." But Gary was watching Lisa, not the teddy bear.

After a minute of agonized silence, Lisa said, "I'm sorry, Grace. You'll have to excuse me for being a little rude, but I was only expecting to see *family* today."

Serena prayed that Steve would not pick up on that remark, but she had a feeling he would not let it pass.

He didn't.

"She's almost family," he said in that same loud voice. "We're getting married."

Lisa glared at Serena.

"Well, you're pretty slick, aren't you?"

"I don't know what you mean," Serena answered slowly.

"I think you do. I think you decided to fuck your way from waitress to wife as soon as my mother died!"

Serena's lips parted, but no sound emerged.

Lisa picked up the teddy bear and hurled it across the room, hitting Serena squarely in the face. The toy fell to the floor, still playing the lullaby.

Serena turned and headed for the door. Steve grabbed her arm.

"Don't run away! Tell her how wrong she is! Tell her we knew each other when we were kids in Brooklyn!"

Serena shook her head violently.

"No. Let me go, Steve." Something in her voice made him release her arm.

"Wait for me downstairs, honey. *Please.* I have a couple of things I want to say to my daughter."

Black eyes glinting with anger, he turned back toward Lisa after Serena left the room.

"Let's get a few things straight, kitten. Grace's no slut. She was my first girlfriend back in Brooklyn, when we were both fourteen years old. She lost her only son in a car accident . . ."

He stopped speaking because Lisa was not listening. She was sobbing, and Gary was holding her in his arms.

Gary looked up and said, "No offense, Dad, but I think you better leave. Lisa hopes to nurse the baby, and she won't be able to do it if she keeps on getting upset like this."

"I'm not trying to upset her, and neither is Grace. We just . . ."

"I'm sorry, but your timing couldn't have been worse. We can talk about this . . . this other thing . . . later."

Steve stood irresolute for a moment, then turned around and headed for the elevator.

CHAPTER 34

It was ten minutes later when the elevator doors opened and Steve came into the lobby. Serena stood up. He took her arm and they walked out to the hospital parking lot without speaking.

As the Cadillac moved toward the exit, Steve broke the silence.

"Let me admit something to you, Grace . . . *Serena*. Lisa was born fifteen years after Cliffie. We never expected to have another child, and I'm afraid we spoiled her a little bit. Maybe a lot. She was such a sweet little girl."

His voice cracked and threatened to shatter. He cleared his throat loudly.

"After you left I talked to them. I told them we just found out we knew each other as kids, but I don't think Lisa wanted to hear what I was saying. Gary heard me, I know he did, but he's worried about his wife. She wants to nurse the baby, but she won't be able to do it if she lets herself get upset like she did this morning."

Her milk won't come in as long as I'm hanging out with her father, Serena translated.

"We have to do what's best for the baby," she said aloud.

He leaned over and patted her hand.

"It's going to take time, honey, but she'll come around."

No, she won't, Serena contradicted him silently. *It'll be Phyllis Abbott all over again.*

Steve heard her silence.

"Sometimes you've got to fight for what you want," he declared.

"I'm not a fighter," she told him as the Cadillac pulled into the King's Feast parking lot. Without another word, she got out of the car and hurried inside to change into her hostess gown. Steve didn't come inside the restaurant for ten or fifteen minutes, and she surmised he must be sitting in the car, trying to pull himself together.

She zipped up her newest hostess gown—silk jersey, the color of the sky in October—not even glancing in the mirror at her reflection. Her body felt as if she'd been beaten with sticks. Her head throbbed like an open wound. When she left the locker room and approached the cash register, Beverly stopped her.

"Grace, what's wrong? You look like a battered butt."

"I feel like a battered butt."

"Talk to me."

Two parties of four chose that moment to walk through the door, the first Sunday lunch customers of the day.

"Talk to you later," Serena promised. She picked up a handful of menus and went to greet the customers.

But Beverly left at eleven, and when Serena was ready to go home at eleven-thirty, Steve was waiting for her.

"Let me drive you home."

"Okay." She was bone tired now, and still hurting. "But you're not going to come in. I just want to go to sleep."

"I know it was a very rough day, Serena, but we need to talk."

She shook her head wearily. "Not tonight, Steve. *Please.* I'm beat."

"Will I see you tomorrow?" She heard the note of anxiety.

"I'll be busy all day. You can call around five, if you want."

Later she lay in bed, sleepless, staring at the ceiling. Was she doing something wrong in her life, or failing to do something right? One deceased son. One divorced husband, one husband lost to emphysema. One flight from an abusive stepdaughter. One escape from an assassin. Another escape from a vindictive co-worker. And now, just when she'd rediscovered a love from her past, a wonderfully fine and decent man, and had been looking forward to spending the rest of her life with him, her wheel of misfortune started spinning again.

One malicious daughter.

She knew Lisa would do anything to eject her from their lives. She might even refuse to let Steve see his grandson if he married her. She knew if that happened, Steve couldn't help but blame her. How could he not? In time, he might come to wish he'd never found her again. She didn't think she could bear that.

Unfortunately, her body couldn't seem to forget what had happened in this bed on the previous night: Steve's strong hands and warm lips caressing every part of her. The tears they'd shed together after the orgasm they'd shared. His words of love and hope for their future together . . .

"It isn't fair!" she said aloud, and let the tears she'd held back all day fall at last. She cried herself to sleep, and dreamed of Eddie. No longer trying to send her a message, he simply held her in his arms. She felt an aura of sorrow surrounding him.

He knows his daughter died, and that she died because she tried to kill me.

In the morning, she got out of bed and looked at herself

in the bathroom mirror. Her eyes were pink and puffy from weeping, and her face felt heavy. Sagging with sadness. She knew what she had to do.

What was it Steve had said? *Sometimes you have to fight for what you want!* But how could she fight a new mother who needs to nurse her baby? How could she put her own dreams ahead of Steve's love for his daughter and grandson?

Fighters stay and fight, non-fighters run away.

When Steve called at five o'clock there was no answer. He called again at five-thirty. At six o'clock he pulled into the parking lot, knocked several times on the door, and finally used the key she'd given him.

The furniture was gone. Serena's clothes were gone. And Serena was gone. There was a note on the kitchen counter. It said: *I love you too much to make you choose between Lisa and me. Please don't come after me. It was too late for us. Serena.*

"Aw, Grace, *Serena,* what have you done?" he roared, stomping around the empty apartment, punching his right fist into his left hand. He pulled his cell phone out of his pocket and dialed.

"Rafferty's Rentals."

"Are you open this evening?" he demanded.

"Yes, sir, until nine."

"My name's Kingsley. I'll be there in five minutes."

When he marched through the door of the rental store, Tim Rafferty took one look at the man's furious face and wondered if he should call his brother-in-law on the Cherry Hill police force.

"Is there a problem, sir?" he asked.

"Did you pick up furniture today for a woman named D'Agostino? The Glenview Apartments, number two-thirty-one?"

"Yeah. The bill was paid. The papers were all in order. What's the problem?"

"When did she call?"

"This morning. It was a rush pickup."

"Did she give you a reason?"

"What're you, a cop? Did she commit a crime or something?"

"No, of course not. I'm just a friend. Did she give a reason for leaving in such a hurry?"

"She just said to . . . wait a second . . . her exact words were, 'I hafta move out of state. It's an emergency.' "

He shrugged. "She was paid through the end of the month, and she ditten ask for no refund."

His next call was to his friend Fred. The investigator. Steve speculated that Serena might have gone to California, because she'd mentioned her cousins in Sacramento a few times.

He described the events of the last twenty-four hours, ending with a question.

"Can you be on the next plane to Sacramento?"

"Didya forget about the bullet I took in my lung? I can't fly no more. My right lung is like a patched inner tube."

"Shit, I did forget. Tell you what . . . I'll go to California. You check out Philadelphia. How does that grab you?"

When he called his son to tell him he was flying to California, and the reason, Cliff's response was so loud and indignant that Steve almost dropped the phone.

"What the hell's wrong with my sister?"

He lowered his voice a bit when he added, "The truth is, Cheryl and I've been hoping you two would get together. You're a perfect couple!"

"Lisa was not quite as enthusiastic," Steve observed dryly. He described the horrific moment when she'd thrown the teddy bear and hit Serena in the face.

"Wait'll I talk to her!" muttered Cliff.

"*No!* You will not say one word to her. She just gave birth two days ago, and if she keeps on getting upset she won't be able to nurse the baby."

"Goddammit, Dad, you and Mom always let her get away with murder! My little sister can do no wrong!"

Steve cringed when he heard the rage in his son's voice.

"She's done wrong this time, Cliff, but there's more than a couple of other people involved here. One of them is my grandson."

"What're you going to do in Sacramento?" Cliff asked.

"Look for Serena's cousins. She might've gone out there."

"Serena?"

"Yeah, her real name is Serena Grace D'Agostino."

Quickly, he told Cliff that they had been junior-high-school sweethearts in Brooklyn, half a century ago. And that they had just discovered it the day before.

And Cliff remembered that the first three digits on the license plate of the sports utility vehicle had been SGD, which she had identified as her maiden initials. Funny that he had never thought to ask her what the *S* stood for.

"Before you hightail it all the way across the country, Dad, why don't you check the airlines first?"

"Fred checked. Nobody by the name of Serena D'Agostino or Grace D'Agostino bought a ticket to California, or anywhere else."

"So why're you flying out there?"

"She might've taken a train. The railroads are not as strict about photo ID as the airlines, so she could've used a different name."

"Ah, Dad . . ." Cliff sighed. "Do you want me to come with you?"

"*Absolutely not!* You've got a brand-new restaurant to run. Beverly's my hostess now, and a trouper, so she can handle the King's Feast for a day or two."

"Does Beverly have any idea where she might've gone?" asked Cliff quickly.

"Not a clue. I already talked to her." He paused for a moment, recalling their conversation. "She knew something was eating Grace—Serena—but they never had a chance to talk about it. Yesterday was Sunday, and you know what Sundays are like."

"Keep me in the loop, Dad, okay? Let me know as soon as you find out anything!"

CHAPTER 35

"Oh, hi, Daddy!" Lisa sounded overjoyed to hear from him. It was as if the ugly scene in the hospital had never happened.

"Hi, kitten. How's everything going, now that you're home with the baby?"

"Great! When're you coming to see him?"

"As soon as I get back from California."

A few seconds' hesitation. "California? Why're you going to California?"

"To look for Serena. *Grace.*"

"When did she go to California?"

"I don't know that that's where she went. She disappeared."

Careful, now. Mustn't upset her.

"The day after we came to see you at the hospital."

"What do you mean she disappeared?"

"She moved out of her apartment and didn't leave a forwarding address."

A long moment of silence.

"Please don't be angry at me for saying this, Daddy," she said at last, "but maybe she did you a favor. It could never have worked out."

"That's what *she* said."

"You talked to her before she left?" Lisa sounded puzzled.

"No, she left me a note." He pulled the scrap of paper out of his shirt pocket and read it aloud to her.

"She told you not to come after her! So why are you doing this?"

"Because I love her."

Another moment of silence stretched between them.

"You don't love her as much as you loved Mom. You *couldn't.*"

It was an angry declaration that sounded like a question, so he answered it.

"I will always love your mother, kitten. Those memories are part of me. But . . ."

"But *what?*"

"People can love more than once in a lifetime."

"What makes you think she's in California?" she asked, making an end run around his last statement.

"She has two cousins in Sacramento, she mentioned them to me a couple of times. Her only family."

"What happens if you find her and she doesn't want to come back?"

Steve let himself laugh for the first and only time that day.

"Trust me. I'll talk her into it."

Three days later, at dusk, Steve walked slowly up the gangplank of the King's Yacht. The attractive middle-aged hostess greeted him warmly.

"Hello, Mr. Kingsley! Your son is in his office . . . or he was a few minutes ago, anyway."

He was still there. He looked up, registering surprise and pleasure, then disappointment as he read the expression on his father's face.

"No luck?"

"No luck." The older man sighed. "I found the cousins. They're a brother and sister, both widowed. They have an upscale Italian restaurant in Sacramento called D'Agostino's. Nice place. I had dinner with them there last night."

"They didn't know where Serena is?"

A short bark of mirthless laughter. "I knew more than they did! They knew her husband died last fall, but they hadn't heard anything from her since then. They were both in shock when I told them all the shit that's been going down."

Cliff was still skeptical. "Do you think they could've been lying to cover up for her?"

Steve shook his head vehemently.

"Son, if those two people were lying, they deserve an Academy Award!"

When he rang the doorbell of the Cherry Hill townhouse, Lisa answered the door. She threw her arms around her father and kissed him on both cheeks.

"Oh, Daddy, it's so good to see you! Gary, look who's here!"

His son-in-law appeared; gave him a welcoming hug and a couple of slaps on the back.

"Is it too late for an old *zayde* to see his grandson?"

"Of course not," exclaimed Lisa. "He's sleeping, but we can go upstairs for a quick peek." She led the way to the nursery. A Winnie-the-Pooh nightlight cast a soft glow.

When Steve approached the white enamel crib where tiny Aaron Michael lay sleeping, he held his breath for a moment.

"Such a beautiful child!" he whispered wonderingly at last. "Healthy, strong."

"Kayn aynhoreh," murmured Lisa, causing both men to smile.

"Can you believe your daughter . . . who's only half-Jewish . . . believes in that old superstitious *dreck?*" asked Gary.

"Why take chances?" Lisa retorted, pointing to the red ribbon tied tightly in a corner of the crib to ward off evil spirits.

"How about a cup of coffee, Dad?" suggested Gary. "One of our neighbors stopped by today to see Aaron, and brought us a coconut custard pie. Your favorite! She baked it herself."

"Twist my arm," said Steve. He'd had nothing to eat since breakfast except for trail mix and coffee on the plane.

They sat around the circular ice-cream table in the kitchen, drinking freshly brewed coffee and eating generous slices of pie.

Lisa confided that they ate almost all their meals in the kitchen. "We only use the dining room for company—and you're not company, Daddy. You're *family,*" she said affectionately.

Steve decided this was the right moment to bring up Serena's name.

"I just got back from California a couple of hours ago," he told them. "I stopped in at Cliffie's place on my way from the airport."

"Oh, how's his restaurant doing?" asked Lisa brightly. *No questions about California.*

"Seems to be doing well." He cleared his throat. "I'm afraid I can't say the same for myself, though."

Lisa pretended to regard him critically. "You look okay to me," she said in the same brittle, let's-not-talk-about-the-forbidden-subject voice.

"I'm not sick, but my trip was unsuccessful," Steve said. He reported what had taken place in Sacramento.

"How about Fred?" Gary asked. "Have you talked to him yet?"

"Yeah, we've been in touch every day. He's been concentrating on restaurants in Philadelphia. So far nothing."

"*Well!* It looks as if she's gone for good," said Lisa in that same chirpy voice.

"Kitten, how long have you known me?" Steve asked her.

She looked puzzled.

"All my life."

"Have you ever known me to give up trying to get what I want?" asked Steve. Without waiting for an answer, he stood up and thanked them both for the coffee and pie.

"And when you're ready to buy a carriage for my grandson, let me know how much it is," he said over his shoulder. "I'd like to pay for it."

His gift for the baby.

As he drove away in his car, he wondered what had happened to the teddy bear Serena had bought for the baby. The one that played Brahms' Lullaby.

The following afternoon, late, Lisa called him at the restaurant.

"Daddy, I have a *huge* favor to ask," she began. "Please, please tell me you'll say yes!"

He chuckled. "Let's hear what it is first."

"Gary's parents are flying in from Tel Aviv the day after tomorrow, and I want you to invite them to stay at your house in Moorestown. You've got plenty of room."

He rubbed his head. "You've got a guest room, kitten. Why aren't they staying with you?"

"That's what they're supposed to do, but I really don't want them to stay here."

"Why not?"

"Well, Gary's father is hard of hearing and he talks so

loud I'm afraid he'll disturb the baby . . . and his mother is so bossy, I know she'll be criticizing me and telling me what to do."

Steve felt his face growing warm. What the hell ever happened to his sweet little girl?

"Listen to me, Lisa," he said. "This is their firstborn grandson, too. Don't you think they're looking forward to staying in their son's home? How often have they come over to visit you since you and Gary got married?"

"They came over two years ago, but I didn't have a baby then!"

"They'll only be here for a week or two. They're nice people, and they both love you. Do you mean to tell me you couldn't put up with a little temporary inconvenience?"

"Oh, I knew you wouldn't understand," cried Lisa, beginning to weep. "Mom would've understood. Mom would've let them stay at your house. Mom would've said . . ."

Steve suspected he was being manipulated.

"Stop right there, kitten. Mom is not here. And if Mom *was* here, she would be ashamed of you."

Careful, now. Don't upset the nursing mother.

"You're not a little girl anymore," he began again in a gentler voice. "You're a grown woman now, with a home, a husband and a child."

"I know that." She sniffled. "But it's gonna be so hard to have company, with a new baby to take care of . . ."

"Leah Barnett has two children of her own. She knows how to take care of a baby. She knows how to cook. She knows how to do laundry. She'll *help* you if you let her."

Then he thought of a good parting shot.

"Remember when you told me I'm not company, I'm *family?* Well, face it—Gary's parents're family, too."

"I have to hang up now, Daddy. Gary just got home from work."

"Okay, kitten. Love you. Think about what I said."

He folded up the phone and rubbed his head distractedly. He'd always thought life would get easier when the kids grew up and got married. Instead, the grown-up problems were bigger and more complex. He couldn't help wondering how Serena would have handled Lisa's request.

A knock on his office door interrupted his thoughts. He called out, "Come in."

"Fred!" He walked around his desk and the two men hugged briefly. They'd known each other since their first year of high school.

"You said you wanted to see me, so here I am."

"Make yourself comfortable." Steve reseated himself behind the desk. "I guess you've pretty much exhausted any leads in Philadelphia."

Fred grinned ruefully. "To say the least. There are quite a few D'Agostinos in South Philadelphia, but none of them seem to know Serena/Grace, and positively, none of them *was* Serena/Grace."

"You already checked her Social Security number on your computer, right?"

"Right. It's too soon for any changes to show up. It still shows you as her current employer, and the Glenview Apartments as her current residence. Got any more bright ideas?"

"Well, we're pretty sure she didn't go to California, and we're pretty sure she didn't go to Philadelphia."

"She could've gone anyplace, you know," Fred put in gloomily.

"Right on. But this is not a young kid. This is a woman over sixty. She grew up in Brooklyn."

"Hmmm. So you want me to give Brooklyn a shot?"

"It couldn't hurt."

Steve's cell phone warbled while he was on his way home from the restaurant. It was after eleven-thirty. He did not recognize the hoarse voice of the male caller, and wondered if it was a wrong number.

He asked uneasily, "Who is this?"

"It's Gary. I just got a call from my sister Rachel. There was a suicide-bombing incident today at a Tel Aviv shopping mall. My parents were there, buying gifts for their new grandson. They were both killed—along with twenty-one other people."

CHAPTER 36

For a few minutes the only audible sound was two men breathing heavily into their telephones; one trying to understand what he had just heard, the other trying to believe what he had just heard himself say.

Finally Steve said, "My God, Gary. *My God!* Who did this?"

"The Islamic Jihad is taking the credit."

After another long moment, Steve asked, "How old is Rachel now? Nineteen?"

"Just turned twenty-two. She's very mature for her age—most Israeli girls are—but she's overwhelmed. I told her we'll be on the next plane."

"You're not taking the baby to Israel!"

Accustomed to being in charge, the staccato words burst out before Steve had a chance to edit them.

"No, Dad, of course not! But Lisa's hysterical. She doesn't want to leave the baby, but she wants to go with me, and I want her with me. We'll just have to find someone to take care of Aaron."

"How about Cheryl? She's family."

"I suggested Cheryl, but Lisa says she has no experience taking care of infants."

"Neither did Lisa until a week ago," Steve reminded him. He could not help but think *Serena would have been the perfect choice.*

"I know, I know. I'm gonna give Cheryl a call in the morning."

"Want me to come over there now?"

"No, please don't. It's been a bloody awful day, and we all need to get some sleep. Come over tomorrow around noon."

When Steve arrived at the townhouse late the following morning, the scene that greeted him was sheer chaos. The bed was not made and the breakfast dishes, still on the kitchen table, indicated that little food had been eaten. Suitcases lay open on the bedroom floor like an obstacle course, and Gary had gone to the drugstore to pick up the medication prescribed by Lisa's gynecologist to dry up her milk. Lisa and the baby were both crying.

Steve took off his jacket and changed the baby's diaper. He sat his daughter down in the nursery rocking chair, handed her the baby and said, "Get a hold of yourself. Feed the baby, or rock him. Talk to him! Sing to him!"

His experience as a father had taught him that babies pick up stress like a magnet picks up iron filings.

He leaned over the rocking chair and stroked the baby's downy head, adding more gently, "He knows something's wrong, dontcha, *tateleh?*"

By the time Gary got back from the drugstore, Steve had rinsed the breakfast dishes, loaded them into the dishwasher, and wiped the table. The baby had been nursed and put down for a nap. Lisa had made the bed.

"Did you talk to Cheryl this morning?" Steve asked, addressing his son-in-law.

"I did, yes. The owner of the shop's giving her a leave of absence."

"That's good," said Steve. "Now tell me your passports are in order."

"Yes, thank God," said Gary. "They're still valid from a

year ago when we went on our vacation to Cancun."

"And you know where they are?"

Gary had dark circles under his eyes, and Steve suspected he had not slept at all.

"They're in a strong box, top shelf in the bedroom closet."

"Go get them right now and put them in your pocket. Do you want me to call the airport and ask about flights?"

"Thanks, Dad, but I did that first thing this morning. We've got two seats on a British Airways flight leaving Philadelphia at six-fifty p.m. today. It gets us into Heathrow at six forty-five tomorrow morning."

"You have to go through London?"

"That's right. Tomorrow morning we board a flight at eight twenty-five, London time, and we should arrive at Ben Gurion Airport around three-thirty in the afternoon."

Steve looked at his watch.

"Okay, now you two kids better start packing those suitcases. Cliff will be here in a couple of hours with his neighbor's truck to pick up all the baby's stuff. Give me the name of your pediatrician, so we can call him and get the right formula to feed the little guy."

At that, Lisa burst into tears again and tried to lie down on the bed. Her father grabbed her arm and pulled her to her feet.

"Hey! I know this is really tough, kitten, but you've got to be tougher. Gary needs you to be strong right now, more than he's ever needed anyone in his life. Don't let him down."

Lisa gulped back a sob and began to fold sweaters and put them into one of the suitcases. Behind her back, Gary and Steve looked at each other. Gary nodded almost imperceptibly, and his eyes telegraphed his thanks.

* * * * *

At three-thirty a pickup truck was in the townhouse driveway, already loaded with Aaron's crib, bureau, changing table, and the rocking chair from the nursery. A big box of Pampers stood next to a large suitcase containing his clothes. With Cliff's arm around her, Cheryl walked carefully down the steps from the townhouse to the waiting truck, holding the baby in her arms. Minutes later, eyes red from weeping, Lisa emerged between her husband and her father. As they walked past the truck, she craned her neck for a last glimpse of her son whimpering in Cheryl's arms. There hadn't been time to purchase a car seat, but Steve assured Lisa he would buy one while they were gone. He had already decided to buy also the best baby carriage he could find and surprise them with it when they got home.

The Cadillac pulled away from the curb and headed for Philadelphia International Airport. In his rearview mirror, Steve watched the pickup truck back slowly out of the driveway and turn north toward Delran. A sullen gray sky slouched over the Delaware Valley as the two vehicles sped toward their different destinations.

Steve watched the London-bound plane until its lights disappeared into the clouds. He trudged back to the garage, and sat in his car for several minutes trying to assimilate all the events that had taken place in the last eighteen hours.

He winced when he recalled Lisa's phone call yesterday afternoon, begging him to let Gary's parents stay at the Moorestown house because of their annoying traits and habits. Guilt is one of life's most destructive emotions, he knew, and he was certain it was exacerbating Lisa's grief and anguish at this hour.

He'd hugged them both before they boarded the plane,

and Gary had whispered in his ear, "We couldn't have done this in eighteen hours without your help, Dad. We can never thank you enough."

Steve slapped him on the back and said, "Just be safe." He knew they were on their way to a country where random tragedies occurred all the time. He would not let himself think about that.

Instead, he thought about his grandson. At least he knew Aaron was safe, living temporarily with Cliff and Cheryl.

And, as he did every day, he thought about Serena, who was still missing.

"Sure, I remember *Serena's Kitchen,*" said Hal Waldman. "My sister and I were in high school then, and my parents used to take us there for dinner every Sunday. The food was awesome. How come you sold the place?"

"I got married and moved away," Serena explained, "but my husband passed away last fall."

"Sorry to hear it."

"And I'd like to open another little restaurant. Do you have any suitable properties to show me?"

"Brooklyn's changed a lot in the last ten, fifteen years, Miz D'Agostino. Big influx of Russians."

She chuckled. "No problem there. My mother taught me how to make beet borscht and stuffed cabbage."

"No kidding. Your mother was Russian?"

"She was Jewish. Her parents were born in Russia."

"Hey, how about that!" the young realtor turned to the menu on his computer screen and began to press buttons on the keyboard. "Let's see what we got here . . ."

Cheryl sat in the guest bedroom where Serena had once slept, rocking the tiny dark-haired baby boy. An empty bottle stood on the floor beside her. She'd remembered to burp him, just as Lisa had told her, and now he was sleeping peacefully in her arms. His body was warm and surprisingly solid, his dark eyelashes rested on rosy cheeks. She hated to put him back in his crib.

She hummed softly. An old Irish lullaby she remembered from her early childhood. *Turra lurra lurra* . . . she knew the melody, but not the rest of the words.

Why couldn't a baby like this one have been born to her and Cliff? The so-called fertility doctors they had consulted in the early years of their marriage had found nothing wrong with either of them. They'd spent thousands of dollars, and tried everything the doctors suggested. She'd taken her temperature every day for months in order to pinpoint her time of ovulation. They had abstained from sex for five days before her fertile time to ensure a maximum sperm count. She had used a saline douche after lovemaking, in case the acidity of her own secretions was killing her husband's sperm.

The culprit was never found. It was almost impossible to believe that a couple who tried so hard did not succeed, but every month her body produced the evidence that she was not pregnant.

And tonight she was holding her sister-in-law's child in her arms. It was pleasurable, but not truly satisfying. Like feeding an hors d'oeuvre to a person who is starving.

"It's not fair," whispered Cheryl as she put the baby back in his crib. She heard his contented murmur as she covered him with the fluffy blue blanket.

CHAPTER 37

Cherry Hill, New Jersey

Steve's cell phone began to play the Toreador Song from *Carmen*, and he unfolded it at once.

"Steve Kingsley here."

"Hey, Steve. It's Fred."

Steve walked into his office, closed the door, and sat down at his desk.

"The news from Brooklyn better be good."

"It's not good, it's not bad. It's nowhere. I've been checking the restaurants. I keep checking the Social Security number, but there still hasn't been any change. She may still be looking for a job."

Steve rubbed his head. "I just got another idea. After she divorced her first husband, she used a trust fund her parents had left her to buy a small restaurant in Brooklyn. When she married again, she sold the business and put the money in a bank. Someplace in Brooklyn, I'd be willing to bet."

"You're saying she might be looking to buy another restaurant?"

"Most likely in Flatbush, where she used to live. It makes sense, the more I think about it. Same as me, she loves the restaurant business. She's a great cook, a good business woman, and . . ."

"And she's got a halo that glows in the dark," joked Fred.

Despite everything that was going on, Steve managed a chuckle.

"Okay, wise guy. Find my angel."

Brooklyn, New York

Hal Waldman unlocked the door and Serena walked into the vacant store.

"It was a beauty shop," he said, switching on lights as they walked through. With a pang, Serena thought of Cheryl. She glanced at her own reflection in one of the mirrors still attached to the wall, remembering the creation of her lovely new hairstyle at Cut, Color & Curl.

"The owner passed away three months ago, and the children are anxious to unload the place," Hal continued, turning to gesture toward the front of the store. "It's an ideal location: a supermarket right across the street, a laundromat, a movie theater, a cleaners and a travel agency. No restaurants in this block."

"It would need a lot of work," Serena observed. "I'd have to buy commercial kitchen equipment . . . tables and chairs . . . vertical blinds . . ."—she glanced down at the floor—". . . and vinyl tiles."

"Why don't you make an offer?" suggested Hal.

Serena nodded thoughtfully.

"This place does have possibilities. Let me think about it."

"Don't wait too long!" Hal warned her. "You can see what a great location it is."

"I'll give you a call tomorrow."

Delran, New Jersey

When the telephone rang at six-thirty in the morning, Cheryl had a feeling it was going to be Lisa.

"Could you get the phone, honey? I'm giving Aaron his bottle."

Cliff fumbled for the phone. "Hullo."

"It's Lisa. I'm sorry to call so early, bro. What time is it there? About seven-thirty?"

"Six-thirty."

"Well, it's one-thirty in the afternoon here, and we just finished lunch. How's everything going? How's my son?"

"Everything's great," Cliff told her. "Cheryl's feeding the baby right now."

"Honey, will you come in here and finish giving him his bottle?" Cheryl called from the makeshift nursery. "I want to talk to Lisa."

"And don't forget to burp him," she added, when Cliff appeared in the doorway.

"I'm sorry I called you guys at feeding time," Lisa apologized when Cheryl picked up the phone. "How's he doing with the formula?"

"Well, let me put it this way," said Cheryl, perching on the edge of the bed, "I'm sure nothing is as good as his mother's milk, but we haven't had any problems with bottle feeding."

"Thank God. We don't need any more problems, do we?"

"No, we certainly don't. So tell me, what's happening in Tel Aviv?"

"Well, the funeral was Sunday, the day after we got here. I never thought anything could be worse than my mother's funeral, but this was worse. Gary had to take charge of everything, because Rachel is like a zombie."

"Of course she is—losing both her parents at the same time, and in such an awful way. What's she gonna do now? Do you think she might come to the U.S.?"

"We told her she's welcome to come and stay with us as long as she wants," Lisa replied, a slight tremor in her voice, "but she said *no way*. She's a student at the Goldschleger School of Dental Medicine, you know."

"I never heard of it."

"It's part of the University of Tel Aviv. We're gonna stay here and help her sell the house, and then she'll go to live with her boyfriend's family."

"Oh, she has a boyfriend!" *No wonder she doesn't want to come to the U.S.* "I guess it must be serious, if she's going to live with his family."

"Yeah, they're unofficially engaged. They're planning to get married as soon as they both finish college."

"Do you have any idea yet when you'll be coming home?"

Cheryl stood up and looked into the other bedroom. Her eyes misted when she saw Cliff changing the baby's diaper.

"I'm not really sure. Gary's parents didn't have a will, so of course he's going nuts trying to straighten out the mess with their estate. He wants to be sure Rachel's education is taken care of, and her wedding."

"So it'll be another week, maybe?" Cheryl prompted.

"Looks that way."

"Let me have the number there, Lisa, so we can keep in touch."

"Give Aaron a kiss for me. And thanks for being such a good sister."

"Sister-in-law," Cheryl reminded her.

"*No*. If I had a sister, she couldn't have done any more

for me than you have." She hesitated a few seconds before adding, "I hope you have a baby of your own one of these days."

"As Cliff would say, from your mouth to God's ear."

Brooklyn, New York

A balding man wearing sunglasses walked into the Mohawk Real Estate office.

"Good afternoon, sir. May I help you?"

"I'm in the market for a small restaurant."

Jesus Christ, thought Hal Waldman. *Two in one day?*

"How small?"

"Around fifteen hundred square feet. A neighborhood eatery, that's all."

"Well, I just showed a very fine property this morning. I can show it to you if you want, but I believe the lady who saw it today is going to make an offer."

Fred Morgenstern did not change expression.

"I'd like to see it."

"Do you have any experience running a restaurant?" asked Hal as they strolled through the premises.

"No, but I'm willing to learn."

Hal could not refrain from saying, "The woman who looked at this property this morning used to own a little restaurant right here in Flatbush. Eleven, twelve years ago."

Fred grinned. "Well, if I outbid her, maybe I can hire her to run it for me."

They both laughed.

Back in the Mohawk office, Hal logged onto his computer and brought the beauty-shop property up on the screen.

"May I have your full name, sir?"

"Frederick Morgenstern." He spelled his last name for the young man.

"And how can I reach you?"

Fred recited his cell-phone number, and suddenly put an elbow on Hal's desk. He used his hand to prop up his head.

"Are you okay, sir?"

"I'm a diabetic. I'm supposed to take insulin by mouth three times a day. I got so interested in this property, I'm afraid I forgot about my second dose. I'm feeling a little woozy. Do you think you could find me a glass of cold water so I can take my medicine?"

"Why, sure!" Hal jumped out of his chair. "We've got a little refrigerator in the back. You want ice in the water?"

"That'd be great." Fred closed his eyes.

As soon as Hal disappeared in the rear of the office, Fred leaned across the desk and read the notation below his own name and number on the computer screen.

As he had expected, it read: Serena D'Agostino, followed by a telephone number. Quickly, he jotted down the number on one of his own business cards and dropped it into his shirt pocket. Reaching in his jacket, he took out a bottle of baby aspirin, shook one into his hand, and put the bottle away.

When Hal rushed back with the glass of ice water, he produced the pink tablet, placed it in his mouth, and gulped the water eagerly. He'd been thirsty, anyway, and his doctor had told him to take a baby aspirin every day to promote a healthy heart.

"You just sit here as long as you need to, Mr. Morgenstern," said Hal anxiously. "Don't try to drive until you feel okay."

"Thanks a million, Hal," said Fred. "You've been a big help."

Delran, New Jersey

At ten thirty-five p.m., Cheryl shuffled from the nursery into the kitchen in her robe and rubber flip-flops. She washed the baby's bottle and put it into the sterilizer, which she used every morning when she made the formula.

She dropped a tea bag into a mug, filled it up with water, and put it in the microwave. She liked to have a cup of herbal tea before going to bed. Cliff wouldn't be home until after midnight, and she was exhausted. Taking care of a new baby was great, but it was harder than working in a beauty shop!

She removed the steaming cup from the microwave and started across the kitchen. Somehow, one of her flip-flops got caught on a bit of the two-sided tape protruding unnoticed from beneath the little hooked rug that Serena/Grace used to call "that nasty little rug." Cheryl lost her balance. Hot tea splashed on the kitchen floor as her arms flailed wildly in an effort to keep herself from falling. The cup fell from her hand and broke. She staggered, still trying to regain her balance, skidded on the wet floor tiles, and fell over the small garbage pail by the sink. She heard a loud crack, and knew the sound had come from her own leg.

She lay on the floor, gasping. Pain, like a red-hot poker, lanced through her right leg, filling her entire body. Her chest heaving, she tried to move and cried out, "*Oh!* God, please help me!" The skin had broken on her lower leg, but instead of blood she saw something white protruding through the opening. With a sense of unreality, she acknowledged that it had to be her shinbone. The pain was excruciating, but she faced the fact that no one, not even God, was going to help her. She was alone. The only other human being in the house was an infant just over two weeks old.

Nauseated and dizzy from the pain, she inched across the kitchen floor and stared up at the yellow wall phone. She tugged on the cord and shook it until the phone dropped into her hands. She dialed her husband's cell-phone number.

When she heard him say, "Cliff Kingsley here," she began to cry. Loud, wracking sobs.

"Cheryl?"

"Yes—" she managed to say.

"What happened? Something happen to Aaron?"

"No, Cliff. It's me." The pain in her leg drove up, up, *up,* squeezing her voice to a wild, wavering wail. "I fell in the kitchen and my leg is broken."

CHAPTER 38

Because Cliff phoned 9-1-1 and his father immediately after receiving Cheryl's call, he, Steve, and the ambulance arrived within minutes of each other. The paramedics applied a splint to Cheryl's leg to prevent further damage to the fractured tibia before lifting her onto the gurney. In the ambulance, an IV was set up to supply saline to her body before she reached the hospital. No further measures would be taken until she was evaluated by the emergency-room physicians.

Cliff followed the ambulance in his new Lincoln Towncar.

Steve remained in the house to clean up the mess on the kitchen floor, and, of course, to baby-sit. He stepped out the back door to drop the offending scatter rug in the trashcan, remembering that Serena had once recounted a discussion she'd had with Cheryl about it. She'd called it a "possible hazard," and Steve had scoffed at her fears and told her she sounded like an old *bubbe*.

Young people just bounce up again when they fall, honey!

He wandered into the baby's room and stared at his sleeping grandson, his eyes clouded with worry. *What in the hell were they going to do about the baby, with Lisa in Israel and Cheryl in the hospital?*

In the living room, he sat down in Cliff's recliner and wondered when the baby's last feeding had taken place. He cursed himself for not asking Cheryl before she was transported to the ambulance.

When his phone began to play the Toreador Song, he said aloud, "What now? An invasion of Martians?"

He opened the phone and barked, "Who is it?"

A man's voice answered, "Ah! The voice with a smile."

He knew at once who was on the other end of the line.

"I haven't got much to smile about right now, Fred."

"You will in about three seconds. I found your angel."

Steve felt a warming sensation that began around his heart and radiated slowly through his body. It was like coming indoors after shoveling snow and finding that someone had lighted a fire in the fireplace.

"Good work, Fred! Have you talked to her?" An embarrassing quiver punctuated the question.

"Nope. Thought you might want to call her yourself."

Tears welled in Steve's eyes. He swallowed hard, tried to speak.

"Bad shit going down in Jersey, Steve?" asked Fred.

"Yeah," he managed to say.

"Talk. I've got a can of beer and plenty of time."

When Steve finished reporting the events of the past week, it was Fred who remained silent. Feeling a little better after his recital, Steve said, "*So?* What're you waiting for? Give me the phone number already."

"King's Way."

"Huh?" Steve was confused momentarily. It sounded like a place he might have owned! He'd expected Serena to answer the phone.

"This is the King's Way Motel. What number are you calling?"

Belatedly, he remembered that Brooklyn was also known as King's County. He cleared his throat.

"Please connect me with Serena D'Agostino."

"One moment please. I'll ring her room."

When he heard her soft voice say hello, Steve's heartbeat thundered in his ears. *Please, God, help me to find the right words.*

"Don't hang up, honey. I need to ask a big favor."

She sounded bewildered. "*Steve!* How did you find me?"

"Fred. Remember him?"

"Oh! The investigator?"

"Yeah. *That* Fred."

"Listen, Steve, I am not coming back to New Jersey. That chapter in my life is over. Tomorrow I'm making an offer on a little restaurant, and I'll be starting a new life here in Flatbush, where I belong."

He detected a quiver in her voice as she continued, "Knowing you was very special to me . . . both times . . . but it wasn't meant to be anything more than a friendship."

Steve shifted the phone to his left hand because his right hand was wet with perspiration.

"I respect your decision, honey, and I'm not gonna try to change your mind. We have a family crisis here at the moment, and I'm only calling you because you're our last hope."

"What? What's happened?"

"Do you remember Gary's parents were supposed to come here?"

"Yes . . ."

"Well, the day before they were supposed to leave, they were killed at a shopping mall in Tel Aviv—"

"They were what? *Killed?*"

"Yeah. It was one of those suicide bombers. Twenty-one other people were killed at the same time."

He heard her gasp.

"Oh, Steve! I read about it in the newspaper, but of course I never *dreamed* . . ."

"Yeah. So Gary and Lisa flew to Israel for the funeral the next day."

"Are they okay?"

"Yeah. But they have to stay a little longer than they expected. There was no will so the estate's a godawful mess, and Gary's sister is a college student there."

"What about the baby?" she asked.

The conversation was proceeding just as he had hoped it would.

"Cheryl took a leave of absence from her job, and she's been taking care of the little guy."

"That sounds like a perfect solution," said Serena, sounding puzzled.

"It was, until tonight. Remember that goddam rug in their kitchen?"

"Oh, *no!*" cried Serena. "I mean, yes, of course I remember that nasty little rug. I tried to tell her . . ."

"I know you did. Well, tonight she slipped on the fucking thing and broke a bone in her lower leg. What they call an open fracture. When I got here the shin bone was sticking out through the skin."

"Oh, my God! *Poor Cheryl!* Where is she now?"

"Riverview Hospital. Cliff is with her."

"And you're at their house?"

"Yeah. Baby-sitting."

"Oh, *Steve!*" She had grasped the problem. "I guess you could hire a nanny."

"Yeah. We could do that . . ."

She said nothing, and he allowed the silence to lengthen.

"But you don't really want to bring in a stranger," she finished the sentence for him.

The conversation seemed to be heading down the home stretch.

"You always seem to know what I'm thinking," he said.

"I'm just a good guesser. You know I'd really like to help you out, Steve, but . . ."

"Fred's up there. In Brooklyn, I mean. He could drive you down here."

"I bought a car," she told him.

"Good. Then you can drive yourself."

"Wait a minute, Steve! I haven't said I'll do this!"

"But you will, won't you? *Please,* Serena!"

"I don't know. Leaving New Jersey was one of the hardest decisions I've ever made, and seeing you again would upset me. Very much."

His heart took off like a rocket at her words, but he was careful to keep his voice businesslike.

"You won't have to see me at all. You'll be busy with Aaron, and I'll be busy at the restaurant."

She'd thought of something else.

"Lisa wouldn't want me taking care of her child!"

"Why don't you let Cliff and me worry about Lisa?"

Another long moment passed, and then, as he had hoped, she crossed the finish line.

"Steve, you always seem to know what *I'm* thinking, too. I've heard too many horror stories about nannies. I'll be there tomorrow morning."

He summoned all his strength to keep the tremor out of his voice when he said, "Thanks, honey."

CHAPTER 39

An April shower was sprinkling South Jersey when Serena's new Toyota pulled up in front of the red-brick bungalow. She did not recognize the butterscotch-yellow Lincoln Towncar in the driveway. She hurried up the front walk, remembering the first time she'd come here. It was three months—no—four months ago. The day of the bus accident. Cheryl had run out of the house to greet her.

No one ran out of the house to greet her today. She rang the doorbell, and a minute later Cliff opened the door.

"Oh, Grace—*Serena*—thank God you're here! We've missed you. Come in."

She stepped through the doorway and he hugged her.

"How's Cheryl?" she asked, shaking the raindrops from her hair.

"She had surgery early this morning. They put some kind of metal rod in her lower leg so the bone can mend."

"Why aren't you at the hospital?" she asked.

"You told Dad you didn't want to see him, so *he's* at the hospital. I told him I'd come as soon as you got here."

She felt him watching her, and knew she was blushing.

"Well, you jump in that beautiful new car . . . that *is* your car in the driveway, isn't it? . . . and get over to the hospital right now. And be sure to give Cheryl my love."

"Any message for Dad?"

She couldn't seem to stop blushing.

"No message."

The brief shower had been replaced by sunshine. Raindrops glittered on the early spring flowers in Cheryl's garden, transforming pink crocuses, red tulips, and purple hyacinths into Mother Nature's jewels.

After the Lincoln Towncar sped away, Serena brought her own car up onto the driveway, carried her suitcases into the house, and tiptoed into the nursery. To her surprise and delight, the baby was awake.

"Well, hello there, Aaron Michael," she said softly. "You're getting to be such a big boy I almost didn't recognize you."

As soon as he heard her voice, his arms and legs beat an enthusiastic tattoo on the crib mattress, and he made a sweet little sound that she chose to regard as a greeting. She put him on the changing table and changed his diaper.

"Shall we go into the kitchen and see whether Uncle Cliff left any bottles in the refrigerator for your lunch?" she asked. He didn't object, so she carried him into the kitchen where her eyes immediately focused on the floor in front of the sink. The rug was gone, of course. Like the barn door that was locked after the horse was stolen.

A magnet on the door of the refrigerator held a scrawled message. It said: "Serena: I made the formula for today. Baby was fed at 8:30 a.m. Cliff." Her watch told her it was now five minutes after twelve. She removed a bottle from the refrigerator and put it in the electric warmer.

As soon as Cliff walked into the hospital room, Steve jumped out of the chair beside Cheryl's bed.

"She's here?"

"Yeah, Dad. She got here about twenty-five minutes ago." He bent over the bed and kissed Cheryl's lips.

"Aaron's in good hands, babe, and Grace . . . *Serena* . . .

sends her love to you. Now tell me how everything went this morning."

"Okay, I guess," she murmured drowsily. "I wasn't awake, you know." She opened her eyes for a moment and smiled. "But I'm glad Serena's here."

Later, after the nurse gave Cheryl a pain injection, which put her to sleep again, the two men walked out to the parking garage together.

"How's the new Lincoln running, kiddo?"

"Great. You know, Dad, I've been thinking about buying a new car for Cheryl. To maybe surprise her when she comes home from the hospital. Whaddya think?"

"I like the idea. What kind of car do you have in mind?"

He thought about Serena's new silver Toyota. He'd given it a once-over before he got in his car and drove to the hospital.

"I was thinking about a Toyota."

Steve nodded, and cleared his throat.

"Good choice. Hey, son, did—uh, did Serena ask about me?"

Cliff shook his head.

"No, Dad. She didn't."

Steve's face did not change expression as he reached his car and unlocked the door.

It's enough, for now, just knowing that she's here.

"See you tonight, son," he called.

Cliff waved and walked on.

That night Cliff placed a midnight call to Tel Aviv. He and his father had discussed strategy during their evening visit to Cheryl and agreed that preemptive phone calls would be the best way to prevent Lisa from finding out that

Cheryl was in the hospital, and that Serena was taking care of her son.

"How's the baby?" was—of course—Lisa's first question.

"Great. Drinks his bottle every three-and-a-half, four hours. Seems to be a happy and healthy little guy."

"Can I talk to Cheryl?" was her next question.

"It's after midnight here, sis. Cheryl says taking care of a new baby is harder than working at the beauty shop."

An appreciative laugh from Lisa. "So she's asleep, I guess."

"Yeah. Sound asleep." He knew that, at least, was the truth.

"Let her sleep. I'll talk to her next time."

Cliff thought he detected a new quality in Lisa's voice, her speech. He tried to define it and couldn't.

"How's everything going there? How's Rachel?"

"Rachel's having a very hard time accepting what's happened. She's angry. Yesterday she was talking about dropping out of college and going back into the army."

"Aw, shit!" Cliff knew that young Israelis were required to serve in the army. He knew also that Rachel had already fulfilled her military obligation.

"She was so lost when we got here that Gary thought she might need psychiatric help, but she seems to have bonded with me. Maybe it's because she knows we just lost Mom in December."

He thought he had identified the new quality in Lisa's voice. She sounded *maternal.*

"So what're you saying? You talked her out of going back into the army?"

"Yes, I did." She sounded proud of her accomplishment. "I convinced her that her parents would not have wanted her to risk her life to avenge their deaths. I told her they would've wanted her to finish college as planned, marry Avi, and maybe add a few leaves to the family tree."

"Hey," said Cliff, a note of pride in his voice, "what happened to Lettuce-head Lisa, the sister I know and love?" He hadn't called her that in years.

She laughed. "I think I left her back in Cherry Hill. Oh, Cliffie, I've seen so much suffering here! Almost every family has lost someone—sometimes more than one—to terrorist attacks. And yet they keep on keeping on. They're invincible!"

Her voice shook with emotion.

"They make me so proud to be a Jew. I've never felt that way before."

Cliff was deeply moved.

"I'm impressed, little sister."

"Hang on, Gary wants to talk to you now."

Gary came on the line and described the bureaucratic red tape he was trying to unravel in order to assure the completion of his sister's education and the essentials of her wedding.

"I guess bureaucratic red tape is a universal affliction," he said, sounding tired.

Then he added, "You wouldn't believe what a godsend Lisa's been. You know I'm twelve years older than Rachel, like you're fifteen years older than Lisa. Well, we're staying at the house, sleeping in my parents' bedroom—and Rachel clings to us, especially to Lisa, as if we were her surrogate parents."

"My dad always says everything happens the way it's supposed to," said Cliff. "You guys were meant to be there for her right now."

"I'm only sorry this is taking so much longer than we anticipated. We'll spend the rest of our lives being grateful to you and Cheryl. It's a load off our minds, knowing that our baby is in such good hands."

The preemptive phone calls continued to preserve the charade. Cliff gave Serena strict instructions not to answer the phone when it rang. If he was calling her, he would let it ring once and hang up, then call right back. The machine would answer any other calls. Serena understood the reason for secrecy, and it made her sad.

Cheryl, who was now a co-conspirator, placed several calls from the hospital on Cliff's cell phone while Cliff or Steve stood guard at the door to ensure that no hospital personnel interrupted the conversations. If she glimpsed a doctor or a nurse attempting to enter her room, she used Aaron as a convenient excuse. *Oh, I have to hang up now . . . can you hear the baby crying?*

One afternoon Steve's cell phone rang just as he was getting off the hospital elevator. Mid-afternoon, halfway between lunch and dinner, seemed an ideal time for him to visit his daughter-in-law. In Israel, it was late evening.

"Steve Kingsley," he barked into the phone.

Right after he'd identified himself, a voice on the hospital's overhead paging system resonated in the hallway.

"Doctor Lerner, Doctor Gordon Lerner, please call the operator."

Lisa's voice said, "Daddy, are you in a hospital?"

How could he deny it?

"Hi, kitten. Yeah, one of my employees fell in the kitchen and broke her leg, so I dropped by to see her."

"That was nice of you."

"Face it, I'm just a nice guy."

Lisa laughed.

"I have good news, Daddy. The house has been sold,

and Gary's got the estate situation pretty well straightened out. It helped a lot that his father's attorney was also a close friend. We should be coming home in a day or two."

"Hey, that *is* good news."

He entered Cheryl's room and sat by her bed, where the phone conversation continued for another ten minutes. Cheryl, who was getting physical therapy every day now, was half asleep. She opened her eyes and smiled when he told her Gary and Lisa would be coming home soon.

CHAPTER 40

"Were you surprised when we called from London yesterday and asked you to meet us at the airport today?"

Steve glanced over his shoulder at his daughter and her husband in the back seat of his car and laughed. "Yeah, I was surprised all right—but it was the kind of surprise I like."

He hadn't had any alcohol since the night of the King's Yacht opening, but right now he was experiencing all the symptoms of a hangover. Although enormously relieved that Lisa and Gary were safe, he had lain awake most of the night after their phone call, trying to decide how he was going to tell them about Cheryl's accident—and the identity of their son's caretaker.

"Oh, it feels so good to be back home!" Lisa squeezed her husband's hand as they pulled away from the curb at the airport and the Philadelphia skyline loomed on the horizon, gilded by midday sunshine.

"I'll take you to your house first," Steve suggested hopefully. He'd called his son's house this morning to let Cliff and Serena know Gary and Lisa were coming home, but no one answered the phone and he'd left no message. Later, he remembered that Cliff had instructed Serena not to answer any call unless it had been preceded by a one-ring-and-hang-up. On his way to the airport, he'd tried again, following that procedure. Again, no one had answered the phone, so neither she nor Cliff would have any idea that Aaron's parents were arriving today.

"No, Daddy! I want to go to Cliff's house first," Lisa insisted. "I can't wait to hold my baby again!"

"Cliff will have to get his neighbor's truck to bring the crib and all the other stuff back to your place, you know." Steve was stalling. "So you may not be able to take him home right away."

"I don't care! I want to see my son!"

As the car sped cross the Delaware River on the Walt Whitman Bridge, Steve tossed a copy of the *Camden County Courier-Post* into the back seat.

"You may be interested in that story at the bottom of page one," he called. In the rearview mirror he saw his son-in-law fold the paper in half to find the article he was referring to.

"Hey, look at this, honey!" Gary exclaimed. "Remember that woman who used to work for your dad, the one who threw the firebomb into Grace's apartment?"

"You're talking about Juliette Black. Sure, I remember her. She was always coming on to Daddy. What's she done now?"

"She's not in a position to do much of anything. She listened to her lawyer and pleaded guilty, but the judge sentenced her to twenty-five years in prison. For attempted murder and felony arson."

"I never liked her," said Lisa. "She didn't fit the image of the King's Feast. She dressed like a call girl, for heaven's sake."

"Yes, that's true, but aside from her wardrobe indiscretions, and her unfortunate tendency to commit murder and arson, she was quite a good hostess," Steve declared with a straight face.

"Oh, Daddy! You have an *awful* sense of humor," Lisa complained, trying not to laugh.

He chuckled. "Yeah, you're right. I guess I won't give up the day job."

"I'm glad the judge didn't fall for her sob story about having to take care of her invalid mother," Gary commented.

"I made *sure* the prosecutor knew that story was bullshit," growled Steve. He hoped Serena had seen today's paper, and read the story.

As the Cadillac turned onto Haines Mill Road, Steve gritted his teeth. He knew he didn't have much time to prepare them for Serena's presence at Cliff's house.

"Hey, kids—while you were in Israel Cheryl had an accident," he began. "Do you remember that little scatter rug in her kitchen?"

"She fell?" Lisa guessed immediately.

Steve nodded.

"She not only fell, she broke a bone in her right leg."

"Was she holding the baby when she fell?"

"No, Lisa, she wasn't. The baby was sound asleep when it happened."

"Could she—uh—how could she take care of Aaron if she broke her leg?"

"She couldn't. In fact, she's still in rehab, but she'll be home soon."

Lisa's voice went up several octaves.

"So who's taking care of my baby?"

"Well, honey, I knew you wouldn't want a stranger taking care of him."

"That's true. So answer my question! *Who's taking care of him?*"

Steve swallowed hard and plunged into ice water.

"Remember before you left, Fred was looking for Grace? Well, he found her living in Brooklyn, and I persuaded her to come back temporarily to take care of Aaron—just until you and Gary got back from Israel."

Lisa rolled her eyes.

"And now the wedding plans are on again, I suppose?"

"No. My persuasive powers aren't what they used to be. She won't even agree to see me."

"And *of course* you haven't tried to change her mind."

"No, I haven't. She only agreed to come down here and take care of your son if I promised to leave her alone."

"Yeah. *Right.*"

He looked in the rearview mirror and saw the skeptical sneer on his daughter's pretty face. His heart crumpled in his chest. Why did she have to be like this?

"Whose car is that in Cliff's driveway?" asked Gary. "It looks like a brand-new Toyota."

"Oh, that must be the car he bought for Cheryl," said Steve, recalling their conversation in the hospital garage. "He wants to surprise her when she gets home from the rehab. We talked about it, and he told me he was probably going to get her a Toyota."

When the Cadillac stopped in front of the red-brick bungalow, Lisa was the first one out of the car. She ran up the front walk and tried to open the door. Finding it locked, she rang the doorbell. The three of them stood on the stoop, waiting. The door remained closed. Lisa rang the doorbell again.

"Don't sweat it, kitten, Cliff gave me a key," said Steve, producing his key ring and inserting the appropriate one into the lock.

Inside the house, Steve headed for the kitchen. Gary and Lisa ran into the makeshift nursery. The white enamel crib was empty, and Lisa shrieked.

"She's kidnapped him! *She's kidnapped my baby!*"

Gary tried to put his arms around her.

"She probably just went shopping, honey."

"Don't try to bullshit me! There are no shops near here. The nearest shopping mall is on Route One Thirty, two miles away! Maybe three!"

Steve walked into the room, frowning.

"Get a hold of yourself, Lisa. Serena is a good person, a gentle person. Wherever they are, he's in good hands. She loves your baby, and she'd love you, too, if you'd let her."

"I don't want her to love me! She's kidnapped my child!" she shouted.

Before they realized what she was going to do, she dashed into the kitchen and dialed 9-1-1. Gary ran after her and grappled with her, trying to get the phone out of her hand.

"My baby's been kidnapped!" she screamed into the phone.

"Give me that phone!" Gary ordered.

They struggled, and Lisa continued to scream.

"They're trying to keep me from reporting it, but my baby is missing, and I know the identity of the person who took him!"

Steve wrenched the phone out of Lisa's hand, and said, "Please disregard this call, operator. There's no emergency here. My daughter has become hysterical for no reason at all."

"Is the child missing or not?" asked the 9-1-1 operator.

"Well, he's not here right now, but . . ."

"May I have your address, please?"

Reluctantly, Steve recited the address. He didn't want it to appear that he was hiding anything.

"Did the person who took him warn you not to call the police?"

"Jesus Christ, lady, my daughter is the only one who thinks the baby was kidnapped! He's probably just . . ."

"How long has the child been missing?" the operator persisted.

"I don't know," Steve admitted. "You see, we just got back . . ."

"Police officers will be there in ten minutes to get a full statement."

"Hey, wait just a goddam minute!" roared Steve, but the line was dead.

Serena, in blue jeans and a pink cable-knit sweater, ambled along Conrow Road beneath a cloudless blue sky. It was the sort of spring day that inspires poets. The azaleas, the forsythia bushes, and the dogwood trees were in full bloom; the sight of all the pink, yellow, and white blossoms lifted her spirits and made her sigh with pleasure. What a good idea it had been to take the baby out in his new carriage. The fresh air had done its work well, and little Aaron was sleeping peacefully.

When she pushed the carriage around the corner onto Haines Mill Road, a police car whizzed past, lights flashing. From the corner, it looked almost as if it had stopped in front of Cliff's house. Frowning, she began to walk a little faster. It *had* stopped in front of Cliff's house, and two officers were getting out of the vehicle!

Had someone tried to rob the place? She was sure she had locked the door when she left. Or had she only thought she did? When she realized Steve's car was parked in front of the police car, she began to run. The carriage wheels rolled rapidly over the sidewalk. As she approached the house, the front door burst open and Lisa darted out, almost falling down the steps in her haste to reach the carriage.

"There she is! *Arrest her!* She kidnapped my baby!"

Gary followed his wife past the police officers—who were standing in the doorway, bemused, as they watched the scenario. Serena stood on the sidewalk, wide-eyed, as Lisa snatched the baby from the carriage. Startled out of a sound sleep, he began to howl.

"It's all right, darling, Mommy's here now!" she crooned, but he continued to scream. Glaring at Serena, she shouted, "What did you do to him? Why is he carrying on like this?"

"He was asleep. I think you may have scared him," Gary, standing behind her, said in a low voice.

"How could I scare him? I'm his mother!"

She turned around to glare at the police officers.

"Why haven't you arrested this woman?" she demanded, pointing at Serena.

"Shut the hell up!" Steve's voice cracked the air like a whip.

Appearing more perplexed than preparing to make an arrest, the officers exchanged glances as Steve strode past them and down the steps. He stopped in front of his daughter.

Lisa had stopped shouting. In all her life, her father had never—ever—told her to shut up.

And he was still talking.

"Listen to me, Lisa, and listen good. I persuaded this woman to drive all the way down from Brooklyn to take care of your son after Cheryl had her accident. She didn't want to come, because she was afraid you wouldn't want her to take care of him, but I talked her into it. And now I'm sorry.

"I'm sorry that I have a daughter who has been so ungrateful and insulting to a woman who only wanted to be her friend. A woman who dropped everything and came here to help us out when we needed help so desperately."

Tears were rolling down Lisa's cheeks. Gary took the wailing baby from her, and carried him into the house. She didn't protest, but stood staring down at the sidewalk.

"I love this woman and she loves me. We were planning to be married, but she called it off and went away because she knew you didn't want her in our family—and she didn't want to make me choose between her and my daughter.

"Well, I have news for you, *daughter*. I've made my choice! I'm going to marry Serena, if she'll still have me. I love Serena, I love you, I love Gary, and I love my grandson. I love all of you! I want us to be a family!

"I thought you learned something over there in Israel. On the phone you told us about all the people who had lost their husbands, their wives, their parents. One of them was your sister-in-law, Rachel! How could you be so compassionate, so understanding with her, and so spiteful and downright mean to Serena? What the hell's the matter with you anyway? Are you so selfish that you—"

"Steve, stop it!"

Serena's sharp command shocked him to silence.

"Please don't cry anymore, Lisa. These nice police officers are going to leave now," Serena said, nodding to them, "and then we're all going to go inside Cliff's house and talk like grown-up people about our future."

EPILOGUE

Philadelphia, Pennsylvania: Two Months Later

It was a blue-and-gold afternoon in June when Steve and Serena were married. A Reform Jewish ceremony at Temple Emanuel in Cherry Hill was followed by a private reception across the river at the King's Yacht.

The King's Feast was closed that day so that all the employees and their families could be guests at the wedding—but Anton insisted on making the wedding cake, an opulent confection featuring white doves and silver butterflies. As he posed proudly beside his creation for photographers covering the wedding, he explained that the dove represents peace and harmony, and the butterfly is a symbol of re-birth . . . a new life.

Steve had insisted on going with Serena when she went to pick out her wedding gown. He told her he was afraid the people at the bridal salon would think, *Get a load of this! A senior citizen bride?*—and end up making her look like Whistler's Mother.

They chose a simple, long-sleeved ivory satin dress with a sweetheart neckline. The fitted bodice was encrusted with pink pearls and silver beads. There was no train, but the skirt flared smoothly from her hips to the floor. She wore silver sandals, and carried a bouquet of white orchids and pink roses. Steve persuaded the florist to create a crown of pink roses for her to wear. *His queen.*

Her only attendant was Cheryl, who had refused to let

her lingering limp deprive her of that role. She wore a satin gown similar to Serena's—except that hers was shell pink. Her bouquet was small, like Cheryl herself, consisting of pink roses and baby's breath.

Steve, and his son Cliff who served as best man, wore dove-gray formal attire with boutonnieres of pink rosebuds. All the men attending the ceremony wore white satin *yarmulkes*.

When Steve and Serena began the traditional first dance together as husband and wife, the song they chose was an old one made popular by Diana Ross and the Supremes: "Someday We'll Be Together."

As the song ended and the assembled wedding guests applauded, the newlyweds stood looking into each other's eyes and smiling. Today was *some sweet day*.

When they began their second dance, Serena lifted her head and whispered in his ear, "I was talking to Cheryl a little while ago in the ladies' room. Did you know she and Cliff are going to Russia in August?"

"Russia! I thought they were going to Disney World," said Steve.

"Maybe they'll go there next year. They're going to Russia to adopt a baby."

Steve whooped, causing the wedding guests watching them to smile.

"How did she ever get my son to agree? He always swore he'd never bring up another man's child."

"I think he caught the fever while Aaron was living in their house."

"Those dirty diapers will do it every time," joked Steve.

He pulled her closer, and both of them were laughing with tears in their eyes as the band began to play another song. Other couples began to join them on the dance floor.

They waved to Serena's D'Agostino cousins from Sacramento, California, who had each brought a guest and were dancing near each other.

A few minutes later Serena said, "Look who's dancing with Beverly!" Steve looked. It was Fred Morgenstern.

"They make a good-looking couple," Steve remarked. "It's about time that old broken-down son of a bitch found himself a nice woman."

Serena smiled. She knew how much Steve loved his old friend.

"Has Fred ever been married?"

"Yeah, once. His wife got a divorce after he took the bullet in his lung. Said she didn't want to spend the rest of her life playing nursemaid."

"Well, good riddance to her!" exclaimed Serena.

Beverly, wearing a very becoming turquoise-blue dress that was one of her hostess gowns, exchanged glances with Serena and winked happily over Fred's shoulder.

The bride and groom walked to the edge of the dance floor, and Steve accepted two flutes of champagne from a passing waiter. He handed one to her, and they stood watching the dancers.

"Would you be offended if we talked a little business today?" he asked.

A change of mood? She sipped at her champagne.

"What kind of business?"

"After we get back from our honeymoon, I think we should drive up to New York and talk to that lawyer who's handling Ed Franklin's estate."

"Why should we do that? Do we need the money?"

"I don't need it. It belongs to you, if you want to claim it."

Serena was quiet for such a long time that he thought she'd decided to veto his suggestion, but at length she looked up at him and said, "You know, darling, that's a good idea."

"I have lots of those."

"I think I'll donate my share of Eddie's estate to Greenpeace." She recalled the day Eddie's will was read, when Phyllis had referred to it as *Green Peas*. "I'm sure he'd be pleased."

She inclined her head slightly as a gentle breeze ruffled her hair, caressed her face. She saw no ceiling fans in the room.

She smiled. A small, secret one.

"Let's sit this one out," Steve suggested, when the band started to play "Green Eyes," a tango. Arm in arm, they strolled back to their table. Seconds later Lisa approached, wearing a salmon-pink silk dress and a tentative smile.

"You're looking lovely today, kitten," said Steve.

"That color is perfect for you, with your dark hair," Serena added.

"Thank you both." She seated herself at the table. "Daddy, I'd like to speak to Serena alone for a few minutes, okay?"

"Okay, sure. I'll go cut in on Fred and Beverly. Watch me make that bum lose his temper."

"I'm beginning to think little boys never grow up," said Serena, giggling as she watched him cross the dance floor and tap Fred on the shoulder.

"Get lost, *klutz,*" she heard Fred say. "You don't know how to tango anyway."

"Oh, is that what you're doing? I thought you had a cramp in your foot."

"Aren't they cute? Like a pair of twelve-year-olds," Serena said. She turned her head, expecting to share a girls-only smile with her new stepdaughter. Lisa was not smiling.

"Is something wrong?" she asked, concerned.

"The only thing that's wrong here is *me,*" said Lisa. "I've been so wrong about you, Serena. I wish I could take back all the terrible things I've said to you. You're so good for my dad. You've made him happier than he's been in years. Since before my mother got sick."

"Well, he makes me happy too." She picked up Lisa's hand and squeezed it. "And you were right to be protective of your dad. He's a very special man. When I first met him at the restaurant—long before I fell in love with him—I respected his loyalty and love for your mother."

Lisa's dark-brown eyes filled with tears. "I never thought I'd say this to you, Serena, but—I know my mother would have liked you."

"Thank you, Lisa," Serena said quietly.

"My little boy is going to need a grandmother as well as a grandfather. I really want us to be a family. Can we start again, and take it one day at a time?"

"That's always the best way, isn't it?" asked Serena Grace Kingsley.

ABOUT THE AUTHOR

Janet Logan attended Goucher College, Towson, Maryland. One of her poems appeared in the *American Poetry Annual* published by the Amherst Society. Two biography stories she wrote for preschool children were published by Field Enterprises in *Childcraft*, an adjunct to *World Books*. *Silver Butterfly* is her first novel. She lives in Hollywood, Florida.